The

PRINCESS

The PRINCESS

★

TREY BAHM

TATE PUBLISHING & *Enterprises*

Published by Tate Publishing & Enterprises, LLC
127 E. Trade Center Terrace | Mustang, Oklahoma 73064 USA
1.888.361.9473 | www.tatepublishing.com

Tate Publishing is committed to excellence in the publishing industry. The company reflects the philosophy established by the founders, based on Psalm 68:11,
"The Lord gave the word and great was the company of those who published it."

Published in the United States of America

ISBN: 978-1-61566-746-8
1. Fiction / Political   2. Fiction / Christian / Suspense
10.03.02

to Mom

ACKNOWLEDGMENTS

I think that by requiring an acknowledgments section at the beginning of the formatting process, a publisher can avoid any possible negativity by the author against its editors. Unfortunately, they also miss out on any praise or must at least wait until the next manuscript or edition. Still, I want to thank the staff of Tate Publishing in advance for their hard work on *The Princess*. Life is an adventure.

God gives us the grace to be grateful, same as his Spirit provides us with prayers to pray. So, the only way I can be grateful is to claim his infinite resources to that purpose. That might begin to cover it.

I want to express this infinite, Spirit-enabled gratitude by singling out those who helped me push this story past the finish line.

I have to start with my former business partner, Jack Klaus, more affectionately known by his wife, his fellow Borgerites and me, as "Rusty." He and I met on Capitol Hill an unbelievable seven years ago. Whereas the relationship initially was one of older brother harassing younger slaphead (I had to explain to him that a career in Congress should not be seen as a stepping-stone to becoming a judge for the Oakland Raiderettes), today he is a sibling of the rarest, closest type. I would be broke on the street instead of broke among friends today if it were not for him. Without him, *The Princess* would not at all be going into production, period. He has truly been Providence's instrument these past three years. Not only have I been utterly dependent upon him; he served a critical role in being one of this novel's first readers. If he doesn't get the byline on the cover, Rusty should at least be considered *The Princess*'s de facto publisher.

I admire Rusty as one of the greatest lovers of truth and common sense I've ever known, and it is rare to see someone with God's hand so mightily upon them.

Next, I have to mention my college roommate, Bryan Strader, MD. Endless phone conversations between Texas and Cincinnati provided *The Princess* with important realism. Moreover, Bryan's genuine care for my well-being in recent years went into some of the relationships expressed in this story. There is a friend who sticks closer than a brother, and Bryan's loyalty has been a vision for me of Christ.

I also want to acknowledge my former supervisor on Capitol Hill, Lou Zickar. Although currently out of government service, Lou made sure I knew that it was okay to be a storyteller, no matter what one did as a day job. A gifted, insightful writer in his own right, I am not sure I know too many people who love their country more than Lou. His idealism has always been an inspiration, his frustrations fully empathetic, and Lou also made sure I knew that an endless pursuit of one's principled beliefs was okay too, whenever DC started to get to me.

There are many others, of course, who have had a direct impact on the Trey who writes over the years and this story today. There were the haters too. But I needed them every bit as much.

All these nods, lifts, and pushes along the way only amount to a fraction of the support from my two biggest fans, Dad and Mom, the latter to whom my first book is dedicated. My dad, Sandy Bahm, was left off, only because he has another one coming his way, Lord willing. It has been Dad who has kept body and soul together financially. It was Dad who discovered Tate Publishing through his church. And it is Dad who does absolutely anything to see that his kids' dreams come true.

My mother, Nancy Bahm, gets the first page for several reasons. First, she loves to read. Her passion for literature goes back to a childhood in rural West Texas during the 1950s when books were as precious as the water. She has taught me the actual delights of a good book, and even though I write fiction, I will only read those books I want, fiction or not.

Second, she enjoys and respects the craft of storytelling. A history and English double-major from Baylor University, Mom possesses a strong sense of good storytelling and its required construction. She always said she wanted to be a book editor. I made sure she got her wish when I finished the first draft.

Third, she loves her country. While Dad has provided me with both the public spirit and skepticism sorely needed for a liberal democracy, Mom gave me the patriotism. And by patriotism, I mean the true God and country kind. We may not always agree on the finer points of a specific policy, but understanding God's special blessings in America comes from Mother's eyes.

There are many other reasons why she's earned the dedication, but I'll finish with this one: her longsuffering. When it comes to my life, she may prefer to emphasize the suffering part of the word. But I think mothers are special, not because they love us unconditionally, but because they innately possess a patience that flows from that same infinite resource that I am claiming makes me grateful. I chafed under her correction when I didn't win some meaningless elementary school costume contest, I saw her weary smile the day I graduated from Greenville Christian School, I watched her cry when I drove off to the Northeast that difficult summer of '98, and I held on to her hand that special day of September 27, 2008.

Thanks, everyone.

June 4, 2009
Allen, Texas

CHAPTER ONE

May 14

Dear God,

Thank you for this day and for the rain. Thank you for our blessed state and nation. Thank you for my husband.

Thank you that it is not a man's world. Thank you that you sent us to help them, and thank you for the joy that your Spirit fills us with and its strength to do so.

Thank you for my work and the busy day ahead. Deliver me from being uncaring toward my staff. Help my talks with Paul to go smoothly when he calls. Protect me from certain thoughts about my ten o'clock meeting. Forgive me of—

Lisa Jeffus cut her morning devotions short by tossing her prayer journal back onto her nightstand, leaping out of bed, and sprinting down the hall as fast as her queasy stomach would let her.

The shower could still be heard through the open door of the master bathroom, and Lisa did not want Bobby to see her. In their four-bedroom house, the regularly unused guest bath provided her with privacy and relief. She had felt a little nauseous the day before during Sunday school, but Lisa dismissed that wave to the extra glass of Chardonnay she had had the night before. But there was that possibility that maybe, finally, the day she and Bobby had been having so much fun working toward had finally arrived.

Lisa, nevertheless, tried to understand why morning sickness had to exist as she knelt before the guest toilet. Her sudden heaves jarred her out of the joyous thoughts of what the disorder signified. Still, she was grateful she hadn't put on her face yet and wouldn't need to retouch her lip liner.

She also thought it was right to protect Bobby from any false hope. A quick stop at the Walgreens on Highway 78 would provide her with a test kit she could use at the office. After another heave, she began to plan for a day that would start late.

Bobby knocked on the guest bath door, which Lisa had managed to get shut in between abdominal constrictions.

"Lisa?" spoke the rich but often reserved voice.

"Yeah! Yes!" Lisa reached up to make sure the door was locked. "I'll be out—"

"I've got to get out to the site early," said Bobby through the door, unhearing what his wife of more than eleven years may have been trying to say, let alone offer as cover. "Sorry. Roger woke me up with a text. It has to be a Starbucks morning for me."

The couple usually started their day together with coffee and bagels at the kitchen table. It was a somewhat strict routine that the busy pair had set up for themselves, as the pastors at Southfork Church had insisted upon "couple time" or "C2" as a relationship preservative.

Lisa quickly excused the change in schedule as she felt another surge of sickness come on. "That's okay! Be careful—"

"I'll call you later. Love you!"

"Love you—," said Lisa, just holding a heave long enough to guess Bobby was out of earshot. Back onto the porcelain altar she went. Relief followed that most horrid of sick motions. She hoped that the post-vomit serenity was a foreshadowing of what would follow the contractions—endorphins or whatever—a wash of ease that made the pain of childbirth bearable. She had a weird feeling that maybe this was the definition of grace. But it smelt so bad.

Within a few minutes, she got her legs back and was opening

the door. What to wear? Ten o'clock was the only face-to-face meeting she had for the day, and that wasn't too formal. She had to look good for that one, but of course, she couldn't look too good. It was still business. She was also a mother now, too, if only in theory. She thought about her black dress with the white-trimmed collar—a flatterer but formal and obscuring. And some new Blahnik pumps would be the perfect accent.

She suddenly reversed her path to the master bedroom—it was too far!—and banged the guest bath door back open as she collapsed with Olympic skill onto the toilet a final time.

The northeastern corner of Dallas County had become a kind of final frontier of suburban America. If one were to think of a suburb in the classic sense as an outlying bedroom community without industry or a major commercial center, the borderless communities of Rowlett, North Garland, and Sachse fit the description. Although a new mall now sprawled along the on and off ramps of the President George Bush Turnpike, even that outdoor retail district had been designed to resemble the small, storefront downtowns that once dotted North Texas.

Filling the prairie along the Turnpike were the old and new tract subdivisions which were a staple of Metroplex living. The Jeffus home was a member of just such a patch of the dream, though more upscale than others. Bobby and Lisa's 3,200 square feet of all-brick gables sat nestled off Highway 78 behind a barrier of assorted hardwoods. The style of the home was completely identical to its neighbors, but considering that the small neighborhood had been carved out of an abandoned, overgrown cow pasture, Lisa believed that their enclave epitomized a core view of hers that wealth and property are the ultimate agents of renewal. They had a Sachse address, and a map would only barely keep them out of Dallas County's hyper affluent neighbor to the north, Collin County.

Bobby Jeffus had crossed over from engineering into management of a recently relocated construction firm. He was a self-made man, having done aluminum-frame construction while working his way through U.T. For Lisa, he was her working man. She had been attracted to him every bit as much for his rugged individualism as his class origins. While she had been given everything, Bobby presented to Lisa the chance to share her life with someone more modest. She quietly admitted to, then overcame, an early desire in their relationship to control her "manservant"—obviously, it was in her nature to be in control—but it only took one incisive complaint by Bobby within the first five months of dating to convict Lisa of her attitude. As unassuming and practical as he was, Bobby was always very prescient in his speech. He seemed to truly understand Lisa, and that was why she loved him.

And Lisa made herself a compliment to Bobby. Known professionally for her ebullience and energy, Lisa was the one who pushed him through the door when he was offered the job in management. For all of his hard rationality, Bobby found in his wife an intelligent risk-taker. Lisa successfully navigated a world that few Americans knew about—let alone understood—in terms of its impact on their daily lives. By starting her own political fundraising firm, Lisa staked a claim in an ever deepening mine that served as the mother lode for modern democracy. Lisa had become part CFO, part vivacious hostess to a growing list of the country's VIPs.

And Bobby's humble persona contributed to Lisa's success by keeping his socialite grounded, when Lisa's ambitions seemed to plan too heavily on a given connection rather than the hard work or required details. Lisa never sought political counsel from him explicitly, but Bobby always had a way of ferreting out from her whether she had actually done her homework before making a decision.

They also looked good standing next to each other. At age thirty-three and standing almost six foot two inches tall, Bobby was far from overweight, but he was beefy. Lisa had never really gained that much weight since college, yet she was full-bodied to begin with. Her height just under five foot nine gave those around her a sense of deference when she walked into a room. She'd styled her thick, reddish-brunette hair shorter since she and Bobby were in school—a kind of natural career hairdo progression—but otherwise, she looked the same whether her last name was Jeffus or Dillon. She and Bobby were both a little too fair to tan, but Lisa's complexion was the envy of her girlfriends.

Lisa was strangely self-conscious about her penetrating, light blue eyes, thinking people might see them and not take her seriously. She got an idea somewhere that light eyes made a woman seem like an airhead, same as being a blonde. She was inseparable from her sunglasses as a result, at times not removing them until she was well inside. Sunglasses were also an indulgence for her. Even before she could afford them out of her own pocket, she never wore a pair that cost less than two hundred dollars.

She only grabbed her wallet and BlackBerry from her purse before entering the drug store. She decided to buy the most expensive pregnancy test kit Walgreens had. The Latina checkout lady smiled as Lisa handed her a twenty-dollar bill. Back outside, she climbed back into her black Tahoe and tossed her essentials back into her purse next to her ubiquitous prayer journal. She cut across the parking lot to a new Starbucks drive-thru, a place where Bobby had probably been less than an hour or so earlier. A funny feeling came over her again, but it wasn't nausea.

Dear God,

Please protect my husband today. In Jesus' name, amen.

She stuttered through traffic down Highway 78 and made a right onto Buckingham. The broad, six-lane street was still quite wet from the sustained spring rains—welcome relief from almost two years of an especially Texan drought. It was a little more direct to stay on 78, but she hated navigating downtown Garland, and the stretch of Highway 66 to Skillman was a kind of bleak industrial zone that dispirited her. Instead, she cut across and skirted the Richardson border then made a final turn onto Audelia south, which fed into Skillman and put her less than ten minutes from the office without any more congestion.

"Is this Cara?" asked Lisa into her phone. Today was the first day for summer interns at the Mockingbird Group, Lisa's firm.

"Yes ma'am," replied the young voice.

"Hey, we are so, so happy you are on the team with us this summer. I really enjoyed talking with you and know we're going to have some fun."

The voice on the other end was excited but a little muffled with intimidation.

"I need you to do me a favor really quick, though."

"Yes, ma'am?"

"Can you simply go around to each person who's there and tell them I'm running late, but that I'll be there really soon? Thanks."

"I'll do it right now, Mrs. Jeffus."

"Please, call me Lisa. I'll be there in a few minutes." Lisa hung up. By now, she was making her way onto Skillman. She couldn't quite escape low-income untidiness along her commute, however, as her office was on the third floor of the Commerce Bank building in North Dallas's Vickery Meadow, a neighborhood in transition. Once the retail nexus of middle-income Dallasites, who lived too far from the Park Cities, Vickery Meadow saw seedy elements overshadow it in the late 1980s in the form of bars, liquor stores, and strip clubs. A haven right before then for Boomer Yuppies with stylish apartments, the Meadow became an immigrant enclave for multiple nationalities once those young professionals got married and moved out to the suburbs.

Lisa rented a two thousand square foot office suite just down the hall from her old boss, a U.S. Congressman. It wasn't all mace-at-the-ready, though. A handful of dumpy bars still lingered, but many liquor stores had either been closed or remodeled along with other retail units. And because of the population density and percentage of children, the city had driven off or was grandfathering out the strip clubs. Still, the owner and founder of the Mockingbird Group hoped one day soon to have four thousand square feet downtown along tony McKinney Avenue, maybe in one of the hot new sky-scrapers her husband was helping to build.

"Good morning," greeted Cara Lawson, the attractive if overly thin SMU intern Lisa had called earlier.

After giving the obliging look at her grandfather's portrait across from the reception desk, Lisa returned Cara's greeting.

"Good morning, Cara."

She knew she needed to be every bit the charismatic general to her junior staff. "Thanks for helping me out. Did you get in okay this morning?"

"Yes, ma'am. Mr..." Cara blurted out in laughter at not being able to remember names. "I'm sorry; the man with blond hair was here already."

"You mean Nate? Oh yes, he's our early bird." Lisa then leaned onto Cara's desk. "I think his hair's more gray than blond, though," she half-whispered, continuing her way in.

"I heard that!" shouted a voice from an office door before Lisa's in the corner. Nate Knight stepped into the central area of the suite while closing a small, metal binder on some papers. It was true that his hair was now significantly grayer than blond, but that belied a very youngish face. He thrust the ream of warm sheets into Lisa's hand as she passed by.

"Clips for the queen bee."

"I told you that we are only to use aviary metaphors around here," commanded Lisa as she switched on the fluorescent lighting of her office. "We are the Mockingbird Group for a reason.

"How do you like my shoes?" she asked rhetorically.

"Isn't that the national bird?" asked Cara, who had gravitated over to the conversation, not sure if she had been dismissed.

Nate snorted, lingering in Lisa's doorway.

"Of Texas, yes," responded Lisa with a smile. Cara returned sheepishly to her desk.

Nate seated himself across from Lisa's desk, Mountain Dew in one hand. "You know," he said, "I still think that Mockingbird has too much mock in it, especially for our business."

"Submit your bill for name change to the committee," quipped Lisa, in one motion setting her BlackBerry onto her desk, tossing her now empty Starbucks cup into the wastebasket, and immediately flipping through the news clips Nate just handed her. She sat down in her burgundy-leather desk chair.

"Looks like Brookshire has indeed drawn an opponent," Nate stated. Lisa was already turning past the copy of the online article from the Tyler Democrat. She continued flipping without looking up.

"That is in fact what my ten o'clock meeting is about."

"Again," grumbled Nate, "your openness and inability to keep secrets overwhelms me. You mean you already knew?"

Lisa smugly smiled at her trusted media expert.

"How?" added Nate with growing frustration.

"Danny Geister," she said.

"He's handling that race?" Nate blurted.

"It is more accurate to say he's been assigned," responded Lisa. "He emailed me Saturday night, before this story ran."

Nate held his tongue for a bit. "Are you sure it's okay to do business with him?"

Lisa raised her eyebrows. "What do you mean? His candidate is doing business with us."

"No," said Nate, "I mean, you know, his reputation?"

"Go back to your office and get to work," chided Lisa, half joking and half irritated.

As Nate was leaving, Lisa checked her desk clock to see that she did end up being almost twenty minutes late. It occurred to her that she hadn't yet seen the rest of the staff this Monday, but her thoughts quickly turned to stepping down the hall and using the pregnancy test kit she had smuggled into her own place of business. She had one VIP to call. She figured she had just enough time before Danny got there. She looked up a number stored in her BlackBerry but picked up her office line to make her call.

"Hi George, this is Lisa. It was good to see you yesterday." Lisa's tone was brisk and every bit as business as her potential contributor.

"Thank you for getting back with me," responded George Masters, a congenial man with a light North Texas accent. Implied in Masters's gratitude was the middle-aged businessman's discomfort with discussing political business in the hallway of Southfork Church, let alone right after Sunday school. "I wanted to make sure I had not maxed out with Paul, but I had something else I wanted to mention to him," Masters explained, heading Lisa off from her mechanical "ask."

"Sure thing," said Lisa.

"We got wind that the House was going to cut the post-op reimbursement under Medicare. I wanted to make sure Paul knew that, so I'm telling you, as well as his DC people."

"I'll definitely make sure he knows," said Lisa, though the most she would or could do was note the issue in her monthly report to Paul on donations. She already visualized herself writing "Medicare provider cuts" on her spreadsheet.

She added an indulgent, "The Speaker just hates those who do the actual health care, doesn't she?"

"Well, I don't know how she expects to—" began Masters on his tirade. This was when Lisa earned her money. She had a headset she normally used when a call went this direction, but her desire to get this one call done so that she could get to the restroom prevented her from setting up her elaborate multitasking technology. She never used the speakerphone, which signaled remote indifference to the other party.

"—and so I'm just alerting Paul to the problem. I know it's tough when we're not in the majority."

"I will sure tell him. Every bit we can do to help moves us toward the day when we are again, though," Lisa "asked" without missing a beat.

"Well I'm going to send another five hundred dollars, which is what I wanted to tell also. I'm still under $2,300, right?"

"You're still in good shape," said Lisa. She had already checked Masters's gifts-to-date on her spreadsheet at home after returning from church the previous afternoon. "You're a true friend, George. I know Paul really, really appreciates it."

"Okay. Thanks," said Masters, abruptly hanging up.

Almost as quickly, Lisa was out the door.

CHAPTER TWO

Dear God,

Let there be a plus sign.

Lisa had her prayer answered. Sure, a blood test awaited, but wholeness filled her heart.

She realized she had been sitting on the toilet of her office building's women's room for almost ten minutes when her schedule came back to mind. But she felt so full, so sure, so hopeful, that it wouldn't have mattered what happened during the rest of the day, even if, God help her, she took the afternoon off. Still, the confidence she felt made her want to spread the news like a good, old-fashioned Baptist preacher. The sweetness of what had happened even seemed to overcome—to compliment—the distant bitterness of losing Mom those years ago.

Lisa returned to her desk with five minutes to spare before her ten o'clock. Before sitting down, she walked over to the shadow-box containing the pink baseball bat that the Texas Rangers owner had given her just last year in honor of her mom. Lisa never forgot the owner's kindness, even after all the phone calls she personally had made to him for a check on behalf of no less than five candidates. The bat had come to symbolize both Mom and success. Lisa wondered if such a symbol were something to be grasped in this life—a grip on grace itself. The hope for a child had been so deep for her and Bobby that the gender was a nonissue, but the slight desire for a boy to one day hold a bat like the one hanging on her office wall stirred Lisa's heart even more.

"Your ten o'clock is here, ma'am." Cara's focused if amateur voice broke Lisa's daydreaming. She turned to see Nate crowding the doorway next to Cara.

"Sure. Just a second, I'll be out," Lisa answered.

Cara immediately returned to the reception area. Nate lingered, trying to get into his boss's business. "You're not going to sit in. I'll shut the door if I have to," said Lisa.

Nate slinked back into his space.

Lisa had normally booted up her computer by now but felt okay that it was still off due to her tardiness. No morning clutter of email and browsing had kept her mind as clear as possible, given the circumstances. Right now, she needed her game face.

She took a deep breath and took comfort in the miracle growing in her womb. Whatever concerns there had been about her mate's virility had been in all likelihood erased just a few minutes ago. She got up from her desk to make her way to the reception area. There was now good reason to separate the pheromones of her ten o'clock from the natural desire to breed and all that goes with it.

"Hi, Danny," Lisa greeted.

He rose up from one of the reception chairs beneath her grandfather's portrait. A stylish khaki suit covered a blood-maroon shirt and broad chest, but the ensemble had a yesterday, almost tired look to it. The suit was wrinkled. In fact, the only real flamboyance was the pair of rattlesnake Tony Lamas that served as the pedestal for Danny's six feet four inches and fetching mane of black hair. He kept his hair cut at the crew level, like a good Republican, but it was so dense that it could not quite escape an inherent waviness. All of that man collided with her newfound grip on childbearing and forced Lisa to cut her eyes sharply away from his—orbs that were as black as primeval Texas crude.

"Momma's gonna buy you a mockingbird," Danny rapped. His voice was weary but had the sublime and dreamy breeziness found only in the tops of East Texas pines.

Keeping it business, Lisa cursorily escorted Danny back into her office. She deftly avoided a fleshy handshake, let alone hug, by playing the encounter casually, as if her old friend had just arrived at her dorm room and they were about to cram for a Lit final. His hands were just too enveloping, and Danny had this habit of offering women he knew his left, which only added to the confusion he blithely cultivated among the opposite sex. As the pair walked through the office suite, Lisa pointed out coffee that was available, still trying to keep the meeting cool.

"No, ma'am. I'm good," said Danny in response to the offer.

Lisa did get a conlike sense at Danny's use of "ma'am."

"Sit down," she said, now back in her office.

She happily noticed that Nate was distracted with his phone as they passed by his doorframe. She smiled at her appointment, but another shot of nausea detached her from her emotions at being in the same space with Danny. She had a moment of wavering confidence, feeling that the slightest touch of sweat may be at her hairline.

"Sorry I didn't shake your hand, Lise," said Danny. "Nails are dirty after changing my brake pads this weekend." So much for thinking she was in control of the meeting.

"Jack-of-all-trades, no matter how old we get," Lisa responded.

"Old is right. I had the worst time gettin' up off my driveway this time. I guess I need Geritol."

Lisa laughed. Danny's humor was as laconic as ever, but his sad, sad eyes—which she dared to look into now that there was a desk between them—made his self-deprecation a little depressing. She felt less intimidated the more she risked studying Danny's face. It was still perfect with its crisp, clean-shaven jaw line and risen nose, but maybe the years and all of his hardships were finally pulling his cheeks down, just below his eyes. His brow also seemed strangely battered. A girl could avoid being fooled by that massively thick black hair, which had not moved one centimeter up that forehead since graduation, because its waviness suggested vanity. Still, one had to be careful about those black eyes—

An unknown number illuminated itself on Lisa's BlackBerry as the gizmo vibrated across her desk.

Danny gave a half-smile. "I just got one of those. I wanted one with a camera."

Fumbling nervously, Lisa hit the ignore button. The embarrassed rush of blood to her head cured Lisa of any more possible nausea.

"How's your dad?" she asked, even though she had only met him once during an A&M versus Texas football game years ago. After a few seconds, the BlackBerry vibrated again to indicate a voicemail had been left.

"He's okay. He has his airplanes." Danny suddenly spoke with a mood that matched his downcast brow.

"And what about, Angelina's her name, right?"

"That's right." Suddenly, Danny's mood became very dark, such that it gave Lisa a shudder. She unexpectedly got the chills. Not wanting to be superstitious, she credited it to the maternal changes, which were no doubt underway within her body.

After a second, Danny strangely seemed okay. He continued talking about his eleven-year-old daughter by saying, "She insists on using her full name, in fact, telling me 'Angie' was no longer acceptable now that she's finishing up the fifth grade. Hopefully, she won't join up with the UN."

"I can't believe how long it's been."

The foreboding pall suddenly rushed back over Danny's countenance. He answered, "It hasn't been long enough."

"But you don't want to hear me sing the blues," he said, the cloud instantly lifting again mysteriously. It was like a switch had been thrown, and now Danny was all business. Lisa was a little perplexed but was eager to get to work.

Danny pulled a CD from his outer suit pocket and set it on Lisa's desk. "This is Brookshire's existing donor list in Excel format.

I'll have a copy of his briefing book to you in a couple weeks. We've got some anti-business votes the opponent made while he was on the Tyler City Council, so that should get you started."

"You've wasted no time," said Lisa. "It's only been a day, since the guy announced."

"He knows he's in trouble. I don't think he's going to win."

"Who? The senator?" Lisa was taken aback by Danny's pronounced lack of confidence in his incumbent candidate, Ben Brookshire.

This was the only consultant in the entire country she knew who had a perfect winning record. Granted, he had less than a dozen races under his belt, but he only ever took on two per cycle. Lisa knew the governor, as well as the Washington people, played their game of divvying up the races among the consultant mafia, and Danny was only sent to the trouble spots; but she also guessed that her widower friend preferred to limit his clients so as to best care for his daughter.

"Yeah. You know I'm not superstitious, but if I had the gift of prophecy, I'd say I'm looking at a mark in the L-column for the first time.

"I don't really care, though. Brookshire's a scumbag."

"Wow," responded Lisa.

"He is. Cheater, philanderer. And this prostitute he married is just awful—controlling, with a new, idiot brother-in-law who's really a Democrat. He had a worthless session this past spring too.

"But both the Mansion and the Lieutenant Governor are pulling out all the stops for him. God bless incumbency."

Lisa had seen and heard this negative spirit come out of Danny before, and she hated it. The attitude made a strong man appear weak. "Tell the governor you're not going to do it."

"I need the money. Which is why you're the fundraiser for the guy. I'm for darn certain going to make sure I get paid." One thing about Danny, he never cursed beyond those words permitted by his youth pastor. Lisa smiled but wanted to talk for a second about something happier. Yet of course, it wouldn't have been right to bring up her pregnancy without telling Bobby first.

"I guess doing general consulting for a state senator in deep East Texas gives you an excuse to fly," she offered, knowing Danny's love for the skies.

"I had to sell my plane."

Lisa now felt worse. The only other way the conversation could go would be a gripe session about the state of the party, and she couldn't decide what she disliked more: negative conversation generally or hearing a once-proud, confident, and happy friend complain about life.

"How's Bobby?" Danny asked.

"He's well," answered Lisa, surprised. "He's getting to be a director for the first time on that new phase of the Court Plaza down in Uptown."

"Cool. A good man," said Danny, who truly admired Bobby, and Lisa knew it.

For all the infatuation she may have had for him, Lisa never really thought Danny felt that physically attracted to her. So compliments from him about her husband she always took as genuine, not polite jealousy.

"I'd love to office down there—even live," she said.

"Not the best place for little kids, though, when that day comes," said Danny as a smile returned to lighten his demeanor.

Lisa felt that hopeful glow return.

"Unless all that new construction down there has run off all the queers," said Danny.

Lisa always forgot that conversations with him could have a rollercoaster effect. She never approved of the lifestyles of her gay relatives, and she hated the tactics of the homosexual lobby, but she still disliked bigoted talk. The disapproval of such speech was part of her natural political instincts.

"Do you know the moment I knew we Republicans would be net losers in our republic—in the long term?" said Danny, unexpectedly eager to pontificate.

"No" said Lisa, feeling she had to be tolerant.

"It was 1992, but it wasn't Clinton's victory that year. Forty-one had come to town after the convention, and our church up in Yale canceled evening service so that we could all go hear him speak.

"I'll never forget it. We walked into the Convention Center from the cemetery side—you know, where they filmed the riot scene of the vets in *Born on the Fourth of July?* Anyway, there was this eerie stillness. There were mounted cops off to the side, and at the doors, these yokels were handing out little pamphlets to those attending the speech. There was a sense that these two groups were expecting some kind of altercation.

"I took a pamphlet and went on in to hear the speech, which was a rehash of the one the president had just given in Houston at the infamous hatefest. I was nineteen—I guess—that was between our freshman and sophomore years.

"I started reading the pamphlet, which was a cheap-looking, wild, and lurid torrent of anti-gay messaging headlined by The Family Defenders or The Families United Group or some such. The paper had some typical stuff about AIDS being God's judgment, etc., but then it went into creepy detail about homosexual behavior, such as fisting and a bunch of other crap."

"Danny!" exclaimed Lisa.

"I have a point, just hang on. At any rate, the speech ended, and all of these big-time Dallas pastors were there. Falwell was there, too, and he begged everyone for contributions to cover the event while at the same time shouting, 'Don't vote your pocketbook, vote your values!' Remember, this was Clinton's first race when Carville was frightening everybody about their jobs.

"But as we left, exiting back out the doors by the cemetery, there were all of these chalk-drawn body outlines on the concrete, like a mass-murder crime scene. Names were written inside each one. What had happened was that during the speech, local AIDS activists had come and set up a very creative protest of 41's funding policies. They waited until the cops, the rednecks were gone, and then en masse quickly drew the body outlines. The names gave them a personal touch. The only signage they left behind was something like, "How many more, Mr. President?" also written in chalk on the sidewalk.

"It occurred to me at that moment that we conservatives may win some battles, but we would lose the war, because we just weren't skilled in the pagan arts. In fact, our reliance on the written word is a fatal flaw. We are like the Pilgrims—people of the Book—who believe reason and persuasion will carry the day like evangelism itself, but when it doesn't, the darkness gets us, and the best we can do is print gross words about our enemies. Liberals, on the other hand, are better at creating an emotional impact using symbols and art. That's one of the reasons why they are naturally allied with visual media like film and TV.

"Don't get me wrong, I wasn't moved by the gays' drawings, but as a whole, I was far more disturbed by those disgusting pamphlets than I was annoyed by a bunch of chalk art. Add to that a more and more apathetic electorate, and all they have to do to us is define us as haters and they win."

Lisa became more concerned about Danny's negativity. He seemed really worse for the wear. She tried to weaken his attitude by flippantly saying, "Sounds like you're letting your work get to you—"

"Lisa—" Nate interrupted, clearly upset, "I'm sorry, but you need to pick up line two right now."

Lisa could sense the panic and picked up her phone.

"Lisa Jeffus." She picked up her BlackBerry and noticed the number that had just come in matched the one currently displayed on her caller ID. After a moment, she broke into tears.

"What's wrong?" Danny demanded.

"That's Bobby's boss ... he's been in an accident of some kind."

CHAPTER THREE

Dear God,

I don't know if I'll remember making this prayer. But I want to record what looks like a long period of dependence on you. I love you, and I know you love me. I am depending on you utterly.

In Jesus' name.

Lisa had been here before. In fact, there was a dull ordinariness, a routine in driving to some famous medical facility, hiking across a hospital parking lot, sliding through the black, metal-framed doors, snaking through a clinical maze to find where you needed to be, and waiting hours on the one guy you needed to talk to even though you had sped to get there.

The familiarity owed to the experience she'd had with her mother. As Lisa and Nate fought through the stoplights on Northwest Highway to Central, then pushed eighty miles per hour south around downtown and back up Stemmons to Parkland Hospital, only the location and sense of emergency were different this time. Danny had even been around back when her mother called her in Washington to inform her of the pending tests. But whereas everyone had gathered at Lisa's rented row house on the Hill, Danny alone now followed in his older model Durango at a matching speed.

Lisa's mind raced about the traumatic nature of what appeared to have occurred to Bobby. She immediately conjured up what she thought of as a worst-case scenario: skull fragments splattered on some slab in Uptown. Cathartically, she backed off of that image by virtue of the fact that Roger, Bobby's boss, stated on the phone earlier that they were about to CT her husband. That obviously meant that there was something to CAT Scan and, obviously, that Bobby was alive.

Dear God,

Please help Bobby to wake up soon, if he is in a coma.

Lisa realized the idea of coma was something with which she was completely unfamiliar.

As she waited roughly two hours in the lounge outside radiology, Lisa found that she didn't mind the rush of family, staff persons, friends, and phone calls bombarding her with the need to know. She remembered how being a hospital drama switchboard passed the time. She knew that initial news about someone's health created that rare moment when people actually listened to you.

Danny didn't hang around for long. Ghostlike, he left. Although some thirty minutes passed, Lisa did notice Danny's absence but knew fully why he dismissed himself. Soon, her BFF would come strolling down the linoleum-lined hallway—someone who simply would not occupy the same space as Danny, which he knew.

Andrea Johnson—a.k.a. "A.J. "—contradicted the tough, partisan mentality most assumed Lisa had, not because A.J. was from the other side, because she was African-American, or because she had an opinionated personality, but because she and Lisa were very intimate friends—the extra-special kind that share their deepest secrets. The openness and vulnerability required for such a relationship were anomalous traits underneath Lisa's exuberant, ultra self-reliant surface.

A.J. and Lisa's closeness went way, way back to their days at University of Texas. For all her big government liberalism, A.J. was deeply prolife, owing to a strict Baptist upbringing. Even though they were both from the Metroplex, the pair met as the first protestors on the beachhead outside the campus clinic when the University of Texas had been selected as a trial site for free distribution of Norplant among the student body. Soon they were joined by campus Right to Life—led by Danny. But A.J. was the real deal. Not only did she care deeply for an unborn baby, but her devotion to God provided a surging morality against the seawall of modern feminism's Gibraltar issue—abortion. A.J. protested Norplant's absolution of personal purity and responsibility more than any side effects it may have had on women's health.

And while Lisa was inspired by Danny's handsome zealotry in those days—he actually got arrested at the Norplant protest—it was A.J.'s morality on life issues that kept Lisa in the pro-life camp. Lisa Dillon, the Republican princess, was no fool when it came to recognizing the pragmatic need of keeping her pro-life credentials immaculate for the future. But the Lisa Dillon who was president of the University of Texas College Republicans was more inclined to put up a Libertarian justification for tolerating a woman's right over her own body. A.J. buttressed the moral angle for Lisa on the grounds of personal responsibility. Sure, A.J. had a touch of Malcolm X-style self-determination in her definition of such a popular conservative concept, but she also never apologized for how she saw things through her faith.

A.J.'s very arrival in the Parkland ER waiting room signaled that an unwavering morality had just entered the universe. The sliding-glass doors seemed to open out of fear. Oblivious to the Latina mother and her restless children already seated at the window, A.J. demanded to know the location of Robert Jeffus, and the pitiful clerk bounced back from her window and onto her computer screen to check for the name. Stunned at the five foot ten Executive Director of the Dallas County Democratic Party standing before her, the clerk trepidly reported Bobby's location and gave A.J. directions to the radiology department.

Her gold bracelets lightly striking each other, A.J. stepped into the radiology waiting room. Lisa and Nate had been joined by Bobby's silent father, Ron. Much to Lisa's relief, her mother-in-law, Brenda, had not yet arrived. Mercifully, Brenda had been visiting her sister several hours away in Corpus Christi. Lisa, Nate, and Ron organized themselves around A.J., but in an instant, she and Lisa embraced.

"He's alive still, right?" asked A.J. She and Lisa had talked about an hour earlier via cell.

"He should be done with the CT scan by now."

"Surgery?"

"I don't know. I have only talked to one real doctor, and that was when I got the first call. The nurse—or whatever he is—has only told me of the CT process here."

"Are you sure he wasn't the radiologist?"

"Yes, you're right!" Only when A.J. had arrived did Lisa crack open the curtain on her fear and uncertainty, as evidenced by her not knowing with whom she'd consulted.

"Hi, Nate," said A.J. quietly.

"Hi."

"Is that Mr. Jeffus?" asked A.J.

"Yes. Brenda's not here," said Lisa.

A.J. gave Lisa a knowing look and then introduced herself to Ron. "You gotten in touch with Bailiff?" she asked Lisa.

"I left a message for him on his cell."

"They're supposed to have votes late tonight," said A.J. Dallas's up-and-coming Democrat powerbroker felt it was okay to divulge information acquired exclusively through her capitol connections. A.J. had surprised many by leaving a plumb post as chief-of-staff to Dallas's lone Democratic congresswoman after the 2006 elections. Although the D's restored majority status in Congress presented a ton of opportunity, there was still an R at the other end of Pennsylvania Avenue, which limited her party's ability to get things done.

But more than that, A.J. had grown tired of DC. The place just hadn't been the same since Lisa and Bobby had left four years earlier.

There were cells, BlackBerrys, texting, and IMing, but she wanted to be home with her friend—her sister. Also, A.J. was wanting to settle down with a good Southern man. She found the DC singles scene self-serving and frustrating. There was an FBI agent she'd dated up in DC, but it didn't last long.

Once back home in Dallas, sure enough, the determined and particular woman found a sweet complement. Curtiss Small was a bachelor minister the same age as A.J., always even-tempered and respectful of his future bride's calling in life. He was as devoted to God as he was with his job as an associate pastor at a gigantic South Dallas mega church. Curtiss and A.J. had been dating for three chaste months.

Lisa was grateful that the mama-bear of her life might actually one day have a home to give and receive love for herself. "How's the Reverend?" she asked.

"He's good," said A.J., smiling. "I told him to come up here when he got the chance. When can you get in to see Bobby?"

Just then, the radiologist reappeared. "Mrs. Jeffus?"

"Yes?"

"I'm afraid it's going to be a while yet. I've talked with the neurosurgeon, and they are still stabilizing your husband. Why don't you sit down, and I'll explain to you what I know. The neurosurgeon will be out shortly."

Lisa got that hollow feeling she had the first few days after her mother died. She felt the blood rush out of her face. A.J. grabbed her as the pair partly sat, partly fell onto some chairs.

A.J. cried.

"Mrs. Jeffus, there are a bunch of complicated terms to describe head injuries and what is happening inside the brain after the kind of trauma experienced by your husband," began the radiologist.

Chapter Four

May 14, Midnight

Dear God,

I hurt and feel empty. Please wake up Bobby.

"Tell me what to do, and I will do it for you," boomed Paul Bailiff, U.S. Representative from the thirty-third district of Texas. Besides not lowering the volume of his voice in the Parkland neural ICU waiting room, Bailiff didn't break stride as he walked in and seated himself next to Lisa, taking her hands in his. He had finally landed at DFW at 11:00 p.m., after having gotten on the first plane he could get out of Reagan National as soon as votes were over. Lisa set her pen down and closed her notebook.

"Thank you for coming." She cried, still amazed that she continued to have tears to shed. Lisa had been alone in the ICU wing now since about 10:00 p.m. She had sent Nate home to his family, and her other staff had come over after hours, bringing in some Whataburger for supper. Brenda, Bobby's mother, had finally arrived but became almost catatonic with the uncertainty about her son's condition. This was yet another act of mercy by God directly, Lisa believed, and Ron was able to handle her until they left. Lisa had told Bobby's parents, who lived a good forty-five minutes from the hospital up in Collin County, that she would take what appeared to be the first watch of many during the coming nights.

Curtiss had indeed arrived later in the evening from his church off Interstate 20 in the south. The large and calming pastor knew exactly how to comfort his friends, and the group prayed for more than an hour together. He and A.J. left, only after Lisa ordered them to do so, around nine.

Lisa also couldn't stand it to have her dearest friend there and to be unable to control the burning desire to tell her about the pregnancy. Besides there being too many people around, she just couldn't do it without telling Bobby first. Above all, she wanted a moment to pray alone. She felt like her pregnancy was a true gift from God, and its accompanying hope provided her with a surge of spiritual energy, which she believed strengthened her to commit any crisis to the Lord at the beginning, as opposed to cowering guiltily upon her knees when things had gotten really bad and one is shamefully at the end of her rope. She knew God would see her through, just as he had comforted her miraculously in the absence of her mother. The sense of his fidelity at this moment was unquestionable.

"I told Lucy to get the guest room ready. You know, we're less than twenty minutes from here," said Bailiff to his former executive assistant in reference to the location of his house near White Rock Lake. Lisa smiled, because her old boss's sincerity was meshed with an obtuse pride he held that he could get anywhere in Dallas from his house in twenty minutes. Even the times this tenet of Bailiff's resulted in a speeding ticket, the congressman would capitalize on the pullover by praising the officer or trooper for his or her professionalism.

He still could not modulate his voice for the hushed space. Bailiff was one of those guys whose every utterance was as if standing next to Cato in the Senate. Moreover, with the drawling baritone one couldn't help but sense that Bailiff's dialect wasn't something of a put-on. It seemed like he had adapted a speaking persona that sought to be more Texan than the Texaniest Texan. But the fact that his speech was always the same volume persuaded everyone—both confidants and voters—that he spoke with an honest tongue.

Lisa took comfort in his offer to stay in White Rock, knowing Bailiff would eagerly provide her with a key for as long as she needed it. She also knew that he gave out offers of help like so many wooden nickels. He so badly wanted to be liked and loved by all. Yet while it gave his DC staff—not to mention his campaign machine—headaches twice over, he always followed through. Such actions made Bailiff come across as insecure, but the fact that he always did what he said pushed his reelection percentages north every term in what had been a swing district when he captured it from a Democrat in '94.

"What did the doctor say?" asked Bailiff.

"Massive head injury," Lisa answered. "The frontal lobes of his brain were impacted. The doctor calls it a cerebral contusion. Other than a shallow abrasion, there was no major bleeding. But he's in a coma."

Bailiff didn't speak. Instead, he released a heavy sigh. He rubbed his eyes.

"I've been taught a new term—an acronym, really," continued Lisa. "GCS, or Glasgow Coma Scale." The doctor said he was going to give me a little chart that reports the different responses a comatose patient can have."

"Was he not wearing a hard hat?"

"Some of the investors had made a surprise inspection, and there weren't enough for everyone. Bobby donated his, thinking he could stay on the ground and field any questions using the walkie-talkie. But his boss called him inside the ground floor for just a second. It was at that second that the steel joist slipped."

Bailiff winced. "So he could wake up at any moment?"

"Apparently so," responded Lisa with her characteristic confidence. "But the doctor was reserved about whatever quality of life he may have."

"You're always so insightful on others," said Bailiff. And now he did whisper, "You know, these doctors try their best to pull the wool over you. They did that when mother got sick."

Then Bailiff's voice returned to its singular pitch. "We've got to get you some help. Still, though, you need to take off as much time as you possibly can."

"Bobby's company is covering everything, and he had a long-term care policy as part of his benefits. All of that will be a big help. His CEO came by later this afternoon and said that he would personally pay all the deductibles out of his own pocket and that the coverage would never expire."

"Roger? I know him," Bailiff said. "He's a good man."

"He seemed very upset. He said he had gotten to know Bobby quite a bit, since he became a manager."

Bailiff and Lisa sat for a few moments quietly.

"Paul," Lisa finally said. She could not keep it in any longer. "I'm pregnant." To her surprise, she felt release instead of more sorrow.

Bailiff simply sat and listened.

"This is so weird. Timing-wise, I mean."

"What did your in-laws say?"

"I haven't told them."

"I'm a little surprised you told your congressman first."

Lisa laughed loudly, using it to escape the pain and anxiety.

"You know I've always thought of you as a daughter," said Bailiff. "I know that sounds a little stale. I also know that I have behaved as a demanding, fussy father many times too. It's a product of my disorganized ambition."

"You once told me I was hired simply because I brought a pen to the interview," said Lisa.

"That's true," confirmed Bailiff. "It signaled to me that you were ready to work, not to mention thoughtful and potentially organized, which as you know is what I have always needed."

"I always believed the real truth was because of who I was related to," Lisa said, tongue-in-cheek.

"Oh yeah, that, too. Your grandfather in heaven, I know, is so proud of you, Lisa. Your mother is also, so much, I know. I don't think I've ever told you this, but your grandfather made me pull over, before I ever drove him one mile. I'll never forget it. Senator Tower and another big donor were with us at an event up in Denton. I had been on your grandfather's campaign for one day. But they all got in that gold '75 Chrysler…"

"I remember that car!" Lisa recalled. "I was only four when he ran for governor, but Granddaddy let me stand up in the front seat. Wow. That huge dash. How unsafe!"

"I was still a UNT student then and had been asked to drive in a pinch, because the senator was coming to town. But we weren't more than a hundred feet down the road when your grandfather made me pull over and tell everyone in the car who I was and what I thought he had to do to win the race. I was twenty years old."

"You've never told me that story," Lisa said. "What did Tower say?"

"You know I don't remember. He likely didn't say anything."

"What did you say?"

"I told him he had to be a Republican." Bailiff paused to recollect the nostalgic moment of his youthful activism. "I told him if he didn't show folks that there was any difference between him and all those conservative Democrats around back then, that there was no point in running. I'll never forget how he looked at me after I said that. His hair was still so dark at age sixty, and he had those dark, dark eyes that suffered no fool. It was a look that conveyed, 'I'm taking in what you say, because what you say is right.' I would get that same look every time my advice proved to be the right thing to do. I also knew then, parked on the side of that highway, that politics was my thing and that I had to serve one day. God confirmed that to me when he saved me after my own mother died in '84. I had some losing races, but God was faithful and finally put me in office. And I owe it all to how God worked through the first Republican-elected governor of Texas since Reconstruction," Bailiff added with a smile. "Our heavenly Father is faithful. It's not much to ask for us to be, too."

"Don't sit here with me all night. One of the Jeffuses will be here soon," Lisa said.

"You pace yourself. If what the doctor says is right, it will only be a matter of time before Bobby is healed. Gripping onto hope in God is our only option."

"Thanks, Paul."

"You call me," said Bailiff, exiting the waiting room.

CHAPTER FIVE

May 15, 7:00 a.m.

Dear God,

Please help Brenda to have peace about this current trial. I can see the worry on her face. I know she needs your comfort.

In Jesus' name. Amen.

Lisa did not appear to have roused at all as she jotted another prayer in her notebook. She had fallen asleep in one of the extendable chairs instead of leaving when Brenda Jeffus arrived shortly after Bailiff left. Lisa's mother-in-law had procured a blanket and pillow from one of the nurses. Lisa woke up in a groggy nervousness with only her hands moving to open her notebook. The rest of her body remained perfectly still under the polyester blanket as she made her prayer.

Brenda had also tried to make herself comfortable across from Lisa on another of the chairs. In spite of still being asleep, the lines of a mother's worry were rippling across her forehead. Problem was that Brenda's were already semi-permanent. Less than a minute after she had received the call from Parkland, Lisa realized that a challenge equal to Bobby's prognosis would be keeping Brenda from browbeating her and everyone around the patient with incessant, nerve-wracking worry.

Her mother-in-law's general anxiety was, naturally, the one personality trait that reliably set Lisa off. Lisa's prayerful commitment to God that he see her through the new crisis contained as much entreaty that Brenda be kept at bay as it did that Bobby be healed. Lisa knew full well why Brenda's worry was the wall between them. Whereas she was the politician who could stomach risk and uncertainty easily—truly, Lisa thrived on it—her mother-in-law was the nagging nebbish who excelled at holding everyone back. Lisa knew this was why Bobby had fallen in love with her; her Machiavellian side was constantly trying to come up with not-so-subtle ways to rub this knowledge in Brenda's furrowed face.

But the evidence of the blanket across her legs served to weaken the daughter-in-law's conspiratorial spirit. Lisa knew Brenda was kind deep down, but all that anxiety on her skin seemed to dry her out and suck the life from all in close proximity. Still, Lisa poured some coffee for the two of them from a freshly brewed pot on a counter inside the waiting room.

"Thanks for coming back down, Brenda," said Lisa gently, standing over her mother-in-law with the aroma wafting out of the cup in her hand.

Brenda shifted awake. There was this fleeting moment when Brenda appeared soft and easy-going, but then she said, "You were supposed to go back to Sachse," without a shred of tenderness in her tone.

"Good morning," muttered Lisa.

"Is Bobby awake? Did I miss something?"

"No ma'am," Lisa quipped defeatedly.

"Well did the doctor come out? Didn't he say he'd be by again at six? What time is it? I hope we didn't miss him!"

"He hasn't been by yet, Brenda."

"Well, where were you? Downstairs getting coffee?" Brenda took a sip from the cup Lisa had given her even as she decried it. "He could have come and gone, and you not know it. He might have seen me sitting over here asleep and thought I was some homeless person—"

"You're too well-dressed, Bren—"

"And went about his day. You should have stayed here or just gone home like you were supposed to. I can't stand this. You know, that surgeon didn't get as good a look at me last night as he did you. I don't think he knows I belong to Bobby!" Only taking sips of the hot liquid caused Brenda to pause.

Lisa sat down, more or less tuning her out. She became sad. Not because she was now stuck with the most annoying wart of them all, but because it was Bobby's patience and practicality that had enabled her to understand and deal with her mother-in-law.

Would Bobby wake up? But more importantly, would he be himself? Would the man she loved so dearly still have those granite shoulders to lean on? Would she have to be the one to lift those shoulders up every day to clean them so that he didn't get bedsores? Where would she get the strength to be calm, to have the calm that only Bobby seemed to have and was so gentle in sharing?

Would her child grow up at the bedside railing of a motionless father?

She began to get weepy, but Lisa expected no care from Brenda. She knew that Brenda's prattling anxiety was a world unto itself; it was Brenda's own private fantasy zone of controlling the uncontrollable. But Lisa had a realization that while Brenda stood two feet away weaving a sticky web of worry with the sole purpose of catching everyone around her in it, at least she was getting it out of her system. The questions Lisa heard shooting through her mind now while sitting in the waiting room were forming her own matrix of anguish.

Lisa thought briefly that her pregnancy would be her secret from Bobby's parents—

"Mrs. Jeffus?" asked a quick-rhythm voice.

"Yes," answered both women.

"I'm Dr. Asitajee." A tall and crisp man in a white exam coat extended his hand toward Lisa. "The neurosurgeon has referred your husband, Bobby, to our group for care. We're a family group that specializes in neurological disorders. May I sit down? I know you're exhausted."

"Please." Lisa was impressed that this sharp, energetic, and frankly handsome individual dropped Bobby's name with such kind familiarity when all of her husband's records rotely identified him as "Jeffus, Robert T." He also improved his standing by locking on to her instead of Brenda when they both responded to the Mrs. Jeffus inquiry. The doctor's dark brown eyes stirred Lisa with trust and inspiration the same way her grandfather's had.

"I'm Brenda Jeffus. I'm Bobby's mother. I'm very upset. I don't think your partner saw me last night," tapped out Lisa's mother-in-law with the striking skill of the world's greatest pianist playing a staccato measure.

"Yes ma'am. I apologize," said Asitajee without ever losing his focus on Lisa. "We're going to have to watch Bobby here for a few more days. The good news is there are no initial signs of internal bleeding. Otherwise, I think the neurosurgeon explained to you how we must now watch for swelling in the brain?"

"Yes," answered Lisa.

"He's still in a coma, but you'll be able to see him shortly," said Asitajee.

Lisa smiled with some relief.

"My group and I will be overseeing his care over what will be some very challenging weeks, maybe even years."

"Yes," said Lisa, "the surgeon last night was very up front with us." Lisa felt she could express her disquiet over the report of last night now that she was in the presence of someone who conveyed competence and hopefulness.

"What do you know yet about extended care for your husband?" asked Asitajee.

"I know that, or I was told that Bobby had a full policy through his work. And other commitments have been made by his employer."

"That's good to hear. You're fortunate," Asitajee said. "The key to any sort of recovery for someone who's suffered a massive impact on the front lobes is long-term care that is constantly attentive. I'll be honest with you. There's home health, then there's home health.

There are rehab facilities, then there are rehab facilities. I know you feel like the world has crashed down on you, but I mention long-term care to you now so that you can begin to mentally pace yourself for what lies ahead."

"I understand," said Lisa.

"Do you have any children?"

Lisa gulped. She just did not want to say anything yet to Brenda, if only because she was currently a source of irritation. Lisa decided that since she hadn't been to the doctor yet, she answered, "No."

"That's probably a good thing, especially for the immediate time period."

Lisa felt a little queasy again, but it was more from foreboding than any lingering morning sickness.

"Someone who's in a coma is simply asleep," continued Asitajee. "We want them with us, but from their point of view, they're having a really long rest. Same goes for those who are PVS. We get upset when we see that their eyes are open, for example, but they don't seem to see us back."

"PVS?" asked Lisa.

"I'm sorry," said Asitajee, "Permanent Vegetative State."

"You guys are worse than the federal government," said Lisa. She wanted the joke to obscure the three most horrible words she thought she had ever heard.

Asitajee chuckled. "I'm afraid you're right. Someone who's had a stroke—or is in SPVS (semi-PVS)," he corrected with a smile, "may be experiencing a little more mental discomfort, but it's with those cases that attentive, stimulating care can make all the difference."

"How long until he wakes up!" blurted Brenda.

"I'm sorry, ma'am, we just don't know," replied Asitajee as he stood up, crossed over to Brenda, and placed his hand on her arm. "And he may not 'wake up' in the sense that it's a new day and time to go to work. It may be a slower, more progressive response of his faculties to his care and other stimuli."

"Thank you, Dr. Asee—I'm sorry—" Lisa gave a gracious grin at not being able to repeat the physician's name.

"No, not at all. It's A-see-ta-gee. It means something like 'teacher from the black village' or 'black teacher.' Here's my card. Call anytime."

"Thank you so much."

"Now, if you'd like to follow me, we'll go see Bobby."

CHAPTER SIX

Dear God,
Though I walk through the valley of the shadow of death,
Thou art with me ...

Lisa hated hospitals. She hated the décor, principally. To her, the look and feel of modern medical facilities were forced serenity. What bothered her particularly about Parkland was that is was a trash bin of taxpayer dollars. The place may resemble a North Dallas mall, but the public money spent masked a cancerous organism where self-reliance, fairness, and self-control were being consumed by the carcinogenic cells of entitlement.

Her own core views on health care included the idea that it was fundamentally not a right. Individuals don't have a right to treatment just by registering 98.6, let alone a right to state-of-the-art treatment. There was something to be said for stabilizing the innocent victim of a car wreck—or a construction accident—on the public's dime when seconds mattered, but after that, it was like anything else; one's health care coverage was a matter of personal responsibility. And the same went for one's kids. She believed that rationing should be adopted and enforced starting with the triage nurse.

Now the experience she was undergoing with Bobby only reinforced her beliefs. Since arriving at Parkland the day before, she expected only to see professionals passing up and down the halls of the massive facility as she took up residence in the neural ICU. While her mother had died at home, Lisa only remembered the strict visitation rules enforced at Baylor Medical Center across town during Carolyn's hospitalizations. Instead, Lisa saw clusters of confused, ignorant citizens and non-citizens at Parkland wondering why their rich doctor wouldn't wave his magic wand. Lisa then realized she shouldn't have been surprised that Dallas County's hospital and the site of JFK's death should be the shrine of the slain president's liberal legacy.

Later the previous day, Lisa, Nate, and the Jeffusses had stepped outside for their supper of emergency Whataburger, where a freeloading congregation of wheelchair-bound chain smokers was taking a break from getting well. She had gotten madder and madder. The only thing preventing her auburnish hair from turning fire red was the fact that Brenda's deep-seated, chattering paranoia kept Lisa speechless.

As Asitajee finally led the two women into the hotel-like depths of the ICU ward, Lisa felt a wave of conviction about her judgment of the hoi polloi. She just wished more people adhered to the gospel of personal responsibility. She and Bobby did. The fact that others were willing to be even more generous toward them at this moment of crisis was God's grace. Finally, Asitajee opened the door on Bobby's room. The ordinariness of the sight was anti-climactic for Lisa.

Save for a bandage gripping Bobby's head—which now appeared bald—it looked like he was simply sleeping in a nicely decorated room among dimly lit computer screens. He had an IV and ventilator, but his body did not seem stressed as it lay in the bed.

"We wanted to give him a few days before we considered a tube," said Asitajee. He professionally proceeded to tread softly as he next asked, "Do you and your husband have a living will?"

Brenda cried as she leaned over the bed onto her son.

Lisa and Asitajee stepped back from the live pieta to have a conversation Lisa was catching on to quite rapidly. As Brenda muttered away in a combination of prayer and entreaty, both to God and Bobby, Lisa discreetly answered Asitajee's question.

"We do, actually. We had it done when Bobby was doing site work exclusively. We have mutual decision-making empowerment in case of incapacitation."

Without needing to ask, Lisa said to the doctor, "When he was in high school, he had an uncle who suffered a bad stroke. Bobby has told me personally and emphatically he would never want to live in a vegetative state."

"We don't need to worry about that just yet," said Asitajee. "Your husband is, if you'll excuse the term, a specimen of a man. He is physiologically strong in so, so many ways—right down to his heart. I also suspect that unlucky brain is made of the same stock. I know you've heard statements—they're cliché, really—that there is so much we don't know about the brain. But it's really true. One of the things I am frequently amazed to witness in my work is the brain's capacity to repair itself—a concept no one held as recently as ten years ago." Asitajee was as auspicious as he was keen.

Lisa did not know why she seemed so suddenly comfortable with Asitajee, but she heard herself asking, "Do you believe in God, Doctor?" She immediately apologized for seeming rude.

Asitajee was unflappable. "I do, as a matter-of-fact. My father was from East India, but my mother is from here. They met at Southern Methodist University."

"We'll be right back, Brenda," said Lisa as she led Asitajee out into the hall. Brenda did not respond.

"I'm pregnant, and I'm terrified," confessed Lisa.

"How far along?" asked Asitajee quickly.

"I only know from a home kit. According to my calendar, I should be six weeks."

For the first time since they had known each other, Asitajee seemed to have no apt words. Finally, he carefully said, "In my mind, there is either a God that has the minutest detail of human lives pre-planned, or there is chaos in the extreme. I wish I had a comforting summary for the reality that is likely somewhere in between."

CHAPTER SEVEN

May 17

Dear God,

Thank you again that Bobby has been able to breathe on his own.
I praise your name.

Bobby didn't stay long in the ICU. For a head injury victim, the
worst is usually over in a few hours, even if comatose, provided the
patient is breathing on his own. Asitajee moved Bobby into a regular
hospital room at Parkland not long after the night nurse noticed
he was breathing normally. The ventilator Bobby had been on had
become superfluous. And while he had been in the ICU for less than
sixty-five hours, to Lisa the time seemed like an even shorter stint
due to the days running together.

Lisa had escaped more morning sickness, although she did feel
slightly nauseated the day before, after another fidgety sleep period
out in the waiting room. She was doubly grateful for the absence
of the vomiting, not just because it was an inconvenience but also
because of any explaining she might have to do.

Brenda remained a tangled knot of worry,
though the constant presence of her husband Ron spared Lisa the role of being
her mother-in-law's piñata. After moving into the regular hospital room, Lisa
could manage Brenda by alternately
claiming and offering up the room's lone

chair for use. As clingy with worry as she was, Brenda still would not stay on her feet for extended periods.

Bobby's prognosis had prompted the insertion of a nasogastric-feeding tube. While still in the ICU, Asitajee ordered that his patient be intubated upon seeing Bobby's strong respirations. Lisa consented, as her trust in Asitajee had grown even more. The talk of the living will vanished. Lisa figured that the doctor had seen far more people wake up or not wake up, and his passion to involuntarily keep Bobby's nutrition up stirred her own optimism that her man would make it.

Still, scenes such as when the nurse would come in to change Bobby's new diapers served to take the wind out of Lisa's sails. The diapers were needed since he couldn't relieve himself, and he had been put on IV fluids shortly after his arrival at the hospital. Instead, he was now drinking and eating with the help of the tube. The first diaper change required that Bobby's heavy lower torso be hoisted up by not one but two male orderlies while the nurse slipped the diaper underneath his buttocks. The sheer limpness of her husband's large thighs caused Lisa to shudder. She for once saw her workman's burliness as a liability, maybe even a hindrance to his recovery. She then feared he might gain weight while he lay in his comatose state, thus causing complications. Asitajee tried to allay her fears by explaining that over time, he would likely lose weight.

"When is the possible time frame during which he might wake up?" asked A.J. She had not come back to the hospital until after Bobby's transfer into the regular room, relying on the phone to stay informed.

"I haven't asked the doctor," said Lisa. "I am afraid of what I might hear. I am making do with his generally positive outlook." Lisa removed some flowers from the window cutout so that A.J. could sit. Until A.J. had arrived for her visit, Lisa had kept the small space cluttered so that Brenda wouldn't set up shop in the space. She wanted only A.J. near her, even though she had been struggling with how to tell her about her pregnancy. A.J. should have been the first person, even before Bailiff. Lisa decided to hold off just another day or two and see if Bobby would wake up.

"It definitely looks less extreme in here," observed A.J. "I can imagine that ICU was getting to you."

"You don't really realize how expensive health care is until you're this deep in it," said Lisa.

"Did you tell me everything was covered?" A.J. asked.

"Yes. The company also wants to pay the deductibles, even though Bobby knew better than to step on site without his hardhat. His boss admitted it was his fault for not having enough hats for everyone.

"Wouldn't it be a Workman's Comp case?" A.J. then asked, her sense of workers' rights coming out.

"That's why the company has stepped up. They knew that Bobby not having his hardhat on would cause issues with the State.

"That's really generous of them." A.J. then cut herself off, not wanting to allude to the long-term costs which likely awaited Bobby's care.

Lisa smiled. Even in the midst of intense stress and weariness, she still had an ideological side that would eek out. She said, "Not all corporations are stingy and evil."

A.J. didn't smile right away.

Lisa sensed A.J.'s stubborn defensiveness. "And you know it," she said to A.J., this time approaching gently and looking her friend in the face.

A.J. finally let down her guard and grinned "What are you doing about work?" she asked. A.J. was the only person with the right to ask this question of Lisa. And the way she asked it clearly meant more in the line of care than concern.

"Why? You know of a Democrat who's about to file on Paul?" Lisa asked, laughing. "Trying to get a leg up while the money girl is down?"

A.J. smiled again. But she was also serious in making sure Lisa wasn't short-changing her responsibility to the situation at hand by stressing about the office. "Is Nate able to help you out?"

"Yes and no," said Lisa, grumbling. "He can handle slam-dunk followups, maybe even the bone-pile, but he will not lift a finger for initial asks."

"You know I only ask because I want to tell you however I can that you don't need to worry about it," said A.J. With gentleness and firmness she added, "I see that to even bring it up starts you in on complaining a little bit."

"It's okay," said Lisa. "Thanks for asking. But, I do think your unusual closeness to the Metroplex's top GOP fundraiser gives you insight into whether or not the other team might have a vulnerability."

A.J. lightened up. Lisa found the shop talk unexpectedly comforting in the midst of the hospital room. To her surprise, when she put her political hat on, she found escape.

A.J.'s previous boss in DC, "Mrs. Evans" as she was known in Dallas, had actually encouraged A.J.'s desire to return home. An appropriator with mid-level seniority, Mrs. Evans would have a little bit of heft with the new Democrat majority. But the Dallas County Democratic machine found itself overwhelmed by the electoral blessings that had come their way during the Midterms. Most of the party operations had been run out of the law office of Oak Cliff's prominent state senator, also an African-American, with a white chairwoman serving as a figurehead without a headquarters staff. Every bit as surprised as *The Dallas Morning News*, the senator had suggested to A.J. and her old boss that she return, knowing that he could no longer handle everything himself. He personally arranged for the Dallas plaintiff's mafia to pony-up the contributions necessary to provide A.J. with a comparable salary. More to the point, the senator, a defense lawyer himself, wanted a buffer between his operation and the newly elected, but barely competent, DA. He needed someone with Beltway toughness to relay his messages to the courthouse.

A.J. and her old boss knew this, but they also knew that they needed someone on the ground, as North Dallas's own influential appropriator, Republican Paul Bailiff, would continue to attempt to control the city and county. In spite of losing his slot in the House Majority, not to mention many allies on the bench and in the Commissioner's Court, Bailiff would retain powerful influence over the Metroplex's federal cash needs with the state's two Republican senators across the Rotunda.

"Can't some of your other staff handle those calls? Or do you still insist on doing everything yourself?" asked A.J.

"My clients hire me," said Lisa. "I haven't found anyone else with my profile to do the job. It's like what the Vice-President might have said after he was picked for the ticket in 2000: 'Having interviewed all the possible candidates, I find no one better qualified than myself.'"

A.J. laughed. Lisa knew she genuinely cared for her. After U.T., they became even closer as their careers progressed. Taking an internship with a longtime Dallas Democrat after the tsunami of '94, A.J. became Lisa's roommate on Capitol Hill the year before she and Bobby married. And during the Jeffuses' early years, it was A.J. more than Bobby who was always on the phone and in the kitchen cooking a host of comfort dinners and desserts while Carolyn Dillon succumbed to the very disease she had been crusading against. A.J. was consumed with anger at what happened to Lisa's mother when she developed untreatable breast cancer. A.J. trusted God, but the sad irony of taking Lisa's only surviving parent in spite of all the money and awareness Carolyn had accumulated against it offended a sharp sense of justice.

But love also accompanied Lisa's political opposite, as A.J. bore up her friend during some exceptionally dark days. A.J. created and managed the Lisa Jeffus support group in DC. For all the city's reliance on the maxim, "who you know," DC can be a profoundly lonely place for the young professional, political pedigree notwithstanding. There's that one person a college graduate knows when they first arrive, but even if a cluster of reliable acquaintances can be formed after a few weeks, one's clique is rarely able or willing to drop everything to help out. A group of true friends takes effort to have in DC and a strong personality like A.J. to keep them together.

As Harry Truman so wisely said, "If you want a friend in Washington, best to get a dog."

A.J.'s plan of action to help Lisa had consisted primarily of making sure a different person called Lisa each day of the week, simply to ask for an update on Carolyn. The Democrat began with an eager group of eight, consisting of six members of Capitol Baptist Church, Danny, and herself. After four months and the summer recess, the only reliable callers left were Danny and her.

A.J. looked over the absolutely still body of Bobby in his bed. She knew fewer people in Dallas who were mutual acquaintances with the Jeffuses, outside of political circles. She considered how that was also ironic; now that they were both "home" in the Metroplex, she and Lisa's connections were fewer and farther between. After what she had heard in recent years, A.J. would never bring Danny in now to help Lisa, even if she knew where he was. "You ever see much of Danny Geister?" she decided to ask.

For a split-second, Lisa had the strange temptation to lie about her new client. "I actually saw him the day of Bobby's accident, believe it or not," she said, feeling more like she was confessing something.

"Oh really?" A.J. became curious. "He running for something?" she asked, although she knew that wasn't the right question.

"No. He's running an East Texas Senator's race. He wasn't too favorable about it." Lisa was dismissive of the entire arrangement.

A.J. knew she had already given Lisa a mild scold for complaining about the office earlier, so she didn't want to become Brenda by voicing her own worries about Danny being back in her friend's world. Still, some intuition had bubbled up. She walked from the window sill over to Bobby and took his hand.

"I'm praying for you, big man," A.J. said. She lightly brushed Bobby's forehead. "God will heal you."

Lisa thought back to the early days of her marriage. She and Bobby hadn't been married two years before her mother had that terrible mammogram. One year, everything was fine. The next year, untreatable cells. Bobby had stood by her every moment, but there were just some aspects of the ordeal he couldn't understand. And his maleness naturally prevented him from meeting a special emotional support need, which A.J. had provided. She was grateful to God that A.J. was here for her now. A.J. provided a special kind of aggressive strength Lisa knew would see her through. If only she could emulate it.

"I better get back down to headquarters," said A.J.

"Sure thing, love," Lisa said. The two hugged and released a tear or two.

"I know he is your rock," said A.J., "so don't forget that all God is probably doing is testing you to make sure only Jesus is your rock."

Lisa nodded in assent.

After A.J. left, Lisa began to wonder more about the baby. She needed a blood test to confirm everything. But how would she tell everyone? It just didn't seem right without Bobby not knowing first. She decided that at the least she would wait to say anything until after the blood test. Although she made sure not to tell anyone, she had gotten an appointment with her gynecologist on the upcoming Tuesday. Maybe by then Bobby would be awake.

CHAPTER EIGHT

May 22

Dear God,

Help the appointment to go well today.
In Jesus' name. Amen.

Lisa never gave up her personal physician in Dallas after she moved out to Sachse. The truth was that Dr. Thorpe, whose office was at Presbyterian, was an old family friend who treated Carolyn and had actually delivered Lisa. She didn't want to start over with someone new after returning home from DC. Even though he was pushing seventy, Dr. Thorpe still delivered babies at 3:00 a.m. He was one of those old-school guys who just wouldn't lay aside his profession.

Lisa went in to Dr. Thorpe's office after she had spent the night up in Sachse. Bobby was still completely comatose. She had spent the weekend considering long-term care for Bobby, though Asitajee was still hopeful on his rounds. She filled in Dr. Thorpe on the accident as the nurse drew her blood. She explained that she would be headed over to Parkland later for yet another afternoon wait.

The physician became very concerned. "Well, you know," Thorpe said, "you should be mindful of the stress of this situation, given the difficulty you and Bobby have had in getting pregnant."

"Yes. We did some tests up in DC,

though, and Bobby had some low counts. I've never miscarried or anything."

"Of course not," said Thorpe, "but if you're anything like you're mother, I know you won't slow down even as your body changes over the next few months." Thorpe was being a little blunt for a gynecologist. Lisa decided it was because he was getting old.

"What kind of changes?" asked Lisa. She had an idea of what would happen to her from friends and family who had babies, but she suddenly wanted to know more, especially since she had to deal with Bobby.

"Well, I don't know how healthy you'll be since you've never been pregnant before. But you'll need to watch out for fatigue, especially during the first trimester. If all goes well, you'll feel better here in a couple of months and hopefully hit a stride."

Lisa felt suddenly afraid. She had a pit in her stomach. Maybe the changes would be bigger than she imagined. What if caring for Bobby infringed on the baby's normal progression? How would she manage work if she became chronically fatigued? She began to sense panic but was immediately filled with the thought that maybe if Bobby were home, at a place where she could work and see after him, everything would be okay. Yes! That was it. If she could make a plan to move him home, she would be in a good place. She would also be ready to nest as her time drew near.

She wanted to get back over to Parkland and see to Bobby's care. She just knew she and her husband were in for a long-term situation. But she knew he was becoming more stable. On the one hand, a long-term coma was bad for obvious reasons. On the other, that may mean that he could be moved home sooner. She had planned to swing by the Mockingbird Group on her way to Parkland this morning for a badly needed check-in, but Lisa decided instead to go straight to Bobby and see where things were and get people motivated.

"Thanks, Dr. Thorpe. It's good to see you again."

"I'll call later with your test results," said Thorpe as Lisa hastily left his office.

A.J. made her way to the Parkland elevators during her lunch hour in the hopes of catching Lisa alone. Lisa had explained to her that the "watch" had evolved into Lisa staying with Bobby during the day with the Jeffuses alternating the nights, usually coming in around 6:00 p.m. Ron had been retired for almost three years, and so he and his worried but non-employed wife had no trouble covering the wee hours. Lisa had been arriving no later than 7:00 a.m., but it was still a question mark as to when the Jeffuses would actually depart. Surprisingly, it was usually Ron more than Brenda who stuck around—even A.J. figured out that all of Brenda's anxiety exhausted her in short order. And while A.J. was fully aware of how Lisa preferred and needed her company to that of her in-laws, she still felt as though she were imposing a bit whenever the victim's parents were at Bobby's side.

Lisa's best friend was going to have a hard time making it back to the hospital before Friday. In addition to work, Curtiss took up most of her spare evenings now, but he had a standing church-related commitment every Friday that made A.J. think she wouldn't be free again until then. She was feeling a bit torn, but A.J. knew that Lisa needed her rest if she were ever away from the hospital, so she didn't bother her at home. She figured the lunch hour would be best for now.

A.J. was therefore disappointed when she came down the hall and discovered that the Jeffuses were still with Bobby, and Lisa absent. She couldn't imagine where Lisa had gone. "Is Lisa all right?" she asked.

"Well, she said she had something else to do," griped Brenda. She had discovered the extra seating on the window cutout. Ron was sleeping on the lone chair. "I can't believe she's thinking of work at a time like this."

A.J. became annoyed. Yes, Lisa should have been at Bobby's side—it had not yet been a week since the accident—but she did have work to put at least one eye on. She had employees who needed her, maybe even the light bill to pay. A.J. was surprised to find herself thinking like a small businesswoman instead of a political operative. "I'm sure it's okay, Mrs. Jeffus."

"It's that Bailiff!" Brenda said. "I like him, but he just asks too much of her."

"Maybe so," said A.J. Yet the operative knew full well the types of responsibilities Lisa had, even though they were borne of an insecure Republican. "But, you know, work is work. We need to pray everything is taken care of in a balanced way."

"Well, I just think there are some times when she should tell him to do it himself," said Brenda.

A.J. decided not to continue the discussion by not answering. She thought it best to choke the oxygen off from the flame.

"Do you know Bailiff even has her taking money from those Orientals up in Plano?" asked Brenda. Obviously, she thought it was all right to make racially-tinted comments with someone who was African-American, as long as it wasn't about that someone's own race. "I don't think it's a good idea for her to be running around with all those people. You know, they're not even really Americans. They are a big part of all the illegal immigration in this country. They are taking over our neighborhood—I don't care if they do vote Republican!"

A.J. bit her tongue against Brenda's rant, tolerating her for two reasons. First, Brenda was upset about her comatose son. Second, A.J. knew she would never change Brenda's mind. Still, the latent bigotry was troublesome. But A.J. had a deeper resentment behind Brenda's remarks—the fact that Bailiff indeed had been very, very successful within the Asian community in his district. Wherever the Thirty-third Congressional District of Texas existed in Dallas County, its boundaries made it eligible for the gerrymandering Hall of Fame. The overall shape of the district made sense as a kind of pie slice that began around White Rock Lake—Bailiff's home—and did its thing around the northern part of the county, then funneled out into the suburbs and rural areas all the way to the Red River.

Bailiff had to absorb some rough, Hispanic neighborhoods southwest of White Rock as well as the mixed neighborhoods of Vickery Meadow and Casa View in exchange for his ultrawhite-bread precincts in Collin County. But overall, TX33 enjoyed a seventy percent Overall Republican Voting Strength rating (or ORVS) thanks to its rural areas beyond the burbs and up along the border.

Yet Bailiff was no slouch when it came to enhancing that ORVS number when he could. The best example was in Ron and Brenda's part of the Metroplex, south Collin County and north Dallas County, a once middle-income suburban region that had become a tight Asian enclave. And by Asian, no less than ten different ethnic groups had settled in the area from throughout that continent. Korea, Laos, the Philippines, Taiwan, Vietnam—each were significantly represented.

While most Republican strategists dismissed these groups as Democratic, usually because they clustered in inner cites, Bailiff realized by vision and necessity that this did not have to be so. Retooling his methods after his first unsuccessful run in 1990, the business executive would spend considerable time talking with restaurant, dry cleaning, and convenience store owners after hours about their operations and what they perceived to be government interference. Bailiff had started doing this in his own neighborhood like a good activist, but it didn't take long for him to realize that virtually every shop owner of Asian descent around Dallas and its suburbs had one thing in common: they lived in either south Collin or in north Dallas County.

Running for office literally opened scores of doors for Bailiff within the Dallas County Asian community. Although most of the different ethnicities kept to themselves, Bailiff actually brought them together in business roundtables and kitchen cabinet meetings. In some cases, men—and they were all men—met their counterparts in another group for the first time as a result of Bailiff's gatherings, and the results were often as positive for the Asian Community at large as they were for Bailiff's own totals. Small but reliable blocs of votes—though not large individually but formidable as a whole—would make their way into Bailiff's column on Election Day. In return, Bailiff would serve as kingmaker in a host of municipal positions. Bailiff had become very proud of his work among this portion of his district.

A.J. was desperate her own party leadership would take notes from the guy. Still, she didn't want to talk politics with someone so irritable and harried like Brenda, let alone prejudiced. She wondered why Lisa didn't clue her in about her whereabouts this morning. After all, she had told her what the watch schedule was.

Lisa finally stepped into Bobby's room around 12:30. "Hey, girl," she said to A.J. She pretended to ignore the Jeffuses. Ron was still asleep, anyway.

"Where have you been?" asked A.J. She hoped she conveyed to Lisa some measure of irritation.

Lisa fumbled with the items in her purse as she tried to come up with a fib. She just wasn't ready to tell A.J. about the baby, and she didn't want to say anything in front of Brenda. "Oh, I was trying to run into the office, but I got caught in some traffic and ended up making a different stop." All of that was true but really foggy. The traffic was the biggest stretch but plausible given Parkland's distance from everything.

"I wasn't sure I'd make it back in here before Friday, so I came on during lunch," A.J. said.

Lisa quickly tuned out everyone in the room, even after the attentiveness required for the obfuscation about her whereabouts. "Has Asitajee made it by, yet? He usually comes in around eleven. I really need to talk to him," she said.

CHAPTER NINE

May 25

Dear God,

We thank you for this day! As we go to the new rehab hospital today, guide us in the decisions we must make. Make the nurses and staff receptive to Bobby's needs. Help him to wake up. Show your mercy on us sinners as we try to discern your will.

In Jesus' name. Amen.

Lisa's persistence with Asitajee had paid off, and within a few more days he agreed with her that Bobby did not need to stay at Parkland. Now, she and Nate were leading an ambulance containing her husband to a rehab hospital across town. Bobby no longer had the bald-looking bandage wrapped on his head, and the hair, which had been shaved during his exam in the ER ten days earlier, had begun to grow back. Nate and his boss had seen the nurse remove the bandage and had been talking about Bobby's downy scalp ever since.

"You know that's what happened to Samson," Nate told Lisa as the pair parked and entered Northeast Dallas Rehabilitation Hospital, a facility just to the west of Greenville Avenue, not far from Central Expressway and much closer to both Jeffuses' homes than Parkland.

Lisa got her umbrella ready. "What?" she asked. The spring rains had shown no sign of letting up.

"When Samson's hair grew back after the Philistines captured him and cut it all off, he got back his supernatural strength and killed all the heathens," explained Nate.

"Yeah. Once he got better, didn't he pull the building down on top of himself? Great analogy, friend," Lisa said.

"Okay. My bad, whatever," said Nate. The pair exited Lisa's SUV and hurried inside.

By now, the admission to the rehab hospital was believed to be only a brief stop on Bobby's recovery. This meant the replacement of the tube in Bobby's nose with a percutaneous endoscopic gastrostomy. Commonly called a PEG, this feeding tube was surgically attached to the abdomen. The simple device enabled the delivery of nutrition straight into the patient's digestive system, thus avoiding the need for the unsightly tube going in through the nose. A nasogastric tube also increased the risk of a respiratory infection. And depending on whenever Bobby would wake up, anyone, including Lisa, could administer nutrition into the PEG. Most often, a protein-rich liquid like Milksure would be drawn into a syringe and then shot into the PEG for a meal. The liquid also served to keep the patient hydrated.

"Well, Samson was a bad boy," said Lisa, asking the rehab hospital receptionist for her husband's room number, "letting Delilah get the better of him."

"True," said Nate, "I know it's not a perfect metaphor. But I was going for the simple return of power aspect. Think of it, Lisa. When Bobby wakes up, it will be like he's taking revenge on death itself!"

Lisa knew Nate was trying to be encouraging in his own way. She had known him now for almost nine years. Bailiff's first communications director had been a Dallas reporter, but the guy couldn't hack it in DC and had to be let go. Nate was not only a media professional, but he had the rare benefit of being both press savvy and enmeshed with Christian conservatives—a group with which Bailiff initially lacked credentials.

Nate was a product of none other than Regent University, the higher education arm of a prominent religious broadcaster's empire. Nate learned communications at a state-of-the-art media facility that doubled as an outlet for an aggressive political news organization. Graduating in 1988 during 41's first presidential run, Nate's own ideals carried the talented copywriter along in religious broadcasting through the early nineties as Christian conservatives matured into a highly organized force within the electorate.

Originally from Oklahoma, Nate fired his resume off to the four Republicans who swept away the Democrats in that state in '94. Hired by a former NFL star from an Oklahoma City-based district, Nate made a name for himself as a good presser, even if a little suspect for his Christian heritage. Like most American reporters, the average DC communications person—Republican or Democrat—is usually rubbed the wrong way by religious zealotry of any form, especially that which emanates from the Christian right. This attitude comes from a combination of general skepticism that is inculcated in journalism departments around the nation, as well as a jadedness, which soon sets in among political people who have had trouble understanding evangelical involvement in politics. Nate sensed this early on but never let it bother him, and his competence and clarity won him respect amongst the GOP press fraternity.

When his home-state boss prepared to step down in keeping with a term limits pledge, Nate was hired by Bailiff and ended up sharing a tiny space in the TX33 office right across from Lisa. Often, such confines fostered tension over who had closer earshot to the Member, but Lisa and Nate had hit it off almost from the start. They were both meticulous in their work habits. Nate was a master of organizing information, and the conciseness he brought to political messaging meant that he never wasted his boss's time.

More importantly, Nate could communicate with and cultivate conservative Christian voters in TX33. While Bailiff had been solidly pro-life his entire career, his years with the Governor Dillon side of the Texas GOP caused the Christian Coalition in the Metroplex to tag him as a "country clubber." On the issues, this was frankly unfair. And Bailiff had been saying he was born again since the mid-eighties. But the big city executive didn't do himself any favors by failing to get out into the rural sections of TX33 and sound out the Christians who had taken over the local party apparatus early in his first run for Congress in 1990. Nate had been brought on to smooth over a rocky history, even though Bailiff eventually found the magic formula that got him elected in '94.

Nate understood the campaign side of the business, and as the Mockingbird Group grew, Lisa eagerly sought someone who could take over some of the operational requirements of her clients so that she could concentrate on the fundraising, her strength and pleasure. Wanting to leave DC with a growing family, Nate jumped at the chance to come on board even though the pay was lateral at best. He left Bailiff in good hands by training his replacement. And Nate knew he could save on his mortgage back in DFW along with a commute that wasn't near as brutal.

The only thing about Nate that occasionally irritated Lisa was his naïveté when it came to processing information/gossip he would receive from a source that was expressly evangelical Christian. In other words, he took at face value whatever a brother—or sister—"in Christ" told him. Lisa wished Nate did have some of that craven criticism that ran in the average journalist's blood, or that at least he wouldn't automatically give believers a free pass. She was a Christian and didn't do so. The difference between them, she decided, was that she had been raised Presbyterian where there was some modicum of privacy amongst the congregation, while Nate, a Southern Baptist, thrived on repeating the lowest details of the prayer chain. This was why she had gotten testy with him two weeks ago when Danny came in for his meeting.

Bobby's room inside Northeast Rehab was clean and serene with wood-paneled walls. Lisa was relieved, fearing the place would be like one of the smelly nursing homes she would visit during elementary school to sing Christmas carols. Her husband was still being unloaded from the ambulance and so hadn't quite made it in yet.

One or two nurses were coming in and out of the space in anticipation of his arrival.

"This will be really good for Bobby," commented Nate. "And, not meaning anything of course, it's close to the office."

Lisa had the exact same thought but knew that for her to articulate it would cast her in a bad light, putting work over family—part of the family. "Yes, it is," said Lisa, "But I still hope he doesn't have to be here long."

"Of course not," said Nate, "but here at least, you're close and can take care of what you need to."

Lisa knew that while Nate had been successfully steering the ship the past two weeks, he was saying that he much preferred Lisa be at the helm. Contribution follow-ups had been put on hold, not just because she was unavailable, but primarily due to Nate's unwillingness to get his hands dirty. For all his tendency to gossip, Nate retained a self-righteousness in never asking someone for a dollar. But Lisa preferred things this way. She felt most in control by being the exclusive contact between client and donor.

"I think I would much rather have Bobby home," Lisa said much more pointedly. While grateful to be out of Parkland, she now felt a restlessness, which was more powerful than the comfort of Bobby's progress. "Being home will be easier with the baby."

"What?" asked Nate.

Lisa flashed Nate a whoops smile.

"Do the Jeffuses know this?" Nate demanded. He did not know Brenda well, but he knew her well enough to know news like this would only be grist for her awful mill.

Lisa saw the Jeffuses coming down the hall. She gave Nate a shush.

"Well, it took us long enough to park! When is it going to stop raining?" rattled Brenda as she and her husband entered Bobby's room. "Where is he? Why isn't he here yet! We thought we were late and that he'd be here already!"

Nate prepared to engage in crisis communications.

"He's coming right now, Brenda," said Lisa. She now heard the wheels of the gurney due to an acquired ability to tune out her mother-in-law.

"Well, it's about time!" Brenda exclaimed.

The nursing director introduced herself to Lisa and made an assuring impression. After about twenty minutes, all the staff had Bobby settled in, and Lisa, Nate, and the Jeffuses settled around his bed.

"We'll be back in about an hour to feed your husband," said the nursing director to Lisa.

"Thank you," Lisa said. She sat down beside Bobby and took his hand.

There was a rare silence even though Brenda was there.

"Maybe I could offer a little prayer for Bobby and us?" said Nate. Although he wasn't part of the blood family, his frequent check-ins on Bobby the past two weeks, as well as his extra hours at the office, had more than earned him the right to minister. Moreover, he considered that only God could stem the family bedlam growing in Lisa's womb.

As if to grant approval, Ron immediately bowed his head. He could have easily been wanting to head off his wife's simmering need to engage in worrisome chatter.

Lisa sat at Bobby's side rubbing his forearm and not closing her eyes. Nate had noticed a strange pall come over Lisa's face the moment the nurses left the room.

"Dear God," began Nate, "surround us with your grace and support us with your—"

Lisa interrupted, "Patience, which we don't have enough of. Give us comfort for a future that troubles us. Spare us both worry and heartache—" Even as she had prayed aloud over her employee and cut him off, Lisa went further in expressing—releasing, really—what was on her heart. The formalized praying she pictured in her head and would have normally written in her prayer journal suddenly broke into wrenching honesty. She lost her decorum of decency.

"I don't understand all the events of the past two weeks, God," Lisa said. "I don't know why I've finally gotten pregnant only to be unable to tell the good news to my husband!"

Brenda made a sound with her mouth, opening her eyes, but the trajectory of Lisa's praying prevented anything more from coming out. Ron and Nate also opened their eyes. Everyone looked at Lisa's face, expecting tears. Instead, an angry-looking, lethal countenance was uttering this prayer of resentment.

"I don't understand any of this. I work hard, I honor my husband and friends, and I've never done anything majorly wrong other than be human, God.

"Why can't Bobby wake up? He's breathing okay; what's the holdup, Lord? And Bobby has been more obedient to you than anyone else I know. Yeah, God, we're all sinners—we get it—but my husband and I are at least decent. And Christ is the center of our life. And so what about trials? If we lived in China, that makes more sense. This doesn't!"

Nate was taken aback by Lisa's frankness, but there was no mistaking that they were her words—he had heard such a bluntness many times before in dealing with candidates and consultants. The spirit was that of her worldly, somewhat ruthless side that had made her a success.

"Let's step out," Nate whispered to Ron and Brenda. He feared Lisa was ready to break down at Bobby's bedside and really did not want her mother-in-law acting up.

Out in the hall, though, Brenda kept silent. The disconcerting moment was finally interrupted by Nate's cell phone. It was Bailiff's number. "Nate Knight," he answered, stepping away from the Jeffuses.

"Hey, Nate, it's Paul. Where's Lisa?" The congressman was insistent.

"Well, we just moved Bobby into the rehab hospital. She's a little busy right at the moment."

"Tell her to call me when she's able."

Nate felt Bailiff was intruding, even if he was the Mockingbird

Group's lead client. "All right, Paul, but I really don't know when that's going to be."

"It's important. The First Lady is about to announce a biotech initiative for Metroplex Children's Hospital, and we're going to capitalize on it," demanded Bailiff.

CHAPTER TEN

May 30, 6:45 a.m.

Dear God,

Please help—

Asitajee interrupted Lisa's prayer at Bobby's bedside. This was his first visit to Bobby during his morning rounds without the patient being at Parkland. Asitajee turned up the motionless Bobby's gown to check the PEG, which remained his patient's only connection to the living.

"Hello," said Lisa, not bothered to set her journal aside. She was experiencing the supplicant's version of writer's block.

"Looks like we've made the move fine," said Asitajee. "He looks pretty good for having just moved across town."

"I actually thought the move would kind of stimulate him somehow," said Lisa with a touch of disappointment.

Asitajee responded to Lisa with his sincere but sharp look of understanding. Owing to Lisa's earlier persistence, Asitajee became aware of a certain willfulness she had. "If Bobby does this well during

transition, we probably won't have to keep him here but for a few weeks," he finally said, offering his best vision of progress.

"Doctor," stated Lisa, finding that frankness again that was part of asking where a donor's check was, "based on what you and so many have told me

70

over the past couple of weeks, I'm kind of wondering what the point of a lengthy stay here would be.

"I mean, why not just get him home?"

Asitajee stared at Bobby's steady stillness.

"I think we all know—I do, at least—," continued Lisa, "after each and every night and day over at Parkland that it's going to be watching and praying from here on out."

Asitajee became uncharacteristically aloof, seeming not to listen.

"Am I not right?" asked Lisa.

Asitajee knew where Lisa was going. He hated to judge her, but as he got to know Lisa—who she was, her business, and the kind of lifestyle she was building—Asitajee felt he could guess that his patient's busy wife found in the hours by the bedside a need to come up with a more convenient plan. The doctor could see family issues on the horizon, the kind that made care of a difficult case like Bobby's that much harder. He respected Lisa and the accomplishments he had heard about, but he could only imagine their burden when added to her pregnancy. He decided to deal with Lisa's determination head on, suggesting, "I think if we monitor him here for a few days, we might be able to discharge him for home."

Then Asitajee's sharpness returned with a look at Lisa. "Though I'm going to insist that a well qualified home health plan be in place as part of the recovery."

For a moment, Lisa sensed the doctor's fangs. But the possibility of establishing a home/office routine around Bobby's care was exactly what she wanted to hear. She was truly sick of hospitals. After watching the rehab hospital's nurses do their thing the previous night, she knew that Bobby could be managed at home and that care could be established with good help. Bobby's boss had affirmed his commitment of all necessary resources for recovery, and Lisa had more than a couple of home health agencies in her fundraising Rolodex she could contact. They were always active on Medicare issues, and she would be proud to throw them some work—it would be good business. She knew politics were always involved.

"Do you have someone you recommend?" she asked Asitajee.

Everyone knew Paul Bailiff was a fundraising machine. More than that, the political class that spanned Austin, DFW, and Washington knew Bailiff's secret, even if replicating it among themselves proved elusive.

And Lisa had known the secret before Bailiff. It had been her grandfather's virtual dying words: Republican donors care about another thing besides taxes.

The trick in fundraising was not only ferreting out from each individual—or more often couple—what that other thing was, but also making sure authenticity accompanied one's interest in it. And the other thing was not so simple as the son's art scholarship or the daughter's state basketball victory. There was always a greater, emotional issue rooted in public policy that stirred the donor. Family or a family member may be involved, but the "another thing" was something that was or could be a catalyst for activism in the donor's life.

And to Lisa's advantage, the best example came from her own life. Her mother never remarried after her father became one of the final casualties of Vietnam in 1973—the final officer to lose his life, in fact, right before Lisa was born. An energetic and forceful personality, Carolyn Dillon didn't pursue a business career, however, other than serve on a couple of corporate boards, which governed her family's oil wealth.

Instead, Carolyn threw herself into charitable fundraising, first for two local Dallas groups then for the National Breast Cancer Foundation. The death of a dear friend was the germination of her another thing, and the charitable activism served as an outlet for the mourning of her lost husband. Yet being a good Republican, Carolyn knew that mere federal dollars for research would not only court dependency and dicta from Washington, they simply weren't enough. At NBCF, Carolyn could keep politics at arm's length yet still be influential.

Carolyn's passionate altruism blended into her motherhood. The truth felt deep in Lisa's heart was that she and her mother had a special place in the world. Lisa had been reared by a single parent of the same gender. She never sorrowed over a father she never knew. Quite the inverse, Lisa knew a world only with Mother. This was a sentiment Lisa came to cherish above anything else, and the exclusive Madonna-and-daughter relationship was something that defined her both consciously and subconsciously. She had long ago concluded that she was indifferent to having either a boy or girl when the time came, but being a parent of one was Lisa's own another thing.

One late summer day, while tagging along with Mom to an NBCF event, eleven-year-old Lisa came to understand, not just the concept of the another thing rule, but its symbiosis with politics. Her mother had assigned her to hand out nametags at a luncheon being held downtown at the Adolphus Hotel. The event was purposefully held there so that a senator could come and speak after participating in the VIP crowd's Main Thing earlier in the day: the 1984 Republican National Convention being held down the street at Reunion Arena. Manning the door, Lisa had been given seventy-one Reagan '84 campaign buttons by the hundred guests for whom she had made nametags.

Young Lisa had to get an empty napkin from the kitchen to hold all the buttons that the massive, uncoordinated conspiracy of donors had provided her. Each doting attendee at her mother's event seemed to think that fatherless Lisa would enjoy a political button. She still kept all seventy-one buttons in a bag in her hope chest—something she knew was irregular for the average girl. But Lisa never saw herself as average; she saw herself as someone who had been given a gift of decoding what it was people cared about and translating that care into action.

Bailiff recognized Lisa's gift not long after he detailed her to his campaign operation in 2003. Relying on consultants and what was essentially a call list generated by them, Bailiff and other smarter incumbents realized that a more controlled, cost-effective means of raising money and tending to the daily requirements of a campaign was needed.

Bailiff always had a leg up in fundraising because, not inaccurately discerned by the Christian Coalition, he was in fact a member of the prestigious Lakewood Country Club in Dallas. He had gotten a job for a major Metroplex utility company in between his service to Governor Dillon in Austin during the late seventies and early eighties and his first run for Congress in 1990. By running with the executive crowd, he had his ready Rolodex.

As the cost of campaigning continued to rise, especially for big-city media, the new campaign model was needed. But the right person for this job was hard to come by, as the profile required not only political savvy and strong organizational skills, but also an iron butt and thick skin for making call, after call, after call. The incumbent also had to manage the overhead needed to support this person at the lowest cost. As a result, many candidates, especially those in big media markets with greater cash needs, set up incentive programs for their managers once the right one had been hired.

Lisa quickly saw how she could work this to her entrepreneurial advantage. Bobby never had any trouble finding work and lovingly followed Lisa wherever she wanted to go. The chance to come home to Texas and run Bailiff's campaign was an opportunity for her to return the favor to her husband when his management job opened up, not to mention get a big house in the Sunbelt. By 2004, back in Dallas but still with no children, Lisa decided to follow the Prayer of Jabez, expand her territory, and help other Republicans. The Mockingbird Group was born using the incentive model Bailiff had set her up with.

She always exceeded her goals, and she shamelessly worked the another thing rule. Bailiff, for instance, would give Lisa five cents of every dollar she raised above different target levels by different dates. Her success was getting noticed in Washington by the end of the '04 cycle, and by the end of '06, she had inked fundraising contracts with two out-of-state governors, a multistate deal for one of the many

Republican presidential candidates, and almost ten local officehold-ers and officeseekers. She ended '06 with a gross of $490,000, raising just over 9 million dollars for her clients. This didn't include straight consulting fees, the bulk of which were being used to pay Nate.

But because Lisa owed her increasing success to the guy who let her branch out in the first place, the modus operandi around the Mockingbird Group was that when Bailiff called, everyone needed to find a stopping place on whatever they were working.

Nate had not told Lisa about Bailiff's call the previous day. Still, he knew what was up. He had never seen Lisa crack out of her happy, bouncing veneer like he had at the rehab hospital. He didn't think she was false or hypocritical; Nate just realized it was unsettling to see someone who always appeared strong come apart, let alone seem to shake their fist at God. He decided such an expression was a threat to his own faith. And of course, it bothered Nate's Christian propriety for Bailiff to want attention when he surely knew Lisa was preoccupied. No amount of fundraising opportunity was worth it until the person you needed was ready, Nate thought.

Nate wandered into the rehab hospital later in the morning, mulling his options. After several minutes, he stepped in front of Bobby's door and saw the nurses feeding him with the PEG while Lisa and now the Jeffuses watched. It was really simple, sure enough. All the nurse did was insert her big syringe, almost the size of a tur-key baster, into a small container of a milklike liquid, draw it up, and then shoot it into the plastic valve-looking device protruding from Bobby's abdomen.

"We make a note here," said one of the nurses, writing on a clip-board, "that he has been fed."

Lisa carefully watched the routine. She only had to acknowledge Nate with a glance as he arrived at Bobby's room. "This is an impor-tant record so that if he were to develop some sort of complication while in his comatose state, we can rule out if the problem is related to a lack of nutrition," said the nurse.

"I'm actually a little hungry, myself," said Nate. "Why don't we go get something to eat."

"There are several good restaurants nearby," said the nurse to Lisa. "I'd encourage you to take a break."

"That sounds good," Nate said straight to Lisa. He could tell she was absolutely wiped out, but she still seemed a little restless. "I vote for Chili's."

CHAPTER ELEVEN

May 30

11:30 a.m.

Dear God,

Thank you for the good transition of Bobby and the hope of him coming home. Please let your will be done.

Lisa completed her prayer entry quickly, exhausted but elated that the block she'd experienced in the morning was gone. The thought crossed her mind that maybe she was thinking more about herself than Bobby when it came to discussing his homecoming with Asitajee, but she dismissed that insensitive notion to fatigue also.

Nate drove silently, even turning off WBAP and Limbaugh's first hour after seeing Lisa immediately open her journal upon sitting in the passenger seat. He felt he needed to get Lisa "back on track" but still had a latent fear that she'd start attacking God again. He filled her in on Bailiff's call.

"Is there a firm that's administering the project—initiative or whatever? Who is doing the actual research?" asked Lisa as she and Nate made the short drive to Chili's. The rain and clouds had cleared out, and Lisa quickly donned her sunglasses after wiping the humid frost from them. "Hospitals typically don't run studies like that by themselves."

"Paul didn't say. And the truth is, his timing made me not interested," said Nate.

Lisa actually found relief in thinking about a fundraising plan instead of one for long-term care. It was, after all, what she did. Before Nate could continue his grumbling, Lisa had dialed Bailiff with her phone.

"Hey, it's Lisa. Call me back," she said into voicemail.

"Find out if there's a firm for me, will you?" she asked Nate. "Once we know that, I can brainstorm about who the First Lady knows. We can also figure out if anyone down here with money is interested. If it's a firm and they're worth their salt, there will be a Web page describing the board or the investors," Lisa said as the pair arrived and entered the restaurant. For a moment, there was no injured husband or growing fetus.

Lisa was well aware that among Christian conservatives, some lingering suspicion remained of whether Bailiff had the true faith. Nowhere was this ambivalence more pronounced than in the rural counties.

Starting in the late 1980s, most rural Republican organizations had been taken over by Christian conservatives. Going back to Goldwater, the only real Republicans in a small town were usually the bank president, the land surveyor, and the Episcopal priest. And while they maintained a fair presence for years, if there ever was a real political conflict with local Democrats—many of whom were already conservative—none of those mentioned were sober enough to want to do anything about it.

Falwell, a slew of broadcasters, and Reagan changed all of that. Falwell printed the literature that ended up in the church bulletin. The broadcasters put together the TV content that was backed up with strong UHF signals. And Reagan simply brought everyone together.

Critical to the takeover was local leadership provided by Baby

Boomers who experienced the Jesus Movement and created a new style of evangelicalism. They had gone off to Bible colleges and seminaries to feed a hungry void of spiritual information. As the bicentennial approached, the thought-out Constitutionalism of these counter-counter culturalists (and culture warriors) motivated them to usher in neoconservatism to the most remote corners of the USA. Taking their cues from Reagan—even after the end of the Cold War—they supported a foreign policy that projected American military strength. Instead of riding a donkey through the city gate, their Jesus rode astride a battle elephant.

But upon returning home from college and settling down, these men and their equally idealistic wives found that they either didn't really want to become preachers or that they were no good at being pastors. To be sure, small towns couldn't financially support their fresh, socio-religious consciousness, unless they were Southern Baptist, and many of them had left their parents' Baptist church to pursue their own faith expression.

In the suburbs, these patriots took on regular jobs and simply voted Republican generally. At the most, they might take over a precinct chair vacancy in one of their sprawling communities. But in rural America, particularly in places like TX33's Black County, they took control. Small-county parties afforded these would-be apostles the chance to express their worldview by actually having a position from which to shape the world around them. Unable to find a vocation that suited their sensibilities in a small town, these born-again neocons often formed their own cottage industries to survive, but they threw themselves into local Republican Party politics.

Those bankers, priests, and Indian chiefs never knew what hit them. As with any group that loses power—however slothfully they may hold it—the old guard, a.k.a. country clubbers, angrily labeled Christian conservatives as radicals.

And the believers returned the favor. With Reagan's unifying absence, as well as that of Soviet Communism, the harmony on economic matters and other policies was made subordinate to social issues, and Christian conservatives regularly cast the stone of "moderate" toward the old guard if they didn't line up. Longstanding Republican Women's Clubs were condemned as covens of abortion. Convention delegates and chairmen who had faithfully kept the GOP name alive in solidly Southern Democratic territory were tossed out during precinct and county conventions with a speed and efficiency that would have astonished Pilate.

The crowning moment of this effort came in 1994 when Newt Gingrich, a small college professor/ideologue elected from just such a rural town, sallied the party forth under the Contract with America by declaring that the existing party leadership in Congress had become comfortable in the minority. The future Speaker's sentiment was not a fresh observation, it was the culmination of decades of activism.

Paul Bailiff had been well aware of these trends and activities throughout North Texas, but his insularity within the Dallas business community spared him much of the rough and tumble, until he made his first bid for office in 1990. His loss in the general election that year, however, was due more to the fact that TX33 was almost wholly contained in Dallas County. After the redistricting of 1991, the rural areas were added. Still, Bailiff lost a second time in 1992, because those rural counties actually kept the incumbent Democrat in office, as he had been pro-life, and the Christian Coalition actually endorsed him over Bailiff.

Running a third time in 1994, Bailiff never forgot that. But instead of adopting a vengeful attitude, Bailiff craftily knew the direction the Party was headed and changed tactics that year. Although willing to exploit the another thing rule, Bailiff had been very private about his faith, primarily because it was linked to the painful memory of his mother's death by leukemia. On the trail in 1994, however, Bailiff talked openly about his conversion experience ten years earlier. In truth, Bailiff had little to say otherwise as he had already ran twice. But in discussing his faith, Christian conservatives realized that he was more or less on their side, even though they colored him with blue-blooded urbanity.

This and heightened anti-government sentiment gave Bailiff the precinct totals he needed to get into office that cycle. In an attempt to quell any doubts about his commitment, he became an aggressive spokesman for the pro-life components of the Contract with America, even appearing on CNN to discuss the first attempt to pass a ban on the partial-birth procedure. In 2000, he went toe-to-toe with a fellow Tejano Republican over the Elian Gonzalez controversy, supporting Christians' desire that the shipwrecked child stay away from Castro at all costs. And in 2005, Bailiff made regular speeches in support of what was a state issue: Texas Proposition 2, which defined marriage as heterosexual and proscriptively blocked any state jurisdiction from approving same-sex unions.

That is not to say the congressman had completely swallowed his pride. Just as surely as social issues became just another part of the House agenda under Tom DeLay, Bailiff knew that over time the Christians would become less of a grassroots force and would grow into another rural-based special interest (like the farmers). This was a natural course. But he had made a secret promise to himself that during the next round of redistricting—no matter what office he held—he would make sure he used all his influence to draw a congressional map that weakened the Christian-controlled, rural counties with pie-shaped districts. All he had to do was survive a couple more primaries. It certainly wasn't that he was anti-Christian; Bailiff simply believed the Coalition types were causing the party to miss good opportunities. As a businesswoman, Lisa somewhat agreed. And besides, it was undemocratic for so much power to reside in their hands.

CHAPTER TWELVE

Nate began his hunt for the Children's Hospital grant with a call to a reporter friend who handled *Metroplex Business Journal's* health beat. This was where Nate served Lisa the best, right after monitoring news around the state and nation about her candidates. Taking his cues from his conversation with Lisa, Nate would then start working leads around town about who did what and at what firm. Although Nate was not from North Texas, his Oklahoma manner and reporter's inquiry usually produced some good nuggets of people data. Canvassing a social landscape was second nature to him, owing to his Baptist upbringing.

It didn't hurt that Nate possessed an enviable network of local journalists from his days as a Hill press guy, but most of his best leads came straight out of the social columns and style sections, both print and online. He also never failed to mine church directories, once he found out a key individual's religious affiliation. And he was completely honest when he represented himself; he usually began a cold conversation with, "I'm Nate Knight, and I represent Congressman Bailiff's reelection campaign," which was of course true.

"How are you, Nate?" answered Joan McClatchie, a woman with a voice as deep as her hair was silver. Joan worked part-time for the Business Journal, covering the medical community. Her chief qualifications for the beat were that her first husband had been a professor at the

University of Texas Southwestern Medical School. She was an aberration in Nate's address book insofar as her contact info had not been acquired during his Hill days; Nate knew Joan because she and his mother had roomed together at Oklahoma State University. The maven had always been an encouragement to him in his journalistic pursuits.

"Why is it that you only call me when you need something?" she said.

"Joan, you know that's not true," Nate corrected playfully. He never felt he had any inherent charm upon which to rely, unlike his boss. Instead, Nate believed his honesty would always carry the moment when he was trolling for news. "I sometimes call others."

"That kind of wit doesn't sound very Baptist," chided Joan. She had long ago abandoned the church for the wine cellar.

"Hey, who directs research out at Metroplex Children's?" Nate asked. Then to head off any mystery about his motives, he laid out his earnest goal. "One of our clients is wanting to reach out to some of those folks for a fundraiser."

"Smart move, whoever that is," responded Joan. "There's a lot of money in that biotech stuff, especially when a new president overturns the stem-cell policy."

Nate did not want to waste time talking issues, so he did not take Joan's bait. He knew she leaned liberal or at least against the president.

"Our client doesn't necessarily want to hit the director up. But we want to help him figure out who is who in that scene down here."

Joan proceeded to meet Nate's goal by revealing a detailed group of local leaders in biotechnology, which included the Children's Hospital director. She even went a step further, telling Nate that if he called a particular pediatrician first, he would find out more than he wanted to know about all the research going on at Children's and elsewhere.

Nate cherished the freshness of information that his honesty broke open. Nate always felt rewarded and, more importantly, clear-minded when he directly asked questions without having to tiptoe around or violate his conscience. He believed he was being a good Christian, executing his work in obedience to God. He was like Daniel in the Bible when he and his friends refused to eat the Babylonians' food and came up with a creative alternative that honored Yahweh.

"Doctor, my name is Nate Knight, and I work with Congressman Paul Bailiff's campaign," Nate said in a later call to the pediatrician Joan had told him about. "The Congressman is interested in learning more about the biotech programs at Children's Hospital and especially about those who are involved with them. If you have a minute, I'd like to know about the research being done at the burn unit."

The evening of Bobby's accident, Bailiff was presented with an opportunity of the kind he thought the party was missing out on due to its Christian Conservative bent. In between votes, a White House Congressional Affairs Assistant told Bailiff that he was under orders by the President to horse trade for a line item in the Labor, Health, and Human Services Appropriations Bill that would fund a special project the First Lady wanted at Metroplex Children's Hospital.

Bailiff had obtained his seat on the House Appropriations Committee his freshman year in Congress thanks to a Texan Majority Leader and Whip. Although the initiative would be supported by what was—for all intents and purposes—an earmark, the assistant and Bailiff knew that with the Democrats in control, there was no need to be hypocritical about member requests. Still, the earmark was not additional spending over the previous year; it was simply language added in the bill's report directing that a certain amount of money go toward "tissue regeneration studies at Metroplex Children's Hospital."

The First Lady had been involved with the pediatric burn unit at the hospital before her husband ran for president and a California-based biotech firm came to her attention as having the best hope for tissue repair. The firm's principals quickly became friends then donors of the First Family. The assistant explained to Bailiff that this initiative would not only bring a cutting-edge stem cell firm to Dallas, but that also the President planned to spend his final years in office supporting budget efforts to grow the project into a bona fide research facility. The First Lady then planned to devote the majority of her time to the facility when they returned home in 2009.

Immediately upon hearing the assistant's pitch, Bailiff felt a warm conviction that helping to bring a stem cell firm to Dallas would be a career milestone. The death of his mother motivated him to get into office and help efforts just such as this one. Although it was initially for children, Bailiff thought ahead to all the fruits of such a facility, even in fighting cancer.

Bailiff of course quickly saw the many other benefits of supporting the initiative. Not only would he purchase valuable capital with the president for carrying his water in a Democratic Congress, but he would also have entrée into a new clique of potential donors: the biotech community. Out-of-state money always made a difference in the coffers, and Bailiff's work in securing the earmark—report language, that is—would only enhance his ability to get that another thing from the breast-cancer crowd at home.

Yet barely had his conversation with the assistant ended when Bailiff's cell phone had gone off in the Capitol and Nate had explained what had happened to Bobby. After another hour of voting, Bailiff had hopped on the first plane to DFW. He knew then that discussing a plan of capitalizing on the Children's grant with Lisa would have been deeply inappropriate at that moment, and he was genuinely concerned about her. He'd planned to call two weeks later at the latest.

CHAPTER THIRTEEN

June 8

Dear God,

I praise your name for this day. We have many hard days ahead, but now Bobby is home. You are ever gracious.

Lisa had been blown away by the change in Brenda's demeanor since she and Ron had received the news of their grandchild. Gone was the hair-trigger edge of anxiety that stood up from her mother-in-law's skin. And not only had Brenda abandoned her fortress of worry, if only because she now had something else to think about, but she also became a powerful ally in the cause to get Bobby home. Brenda understood fully both the practical and instinctual motives for Lisa to get the expecting father home. To that end, Lisa's in-laws became assets instead of liabilities.

The elder Jeffuses paid dividends for Bobby's homecoming. Brenda and Ron took the day of and the day before Bobby's return to clean and prepare the house in Sachse for his special needs. Although fairly neat to begin with, the dust had collected around the place in the weeks since the accident. Moreover, the guest bedroom had to be rearranged for Bobby's bed and support equipment. Ron had made the new medical furniture his personal mission. He had a handyman nature that was the genetic parent to Bobby's construction aptitude. He made

86

sure that all the equipment was assembled properly, organizing its delivery for that day before his son's arrival and directing the most efficient setup of various medical tables and trees according to how he observed their layout in the rehab hospital.

Meanwhile, Brenda armed herself with a cleaning caddy full of 409, Windex, Pledge, and rags. After a day's devotion, the house had never been cleaner. Lisa had absolutely no issues with her mother-in-law doing the Rhoda thing. It kept Brenda occupied.

The ambulance pulled quietly into the Jeffus home in Sachse around 11:30 a.m. Only A.J. had joined the family for the home-coming; it was one of those moments that, while she'd received many offers of help, Lisa only wanted her closest friend with her. There were too many difficult things she felt needed to stay within the propriety of the family. An exception was Curtiss, who A.J. had co-opted into the return as a sort of required clerical presence.

As the EMTs rolled Bobby's large, sheeted body over the bumpy threshold, Lisa had kind of a dead, despairing feeling come over her. She had this strange sense that an unwelcome guest was arriving. She felt guilty as a result, but she was curious to identify the emotions as the same that had caused her to blurt out her frustrated prayer at the rehab hospital. As she led the EMTs down the hallway, past the guest bathroom, she somewhat hastily pointed out the new hospital bed then made a quick retreat into the room that would become the baby's.

Dear God,

I feel conflict. Forgive me of any selfish desire.

A.J. found Lisa lingering in the doorway of the room that would become the nursery. She was still in the dark about her friend's pregnancy. She had assigned Curtiss and herself lunch duty, making her signature tuna sandwiches while wearing an apron over her navy suit. A.J. saw that Lisa was unsettled.

"Overwhelmed?" she asked her friend.

Lisa didn't tear up but showed that same stiff reaction to the situation, which had occurred during her prayer with Nate at the rehab hospital. A.J. noticed reactionary anger in Lisa's face.

"Is it all right to be mad? I am now just really mad," said Lisa.

"Of course it is." A.J. assured. "I'm mad. I've been mad. You're going through a natural grief process even though no one has died. You're at an anger phase.

"Bobby can only get better," she asserted.

Lisa responded with some incredulity on her face to her friend's words. While she had told Asitajee, Bailiff, and Nate about the baby and the Elder Jeffuses had heard about it during her nervous prayer, she still had been tight lipped about it, not discussing it with anyone. She felt she was betraying her closest friend. "A.J.—"

"Lisa?" asked Brenda loudly, coming down the hall. "The nurse is here." Asitajee had helped Lisa schedule the arrival of the home-health nurse in conjunction with Bobby. Lisa and A.J. followed Brenda back out to the front of the house.

"I'm Sharon McAnnas," said a stout, fiftyish woman with a gray and brunette perm. She had a stylish Kohl's look today for the first appointment, but Sharon's bricklike build belied most feminine forms. Later visits in scrubs would serve to further obscure what curves Sharon had. She was open and gregarious, but Lisa did not pick up on any sort of gushing sweetness that she thought was the stock-in-trade of home nurses.

Asitajee's recommendation had been the Home Health Agency of none other than George Masters. Lisa was elated and knew she could communicate easily with Masters. She identified the recommendation as nothing less than God's grace. She felt comfortable with his professionalism and knew that their political relationship wouldn't get in the way of Bobby's care. Masters lived up in southern Black County and out of the Metroplex. He was, in fact, the GOP Chairman for Black County. But Lisa figured if he traveled thirty minutes for church, it was no problem for his agency to serve down on the edge of Dallas County.

"Good to meet you." Lisa heard herself mumbling.

"How are you feeling, darlin'?" asked Sharon. Suddenly the doting–nurse voice came out, laden with Southern syrup tapped from the tree of a trailer park. "My nursing director told me yew were pregnant."

"What!" shrieked A.J.

So much for a doctor's confidence, Lisa thought. "I'm sorry." Lisa felt run down. She walked into the future nursery and sat on the double bed inside. All of her exuberance was gone. She was having trouble thinking. Sharon and A.J. were on her heels.

"Darlin,' I know you've got to be tired. Got to be. Don't you worry about your husband. We'll get him comfortable," said Sharon, leading Lisa to lean back on the bed as A.J. looked on.

Lisa looked into A.J.'s face momentarily. Clearly, a breach of trust had occurred, but she lacked the strength to sandbag the levee.

"We have some lunch almost ready," A.J. announced, going back to the kitchen.

Lisa realized she only had the mental strength to know she didn't have any strength at all as a result of the past three weeks. She drifted off to sleep.

Nate's cell vibrated on his desk as he reviewed *The Drudge Report* on his computer screen. He recognized that the number was Bailiff's.

"Yes, Paul," he answered.

Bailiff had always allowed, even insisted, his staff call him by his first name. He said it helped him feel grounded. Former staffers could retain the privilege.

"Nate," Bailiff commanded with his baritone over the airwaves, "is Lisa there? Weren't they bringing Bobby home today?"

"Yes, sir. But I am pretty sure she won't be in the office. Did you try her cell?"

"No, it's okay. She had emailed me an initial list she had put together for a biotech event. Did you have a hand in that?"

"Yes, sir. I actually put that list together, and she wanted me to send it from her email while she was busy with Bobby. I discovered the firm down at Children's administering the grant. That's the CEO's name there at the top."

"I saw that. Great work. Your sleuthing spared me a call to the East Wing and a capital expense in finding that out," Bailiff said. He then altered his tone, if not his volume, "Nate, I'm really glad you're handling this, because of Lisa. I think that with all that's on her plate—you knew she was pregnant, right?"

"Yes."

"I think that with all she has going on, maybe you and I along with my chief of staff can get this group together and begin the relationship."

Nate had never seen himself as a fundraiser. Not only did he think of it as "dirty work," it was also a tedious process of endless phone calls that interfered with his news-junkie habit. But he was willing to try, if only to help his boss keep the business going.

"Let me know how I can help."

"Okay. I'm going to put a call in to this CEO fella, this Dr. Ranzim, and I'll be back in touch with you about how to proceed."

"Yes, sir."

"I also wanted to let you know I'll be out at the Black County GOP monthly meeting this Tuesday, if you'd like to come along."

"Sure thing," Nate answered. He knew full well why Bailiff wanted him there. He made a mental note to get the congressman a list of recent bestsellers among evangelicals. Nate heard the other end of the line go dead. Bailiff moved quickly on his action items.

Lisa slowly opened her eyes to see A.J. seated on the foot of the bed. It was raining again, and the low light from the window indicated that it was fast becoming evening.

Lisa was restless from the searing impression of a last-minute dream. There had been a happy feeling of positive images, then a hard, ultra-vivid memory of when Bobby first spoke to her. In the dream, he was his old self but wearing a hospital gown. They were walking along a sidewalk of the University of Texas campus on a cloudy day, although her personal memory of their first meeting was in reality a sunny day. She concluded the dark, almost gloomy sky in the dream came from the constantly overcast days of the current spring.

"What is your name?" asked Bobby in that matter-of-fact way. "You have the sharpest eyes."

Then she woke up.

"How long was I asleep?"

"Seven hours," answered A.J.

"You've been here that long?"

"Curtiss is still here. He's a good man. The nurse left around three. I think Bobby is in good hands."

Lisa sat up on the bed, nearer to her friend. "I'm really sorry about not telling you."

"I asked Mrs. Jeffus about it. She said you only mentioned it but have been completely unwilling to talk about it." Then A.J. looked pleadingly at Lisa and said, "I don't get that."

"You know how hard it has been for Bobby and me to get pregnant. I just wanted him to know first, thinking he would wake up. The Jeffuses only heard about it because they were in the room praying with me."

"Don't you really think he'll get better?" asked A.J.

"I'm frustrated. But Asitajee seems so hopeful."

"Well, it will take awhile. I am really hurt, Lise, not because you haven't told me but because you don't seem to be realistic about the situation. It's your only real character flaw, girl. If you have some sort of plan or expectation in your mind, you tend to forget what you have to do pragmatically to get there. Which means you don't communicate about everything. You are being too self-reliant."

Lisa yawned, still groggy. "Yes, ma'am. You know, I feel kinda weird about the baby. I mean, I'm excited and all, but it's just not what I expected."

"Obviously!" A.J. said.

"No—what I mean is that, Bobby's accident or no, having a baby is kind of anti-climactic. I don't feel that I'm achieving any kind of fulfillment, as a woman or whatever. I mean, I'm just having a baby."

"This is a big deal, though, girl—"

"I know," Lisa said, frustrated. "Maybe my attitude will change as I get further along."

"I bet it will," said A.J. as she embraced her friend. "Dear God," she prayed, "help us to see all the grace around us."

"Amen," they both said.

"Curtiss has to go, but I will stay tonight if—"

"No, no," insisted Lisa as both women stood up. "Y'all have been good enough to let me rest. Now I'll be wired for a bit, and I want to simply spend the evening alone with Bobby. I have to get used to this new situation—how's that for being practical?" she said with a smile.

Lisa received a hug from Curtiss. "I have a cousin who does medical massage therapy," he offered. "We can put you in touch with him."

"Thanks. That might be good," Lisa said. The summer rain picked up heavily, but with an enormous umbrella and a sprint, A.J. and Curtiss got out to the sidewalk and into his blue BMW.

Seated in his Durango a house away, Danny recognized A.J. as the couple clung to each other and made their dash through the downpour. Danny didn't know Curtiss but correctly assumed he was A.J.'s boyfriend as he shut the door for her then came around to the driver's side of the BMW. Neither Curtiss nor A.J. noticed him parked a slight distance to their rear as they fought the rain with their umbrella.

Danny noted the vehicle model as well as the license plate, which read: WWBOD. He figured whoever A.J. was dating was a kindred spirit, supporting Senator Bartin Oltan's early presidential candidacy. He thought the plate was cute and felt justified in his theory that liberals were just plain better at the visual gimmickry.

Already wearing raingear, Danny stepped out of his SUV confident that only Lisa remained in the house. He was oblivious to the heavy drops as he approached the door. Some distant thunder pealed. He rang the door bell.

Lisa still hadn't gone in to check on Bobby, instead going into the kitchen to pour herself a Dr. Pepper as a boost to her blood sugar. Glass in hand, she answered the door. "Hi! Come in!" Danny stepped in, dripping wet, and shut the door behind him. "What are you doing here?" She felt a rush far greater than any soda could give.

"Sorry, I don't plan to stay," Danny said. "I just wanted to make sure he got home okay."

"How did you know?"

"Come on, Lise," said Danny with a smile.

"No, I mean it. How did you figure it out?" Lisa asked, now somewhat nervous. Danny's possible motives for coming over to her house raced through her mind.

As he took off his rain jacket and hung it on a doorknob over the entry tile, he explained, "I called Parkland. They said he was discharged to a rehab hospital but wouldn't say which one. I made a guess of three up this way, finally found Northeast, which said he'd been sent home."

So much for patient privacy, too, Lisa thought. She remained very curious about why Danny appeared. She knew that slipping around was his way, but why was he up here?

"Are you on your way out to Yale?"

"Nice place."

"I don't guess you've ever visited us since we moved back. You want a tour?"

"Where's Bobby? I have something for him. Do you have a CD player?"

"Uh, yes. Just a minute." Lisa walked quickly out into the garage where she retrieved the squatty boom box Bobby kept on his workbench. Maybe Danny was just there to pay his regards. By the time she and Bobby had gotten serious during college, Danny was doing other things, working on races around the state even though he had not quite graduated. As a result, Danny and Bobby only met a few times and never bonded. Clearly, he was concerned as much about her, Lisa concluded. Maybe he did have some feelings down deep in there for her. Maybe she shouldn't make too much of it. She met Danny in the living room and led him down the hall to the guest room, radio in hand.

Bobby still lay in the bed utterly motionless. She busied herself with plugging in the radio. The room was lit only by the low setting of a cheap three-way floor lamp brought in by Ron per the rehab therapist's recommendation. Bobby's father had positioned the bulky hospital bed dead center in the room so that anyone could get on any side of it. But in doing so, the bed dominated the space—left narrow lanes between it and the walls—and forced Lisa to walk around it to get anywhere. The nurse's touch had been applied to the patient and space with a professional-looking bed made around her husband's body. In addition, all the necessary medical supplies had been neatly organized on the tables. As she placed the radio on the top of an unused chest of drawers, Lisa saw Sharon's business card along with some notes. There was Masters' Christian fish logo embossed in red. Lisa decided she would need to call Nurse McAnnas soon to get a handle on the feeding schedule.

"I brought him something that I think will stimulate his brain," said Danny as he crossed into the room. As he turned to come around the bed, Lisa noticed that the denim-style shirt he was wearing was completely soaked in the back. Standing directly in front of her, he produced a CD case with a disk marked in black Marksalot: Texas Fight.

"You are soaking wet! Bobby has a T-shirt back here I can loan you," she said, hustling back out of the room. That go-getter hostess side of her bubbled up.

Danny placed the CD into the player, and the brassy, kinetic sounds of the University of Texas marching band blared into the room. Danny quickly lowered the volume and then unbuttoned his shirt. He pulled it off his broad shoulders right as Lisa reentered.

The sight of Danny's chest sent an unexpected shock down Lisa's spine. She forced her eyes onto Bobby in the bed as she tried to coolly walk back around to the chest of drawers. Between the sudden sexual tension and "The Eyes of Texas", she released a burst of laughter.

Danny smiled, taking the T-shirt from Lisa. "Pretty cool, huh?" he drawled.

Seeing the shirt go on, Lisa felt it was safe to remove her gaze from the motionless lump of her husband's body. She looked at Danny with a goofy smile.

"Thanks for the shirt." Thunder rattled the room's window. "You know, I know we're not gonna be judged any more by a flood like Noah had, but I still think too much rain is a sign God doesn't like something—especially here in Texas, where it's supposed to quit raining in the summer."

"What about drought? That's biblical judgment too," observed Lisa. Her Southfork Church small group had studied the life of Elijah back during the winter quarter. "So which is it, Mr. Preacherman?" For a moment, the pair were kidding like it was college all over again.

"Aw, sister, God straightens us any way he can," he said, smiling. Then that dark pall suddenly rushed over him. Lisa felt a chill. "When there are extremes, that is the sign of disfavor."

Lisa felt her mind swing from wanting Danny to leave to seizing him in an embrace. She wanted to dismiss her uncertainty to exhaustion but knew she couldn't, after just having a long, long power nap. There was something unsettled in her heart…something fundamentally disturbed. The music stopped. She thought of her pregnancy, hoping the information would somehow provide an emergency defense.

"Texas Fight" came out of the CD player.

"Need to get up to Black County. I told Angelina I'd help her with her long division," said Danny. He exited the room.

Lisa didn't follow him out.

CHAPTER FOURTEEN

Nate pulled up to the Black County Criminal Justice Center but parked well away from its entrance. He saw Bailiff already working one or two of the party faithful outside. At the congressman's side was a clueless suburbanite woman/child, no doubt one of this summer's TX33 district interns. The poor girl was way overdressed for the event, wearing an Ann Taylor suit among a small forest of Wranglers. Nate saw his opportunity to catch Bailiff and slip a small index card into his hand before entering the event.

"Hey, glad you could make it," remarked Bailiff as he took the short list of Christian bestsellers from his old flack. Bailiff resumed a conversation he was having as he effortlessly walked into the building, never allowing the constituent to feel he had anything but his congressman's undivided attention. Inside a lecture room, Nate took a seat in the back.

George Masters called the meeting to order. Even though the red-skinned chairman was pushing sixty, he didn't look a day over forty-five, owing to both a head of solid brown hair and a trim build. Once a pastor, Masters had no trouble leading a group of people. Although he held a degree from Dallas Theological Seminary, he felt he had "lost his calling" and later took a job managing a doctor's office. A few years later, he started his home health agency using his name and the Ichthus fish logo. He made a lot of money in the late eighties and early nineties and stayed profitable even during the Balanced Budget Act cuts after the Republicans took over.

Masters's current tenure as Black County GOP chairman was really only that of custodial role. He took back the reigns during 2006 when the then chairman (a program manager from the county's big-defense contractor) got transferred to a job in Canada. Masters was typical of local GOP bosses who had mellowed from their Christian Coalition activist days and taken a sort of golden-years attitude now that they had an iron grip on the state machinery. Still, Masters never hesitated to do the party's grunt work, knowing its importance. He also felt a little insecure over the fact that the Christian Coalition had endorsed Bailiff's opponent back in 1992. He wanted to stay in a relevant position as a county chairman in order to retain his value and access to Bailiff, as well as amend any loyalty issues. Bailiff kept Masters on his short list of confidants for the same reason. While speaking to the Black County GOP's monthly meeting was a regular stop on his schedule, Bailiff generally came calling when Masters had something afoot.

After a prayer and the pledges, Masters introduced Bailiff, who gave a standard, off-the-cuff legislative update. With the current Speaker in charge, pretty much all of it was bad news. Yet there was something about Bailiff's down-home delivery that prevented his rambling update about card check and climate change from sufficiently alarming the base voters in the room. Bailiff conspicuously left out any comments on the effort to stop congressional earmarking. Nate observed a certain resignation in the room; a spirit made worse when Bailiff conveyed unencouraging news about the prospects of retaining the White House.

"What about stem-cell research?" asked Masters somewhat suddenly.

"What about it?" asked Bailiff.

"Well, we know a Democratic president, God forbid, will sign whatever bill Congress puts out to overturn the existing policy. If that happens, embryos will be murdered at a rate that will make Auschwitz look like a Kindergarten."

"I support the existing ban on new-cell lines," said Bailiff, quickly staking his ground. "And I will vote against any effort to expand that. As a member of the Appropriations Committee, I will also oppose federal funding of embryonic stem cell research."

"But what are you gonna do to stop it?" asserted a voice near the back, not far from where Nate seated himself. "We know all about how you people can say no but then reap the benefits. How can we stop embryonic stem cell research completely? Will you stand up to Michael J. Fox? Will you say no to the Juvenile Diabetes Foundation?"

Bailiff knew he should have known better that to underestimate what his constituents knew. He attempted to change the subject with, "I will do my best to stop it. And there are other battles to fight." He then segued into some more of the conservative agenda that didn't have a prayer of being considered. Finally, Masters stepped in to free Bailiff from the sights of the firing squad. He then ended the meeting after some announcements.

Masters took Bailiff's hand and joked with him about putting him on the spot.

"Have you read Keith Kenner's new book?" asked Bailiff. "I heard it is good."

Masters lit up. He always saw Bailiff's interest in spiritual things as an encouragement. While he had felt the believer's bond between them, Masters always saw Bailiff as someone who needed guidance in the dark world of the Beltway. "I have a copy in my car. Let me go get it for you right now!" Bailiff then reached out to shake another hand.

June 12, 10:00 a.m.

Dear God,

I'm feeling a little besieged. Guide me through this day with your grace.

Lisa feared her prayers were going stale. What was grace, anyway? Her pastor, Keith Kenner up at Southfork, described it as God's goodness in spite of sinfulness. Still, remembering this only rang hollow with Lisa. She wondered what the true meaning of grace was. Just having a baby? Maybe carrying life in the midst of a trial, like with Bobby. If so, that seemed heavy-handed. How are people lifted up by God's goodness? She felt discouraged as she thought that so much of what had been presented to her as the Christian life was simply that which enabled goodness and decency—something that was supposed to be the fruit of a changed life.

But a life changed from what? She had anything but a so-called "Damascus Road" conversion. She never murdered, cheated on, or lied to anybody, even when politics lends itself to exaggeration and dishonesty the way fast food lends itself to a heart attack. Then she remembered the comfort from God she experienced during her mother's cancer. Although she attended InterVarsity meetings at University of Texas, she drifted away from regular church attendance those early years in D.C. But her mother's illness brought her to her knees and got her into Capitol Baptist Church and its leadership under a young, articulate pastor. It was there Lisa first heard about the concept of grace and came to a conclusion in her mind that she was a sinner in need of salvation through Jesus' sacrifice. While she later confessed her conversion to the pastor and his wife, the all-consuming end stages of her mother's cancer interrupted her regular attendance yet again. Still, she wanted to be near God's people and the spirit of grace they fostered.

She found that fellowship at Southfork Church upon returning home. For Bobby, both attendance at Capitol Baptist and Southfork were simple continuity from his own upbringing in a large, conservative Southern Baptist Church. Yet he was loath to be too involved. In contrast, Lisa wanted to participate and more often than not attended one of the many small groups that had broken out within the North Dallas megachurch. She knew the fellowship was in what the Gospel of John called "in spirit and truth." As she reflected on

the goodness shown her by the body of Christ during those difficult years, during and after which her mother died, she remembered
God's grace was something that was conveyed when one was in spirit
and truth; emotions were the deceiver.

Lisa put her prayer journal aside on her desk. She was grateful to
get back into the office after a regular commute. Sharon McAnnas
had arrived right on time that morning, and Lisa made her commute
as if nothing had changed. She had been in and out of the office, of
course, over the past few weeks when she could get away from the
hospital. But today started off normally. Maybe that was what grace
meant: getting back to normal.

Nate entered Lisa's office with a hardcopy of a spreadsheet and
sat across from Lisa at her desk. "Getting back to normal?" He asked
telepathically.

Lisa smiled, then yawned. "Still tired. I feel like I'm sleeping for
two people."

"I went out to Black County with Paul last night," Nate stated,
half confessing, half informing his boss of the new role he seemed
to be walking into.

"Really?"

"I want to tell you that Bailiff asked me to work with him on the
biotech list." Nate seemed to want to preempt any line of inquiry.

"That's good," said Lisa to Nate's surprise. "Maybe I can finally
get you down into the slave galley with the rest of us."

Nate smiled.

"Was George there?"

"Masters? Oh yes," answered Nate.

"He's doing Bobby's home health. So far, I'm impressed."

"Is someone there twenty-four hours?"

"No…just from eight until eight, right now. We built some
overlap into the evening in case I'm late and until I get the hang
of feeding and changing him before night. We have two shifts that
change at two. I'm supposed to go home and meet the afternoon
nurse here in a little bit."

"Are you … how are you going to manage it when you get further along with the baby?" asked Nate somewhat sheepishly.

"I'll still have the help. I mean, coverage or money is not at all an issue," said Lisa, staring off a bit. She latched onto the pink baseball bat on the wall for a second.

Nate wasn't sure Lisa was completely engaged with him. He held his spreadsheet out for Lisa to see. "Well, I wanted to show you the list we had worked up for the biotech folks Bailiff wanted to go after. They're all in California, with a pair of director types up in the Boston area—"

"Who did you find out in Texas would qualify as the 'biotech community'?" interrupted Lisa.

"We have some good leads. Bailiff went ahead this weekend and called the CEO of this firm, a Dr. Joseph Ranzim. He told me last night after the meeting that they had a good conversation. He said this firm has some technologies under development that can regenerate skin that has been burned."

"Regeneration?" Lisa repeated. "That sounds like stem-cell technology to me."

Nate paused, nodding. "Bailiff didn't say. You know, it's funny, someone in the GOP meeting last night carped out against stem-cell research."

"What did Paul do?"

"He said as a member of the Appropriations Committee, he would not vote to fund it."

"Yeah, but the way things are now, and if a Democrat gets in the White House, his no vote won't matter."

"Funny … that's what this person at the meeting said, in so many words."

"Do these people want anything specific, like an earmark or something? The biotech people," Lisa clarified.

Nate grinned again. "I guess that's why they pay you the big money," he said.

"Find out just to make sure. Our job is to get the dollars, but I don't think anyone on Bailiff's staff is going to be tuned in to what this bunch wants, if anything."

"Sure thing. But I think that's also why Bailiff is being so aggressive in starting a relationship with them now, before there are any policy changes or tricky votes."

"Yes, but check with Bailiff the next time you talk to him, or I will. The only thing worse than taking money from someone we don't agree with is having to give it back," Lisa quipped.

"One other thing," said Nate. "Bailiff is acting like he wants to go ahead and set up an event for these people. He says they're coming to town in a couple of weeks to visit Children's Hospital."

"Aha! What we do best! What day?" At the thought of assembling a bona fide event, Lisa came down out of her thoughts and into party planning. She perked up.

"June 29. They arrive at DFW around 12:00 p.m. Daylight, and then they have their meetings out at Children's." Nate realized he was getting into the nitty-gritty of handling contributors, not merely collecting information on them for his boss's fund solicitation, or "ask."

"Great. We'll go ahead and plan for that." As Nate exited, Lisa began to compose an email to her staff person who handled organizing events. An Instant Message popped up on her screen from A.J.: "Baby expo at Market Hall, June 30. We are there! ;)"

Lisa smiled. "Sounds great!" she replied. In her email, she asked her staffer for a standard setup: cocktails and dinner for twenty. Instead of the standard location at the Crescent in Uptown, however, she instructed her staffer to price a suite at the new Hotel Palomar, which had just opened up on Mockingbird across from the DART station and over Central Expressway from Southern Methodist University. She wanted a dining venue that overlooked campus, as well as one with more contemporary décor. While there were risks to holding an event at a new place for first time donors, Lisa thought the academic backdrop would signal to these biotechies, as she came to call them, that Bailiff cared deeply about their intellectual purpose as well as their business program.

"Stephanie Knight told me she wants to plan a shower. What's she like?" continued A.J.'s Instant Messaging.

"A gun-toting, Bible-quoting, president-loving soccer mom who loves babies—you'll get along famously."

"I can't wait ;) Another chance to convert someone to 'our side.'"

Lisa realized how fortunate the world was that even with her opinions, A.J. truly respected those who felt deeply about their beliefs. Lisa swore to herself that she would never let another breach in their friendship happen again.

Lisa composed a second email to "ALL STAFF." Whenever the Mockingbird Group shifted into event planning mode, she made a general announcement to everyone so that no matter who you were or what you were working on, the completion of the event had to take priority. The "ALL STAFF" email also served to help everyone save the date, in case all hands were needed. A small-dinner event likely wouldn't require all hands on deck, but Lisa thought it built team spirit for the group to have an event date firmly fixed in mind.

While two of her staffers went to work on the hotel and food, she and the intern, Cara, would compile the call list and begin dialing for RSVPs. Since they were dealing with a specific group of people coming to town for a specific purpose, less time would be needed on making calls. But Lisa wanted to try to include some of the biotech leaders from DFW, even if they were from competing hospitals. The final list would be subject to Bailiff's approval, but compiling a list early—even a short one—served to: (a) save time later; (b) show the client (Bailiff in this case) that there was more money out there locally on this and related issues; and (c) commit the group to other fundraising opportunities. Any potential donor was a potential commission. It was basic dollars and sense.

Back in his office, Nate began to think more about the fact that he could well be finding himself starting relationships with these contributors, and Lisa's direction that he find out all he could about any stem-cell issues with this group was not a crass covering of the bases for him. Nate could not fathom partnering in any way with those whose hubris put them above the ethical considerations of harvesting human beings, let alone asking these modern day Dr. Frankensteins for money.

Nate decided to do some in-depth Net-stalking on Joseph Ranzim. His first searches were mainly pabulum from Ranzim's firm's Web site, as well as those of other medical and academic institutions with which he was affiliated. Other listings were online documents and lengthy, arcane articles related to science and biotechnology. Nate quickly jumped to page result fifteen and saw no references to Ranzim. Backtracking a bit, he saw that uninterrupted page rankings of Dr. Joseph Ranzim stopped at about page result eleven. Nate dug in to examine every single link. His conscience was heating up and would not let him do otherwise.

Lisa was confident the biotech event could be organized by week's end, but it would take some effort. The commute earlier back home to meet the afternoon nurse ate almost two hours out of the day, but Lisa was pretty sure there wouldn't be many of those. She knew, as did everyone including the elder Jeffuses, that the nurses were there so that she could continue with her routine. Besides, after seeing the afternoon nurse do a bed change, Lisa knew these trained professionals were far better to her husband than she could be. She believed that planning the biotech event, while short notice, was God's providence in enabling her and her staff to get back into the game after almost a month of disruption. She was grateful for the trial and knew that by his grace she'd stay successful.

CHAPTER FIFTEEN

June 15

Dear God,

Thank you for getting me through the week. Thank you for Bobby's nurses and the home-health agency. God bless George Masters. Help us to have a good weekend.

In Jesus' name. Amen.

Quitting time on Friday arrived at the Mockingbird Group. The week had indeed gone well. Lisa was still worn down (she felt as though a space alien had taken control of her body), but Bobby was home and she felt caught up at work. With Nate's erstwhile uninterested help, they had successfully planned a small contributor event on the fly.

Best of all, she felt she had fully patched things up with A.J., as her friend found the Baby Expo and made plans for the two of them to go. Lisa thought it would be nice to work hard over the next couple of weeks, have her event, and then spend a special afternoon with her BFF, during which the new baby would be celebrated. She cherished the thought of being able to attend an event in which she was the VIP.

Lisa had made this last entry into her prayer journal out of a concern that she might not have time once she got home for the weekend. With her staff gone, she sat silently in her office writing. Outside her window, she watched the rain pick up yet again. She had never seen rain like it had been doing all spring in Texas. Her grandfather—less than a generation removed from the Dust Bowl—would have called all the rain a "drought buster."

Lisa took comfort in the occasional memory of her grandfather, a man whom she considered both wise and tough, a man unafraid to fight for his convictions and for reforms. She remembered how, in private conversations, Grandfather Dillon would lambaste Richard Nixon over his secrecy and corruption. In later years, she was struck by how little he cared for party loyalty when wrongdoing was in the mix. His integrity plus his strength were key in his election victory in 1978. In her mind, he was Carter plus Reagan—an honest man who wasn't afraid to take on the big enemies.

She packed up her prayer journal and Blackberry to make her way out. Passing back toward the front, she let out a gasp to see Danny leaning against the reception desk, holding yet another CD.

"You are so sneaky! Why do you do this!" She set her purse down on the desk. "How did you get in?"

"Door was unlocked."

"I guess Cara was the last to leave. We don't give our interns keys."

"Just like on the Hill."

"I mean it! You scared me." Lisa was about as mad as her jovial personality would permit her.

"How ya feeling?"

Lisa realized Danny didn't know about her pregnancy, but she still had a good defense if she appeared not to have a spring in her step. "Better. Tired. But I can see a routine settling in with Bobby."

"I didn't want to come by the house, but here's Brookshire's briefing book." Danny extended his hand with the CD. "Better late than never."

"Whose?" Lisa looked up at Danny, still slightly annoyed.

"The Tyler Senator, remember?"

"Oh, right! I'm sorry. A lot going on. Why didn't you just mail it?"

Danny shifted off the desk, looking into Lisa's face. She felt a small rush. "I guess I'm just a little too old-school paranoid that someone will intercept my data."

"I've got a couple hours. You wanna get a burger?" Lisa heard herself ask.

It was a very short drive to Keller's drive-in, although the tangle of traffic lights where Abrams and Skillman met in Vickery Meadow added a couple of minutes. Lisa and Danny didn't have to risk getting wet at the longstanding dive, as its covered parking afforded the only seating. Danny hopped from his Durango into the passenger seat of Lisa's Tahoe. Lisa felt that keeping things away from a dining table would honor propriety and that remaining in the driver's seat conveyed to Danny the requirement of her departure. Lisa ordered enough supper for a ship of sailors, while Danny purchased a grilled cheese with water from the pancho-clad carhop.

In spite of the on-and-off rain, Friday night along Northwest Highway was getting going around and beside the drive-in. Covered in black, shiny raingear, knots of bikers rumbled and popped their chrome into park under any available covered space. Amid the mufflers, Danny and Lisa reminisced for a few minutes, making small talk.

"You know, I need to ask you, did they actually book you when you got arrested during the Norplant protest?" asked Lisa. "I know they let you out only six hours later."

"Well, they did. But I kid you not, the film got messed up some way, and it didn't make an impression."

"Really? Weird. That's just as well. Any mug shot that might be out there … even one taken during legitimate protest … is impossible to overcome these days. Who knew the Internet would be what it is today back then, huh?" said Lisa in between bites of French fries. She had perfected the art of keeping her makeup more or less intact while engorging on greasy food. This was done by breaking up food like fries into small pieces. These bites of potato-flavored oil were then carefully eaten.

"Yeah, all the technology. Too bad our people can't seem to make it work for them."

"I think that has to do with your pagan visual theory. I thought about it some more," explained Lisa, "and one of the biggest problems we have is that middle-aged white guys are just uninteresting to look at. It's a fundamental problem, really, and it doesn't matter if they're on a flyer or on a Web site. It's government by Elmer Fudd."

Danny laughed. Lisa was glad to see the old joy of her friend. She knew his pain, even though he never discussed the untimely death of his wife. She also knew his burdens, suddenly having to raise a daughter. She was glad the circumstances forced him out of the rat race of the Beltway and back home where his family could help—kind of God working through inconvenience.

"How often do your in-laws see Angelina?"

There was that sudden, dark chill again! Lisa felt very uneasy as Danny's mood turned on a dime.

"Look," declared Lisa, reaching across the SUV console and taking Danny's greasy hands, "I am tired of being spooked every time your family or whatever is mentioned. Have you ever talked with anybody about all that?"

Danny let Lisa hold his hands, but she sensed his conflict. He finally answered, "What is there to talk about?"

"Well, for one, I think you haven't grieved all the way over that car accident or whatever. I know you well enough to know that you'll bottle it up—"

Danny suddenly interrupted Lisa by saying, "It is best it stay in as tight a bottle as possible." He opened the Tahoe door to make one of his customary abrupt exits. Lisa caught him on his bicep.

"Listen!" Danny demanded, shooting Lisa a look that could kill. "There is too much information out there that you just can't handle. You're just a pretty, green-eyeshade beggar working for a whole cabal of beggars."

"What?" Lisa didn't see what politics had to do with Danny's personal tragedies. She regrouped. "Please let me help you," she argued with the full force of her spirit.

She looked Danny full in the face. "I ... I want to help you. You and I are kindred spirits of a sort, and I know I can help you."

The rain began to pick up again. Danny broke away. He pushed his way past some bikers crowded under the canopy then bent his tall frame back into his Durango.

Lisa watched Danny pull out onto Northwest Highway and head west. After a few moments she realized she was alone, as the Tahoe remained parked at a place with increasingly rough-looking patrons. She watched some cheap, paunchy women throw themselves at some of the bikers. As she restarted the engine, she thought that illicit was too commendable a term to describe the gathering clientele at the drive-in; trashy was more appropriate.

Between the low-lifes she left at Keller's, and Danny's berating, Lisa became very vexed on her commute back north. She wanted to call A.J., but she knew full well what A.J.'s opinion of Danny was and what she'd likely say if Lisa admitted to her that she had just had a burger with him. She hit the speed dial number on her phone. In the same instant she hit the stop button. She didn't want to be lectured. She sensed that she might be playing with fire.

Carrie Underwood played on the radio, although Lisa was not listening. She wondered how she could get to Danny to get him to break open. Maybe she couldn't ease his pain, but if she could just get him to a place where he could get help and be open to God's grace, then perhaps that was why God had put him back in her life at this time.

Lisa wondered again about Bobby's accident and the timing with the pregnancy. Some things about God's timing made sense; this sure didn't. She realized she wouldn't be home in time to feed Bobby. She had failed to get the afternoon nurse's phone number, and Lisa and Bobby didn't keep a landline. She hoped the nurse would stay until she got there. That was the agency policy, but they hadn't really put a late evening for Lisa to the test.

Lisa pulled into her garage and clicked the door shut. The house was deathly quiet as she entered through the kitchen door. She called the afternoon nurse's name. She called again, setting her purse on the kitchen table while making her way toward Bobby's room.

Bobby still slept, undisturbed but with clean bedding around him. Lisa had memorized the layout of the room over recent days, as she and the nurses practiced their care of her husband. On the chest of drawers, a slip of paper stood out, which Lisa retrieved after walking around the bed. The paper was a note of apology from Jenny for leaving early, but she had a family emergency. It stated that Bobby had not yet been fed.

Nearing 8:30 p.m., Lisa quickly retrieved the syringe for the PEG and drew up the remaining contents of a Milksure can already available on the bedside table. She injected the liquid into the PEG tube. Lisa heard her BlackBerry ring from the kitchen. She had always used vibrate mode but switched it back to loud once Bobby was home so that she wouldn't miss a call. She thought it was odd that someone would call her on Friday evening, so she hurried to get it.

Danny's number illuminated the screen. She answered his call.

"Hey, Lise. I…uh—," stammered Danny, "I, uh, wanted to tell you I'm sorry. I know you care, and I appreciate it."

Why couldn't he have said this in person, Lisa thought. "It's okay. I—"

Danny interrupted, but Lisa couldn't tell if it was the connection or control on his part. "I actually had talked with someone about everything that happened those years ago through my church back home. It helped. But I just have this pain I have to live with and deal with. I'll be all right."

"Yes, but Danny," asserted Lisa, "it's not good just to cope with it, even. I think so, at least. With Mom, there's no telling how many different people—an army of people in work, at church, everywhere—who I just talked to. And yeah, the truth is, I still miss her awfully. I just do. But this sneaky, isolated life is no good for you. You should think about moving closer in, getting involved in a church."

"Where, Southfork? Huh!"

"Danny, come on. You're being judgmental."

"Maybe so. But I need Mom's and Dad's help with Angelina right now with all this traveling—maybe in a couple more years, when she's a little more independent."

"Well, I think you should think about yourself a little more." Lisa heard a pause come over the touchy connection. "You need to think about yourself so that you can best help Angelina."

The pause remained. "Danny?" Lisa asked.

"Yes. Thanks, that's good advice. I really appreciate talking to you and your reaching out. Do you have any help this weekend, or are you solo with the big guy?"

"Yes. The main nurse comes tomorrow from ten until three, then the same Sunday. It's supposed to be so that I can have a break, whatever."

"It's that tiring, waiting on a sleeping dude?"

Lisa laughed. "No, no. Actually, I should tell you that I'm pregnant."

"Really? Wow! Congrats!"

"Thanks."

"Well, is everything all right? I know you and the big guy have had some challenges. Are all systems go?"

"So far. I'm about two months along. I have appointments every month. And other than getting tired, I feel pretty good."

"Wow. That's really good. It'll bolster your pro-life credentials." Lisa smiled.

"Keep me updated, will you?" asked Danny. "I want to know it's going okay. Let me know if I can help with that, too. Not sure what I can do, but just lemme know."

"You bet."

There was another pause.

"Well, you have a nice evening, Mockin'bird."

"Good-night, Danny." Lisa ended the call.

CHAPTER SIXTEEN

June 16

Dear God,

Lisa drew a blank again, trying to pray. The morning light was pale in a way that signaled enduring overcast skies. She decided she would go into Bobby's room to check on him. She hoped that once there her prayer block would break.

This was the first time she truly felt alone with her comatose husband. Each previous day, Sharon and her largeness had arrived shortly after Lisa arose and was in the middle of her morning routine, what there was of it. This Saturday, with the room cool from the early morning cloudiness, Lisa felt the brunt of how things had changed. Even before coming home, Bobby and she had been surrounded by a nonstop hustle of people—nurses, orderlies, doctors, caregivers, technicians, family, friends, nutritionists, and assistants of every conceivable sort.

Now, it was just the lonely couple and half at that. Lisa began to cry, alone. It was that hard weeping borne of deep sorrow. She went back into the master bedroom and crashed back onto Bobby's side of the unmade bed, unable to stop crying. The memories of her mother flooded her. The happy times with her grandfather watching election night returns rushed into her mind. She was overcome with the bittersweetness of her life.

She never saw herself as carrying a burden, but she began to question again all that had happened. She reached back for her prayer journal and began writing/praying furiously.

Dear God–

I already told you I don't understand any of this. I am sad and angry. I'm still sad and angry.

She stared out at the window. Some rain began to fall against the glass.

Am I supposed to wait nine months and then Bobby will wake up? Is that it? Am I just supposed to hang on, and then he'll wake up? If you have chosen to keep Bobby asleep, can I at least have some guidance?

The thought jolted through her to reach for her Bible and to look for answers. By her bedside, she read it occasionally but not regularly. A twinge of guilt over not "being in the Word" pricked her conscience.

Still, she randomly flipped through the crackling pages. She rushed to her most-favorite passage, 1 Corinthians 13. As she started reading verse one; however, her eyes fell across the open pages to the end of chapter eleven and read:

"For he who eats and drinks in an unworthy manner eats and drinks judgment to himself, not discerning the Lord's body. For this reason, many are weak and sick among you, and many sleep."

Not what she wanted to read.

She closed her Bible, frustrated. Her phone rang. It was A.J.

"Hey, did you get home okay last night?"

"Yes, thanks for asking. I just came home, fed Bobby, and went to bed early. What did you and Curtiss end up doing?"

"We didn't go out. He has that standing commitment on Fridays. He told me for the first time, though, that it was some kind of drug ministry they're doing down at his church. It was just as well, my chairwoman and I ended up going to dinner."

"Any word from DC on if they're going to get a deal on that immigration bill?"

"I don't know. Still has to get through the House, and from what I know of the Speaker, it will look completely different."

"I actually have a couple of donors who are interested. They're lawyers who want to cash in on the temporary visa piece."

"Are you kidding me? Every law firm on the block in Oak Cliff is ready to hang out a 'Get your Z visa here' sign. But that doesn't stop your old boss from breathing bigoted fire," chided A.J.

"What are you talking about?"

"Did you read *The News* this morning yet?"

"No, not yet. I'm not in front of my computer."

"Well, he told the editorial board that he resented Senator McBride's comments that those who opposed the bill were bigots."

"Well, that doesn't make him one."

"Whatever," said A.J. with a laugh. "Hey, I didn't mean to talk politics with you, but I was wondering what the doctor said about Bobby getting some massage therapy."

"Are you kidding, I can't haul him out of here—"

"No, girl. They come to you. Remember, Curtiss has a cousin who is a licensed medical-massage therapist? He will come to your house."

"I guess it's all right. The nurse will be here in a little while, and I'll ask her."

"Well, I have his number. He's a great guy, too. I've met him. He's blind, actually, and this is how he earns his living."

"Blind? How will he get to our house?"

"He has a driver who drives him around. That's no problem. He's very good. Curtiss has him give him massages."

"Sure. Text me his number."

"Okay. And hey, hang in there, Lise. We are all praying for you. You have so much to look forward to!"

A.J.'s words didn't seem to pick Lisa up, but she acknowledged her friend's kindness. She also knew that A.J. felt she did her best when she took action. It was the behavioral component to a heart fully committed to liberalism.

Lisa fixed herself breakfast and then took a hot shower. After drying off, she noticed a voicemail on her BlackBerry. It was Nate: "Hey, I'm sorry to bother you today, but Bailiff is all worked up about something Masters told him last night at some wedding dinner he went to. Gimme a call when you get a chance."

Lisa finished dressing when the doorbell rang. Sharon had arrived for her Saturday shift.

"How are you?" said Lisa, opening the door but keeping her BlackBerry to her ear at the same time. Sharon smiled but was slightly put off by Lisa's preoccupation. Sharon strode back down the hall to Bobby's room.

"Nate?" asked Lisa when her call connected.

"Hey. I'm sorry again," said Nate.

"What's up?" After a second, Lisa followed Sharon into Bobby's room. She observed Sharon check the feeding chart first thing.

Nate said, "I think Masters heard some pediatrician tell him that the burn unit at Children's was getting federal funding for stem-cell-tissue research. He then told Bailiff about it last night at a rehearsal dinner the two happened to both be attending up in McKinney."

"I hope it wasn't one of the doctors I talked to!"

Sharon appeared to pause as she looked at the chart. Lisa shuddered at remembering she hadn't fed Bobby yet this morning as Nate chatted away. "Listen, I need to call you back. Did you find out if it was embryonic or adult stem cells?" Out of the corner of her eye, Lisa noticed Sharon perk her ears.

"No—"

"Find that out and call me later. Bye," said Lisa curtly. "I have not had the chance to feed him yet this morning," Lisa immediately declared.

"Oh, that's okay, sweetheart," answered Sharon. "I don't mean to interrupt you. Did you feed him last night?"

"Yes," replied Lisa, slightly guarded.

Sharon marked the space on Bobby's feeding chart. "Great. Be sure and note it here when you do."

"Ahh … I'm sorry! Completely forgot!"

"That's fine, sugar. All of this takes a lot of time to get right. Now, I'll go ahead and feed him now if that's all right. I don't mean to be nosy, but sounds like you have a serious matter you're dealing with."

The down home name-calling rubbed Lisa a little bit the wrong way—Sharon seemed a little fake with it—but she wanted everyone to relax. The morning's slight dreariness now seemed like a fleeting serenity as she and the nurse became busy with Bobby.

He was so dishearteningly still. He just lay there, absolutely immobile. His skin had a good color, but otherwise, it just didn't seem like Bobby.

"George said you used to work in Washington, DC?" asked Sharon.

"Yes," answered Lisa.

"I bet that was exciting," said Sharon.

"Yes, I enjoyed it. But it's good to be back home." Her answer was somewhat rote; people often asked her about DC as if she had once visited Oz.

Sharon completed the feeding. "And now you're a consultant, is that right?"

"Yes." Lisa didn't feel talkative. She sensed Sharon was rooting around for something. She regretted talking to Nate when Sharon would overhear the conversation. She decided to head off the interrogation.

"We do consulting and fundraising. That was my top consultant on the phone, in fact. We're trying to make sure of an issue on stem cells."

"Oh, God bless you," gushed Sharon, reaching out to Lisa. "You know, I would do anything to save just one unborn life. I can't believe people would—"

Here came one of those moments where Lisa would normally put on her headset and multitask, except she was in her own home. She was smart enough to know that it was more about letting Sharon talk instead of her affirming anything. But of course, she went on and on and on, straight off the National Right to Life talking points. Sure, she was deadly sincere, but Lisa felt there was something to be said for the deciding class figuring out an issue versus letting it bounce around the masses.

People like Sharon represented the rambling class, in Lisa's mind. They had their ideals, and they were true to them; but they completely lacked the ability to shape the world according to them. They were people of any political philosophy, who thought that to effect change was simply to hold an opinion, but the truth was that they were both unwilling and incapable of getting their hands dirty when a given policy required hard work or tough decisions. Hence, when they rambled about an idea, they actually felt they were being helpful.

"And I just thank the Lord for Fox News. Where would we be without them? Do you watch Fox News?"

"No, I haven't, not lately," said Lisa with a forced smile.

"You should. It's so good." While Sharon had been off on her monologue, she had successfully checked Bobby's blood pressure and temperature. "Your husband is so strong, Lisa. I just know that with the help of Jesus, he'll pull through."

Lisa had no idea why evoking the name of Jesus Christ irritated her all of a sudden. Her mind cynically asked—almost out of nowhere—why Jesus didn't keep that steel joist in place. "Excuse me, Sharon, but I need to go to the restroom." Lisa didn't hear Sharon's "Oh sure, honey" as she hustled into the guest bath.

Lisa shut the door and sat on the toilet. Why this rush of negative emotions? Why did life seem so spoiled and tedious? She felt that angry flood again but shed some tears with the emotion this time. She dreaded the thought of spending the rest of the day with

Sharon. Where could she go? What valid errands did she have to run? What errands could she make up? Maybe she could just go for a drive, out and away. But to where? She opened the door, running the water and rinsing any tears off her face. Her sharp blue eyes were cracked up with red. She didn't want Sharon to see her and give her the aw-shucks treatment.

"Is there anything you need, Sharon?" she asked, standing in the doorway to Bobby's room.

"No, honey, are you going out?"

Before letting herself be annoyed at the question, she quickly explained, "Yes, I'm short on Dr. Peppers."

"Okay. I'll be here."

"I'll bring you some lunch," Lisa said, walking back to her bedroom to get her shoes. She felt guilty for being terse, but Lisa wasn't interested in taking orders, even if it was just for a barbeque sandwich.

She cranked up her Tahoe and drove out of her subdivision to Highway 78. She just wanted to drive. She knew she wasn't running from anything—she loved her husband—but she just needed to clear her head.

Twenty minutes into her drive, she began to move out of the Metroplex. She was well through Collin County almost into Black County, but now the towns were free-standing, absent tract-home subdivisions that clung to old farming towns like barnacles to a rotting board.

Her thoughts turned to Danny. He grew up in a small North Texas town that had lost its bygone cotton farming glory, Yale. His mother and dad were more or less salt-of-the-earth people, she, working out of the home while Mr. Geister progressed steadily up the ladder of one of the nation's premier defense contractors. Mr. Geister was not a native of North Texas, instead coming from the Texas Hill Country and graduating with honors in aerospace engineering from Texas A&M.

Ten years after working at the contractor's plant in Yale, Mr.

Geister received the opportunity of a lifetime by being selected to work an Air Force contract in South Korea. The opportunity put Geister on the fast track for Program Director, but it also meant three years overseas for the family. Danny and his sisters were uprooted from their friends. But while his sisters rebelled, Danny retreated into a world of stringent, evangelical-religious expression supported by a Reaganite determination to rid the earth of atheistic Communism.

Danny did embrace a subtle rebellion against his father by selecting the bitter rival of his old man for a college, UT. However, Austin would prove to be too great of a culture shock for the teenager just returned from Korea. He majored in political science but partied hard until one Sunday he awoke with a hangover and began attending a Charismatic church across town. He would never drink again, and his spiritual energy found an outlet in the campus right-to-life movement.

It was there he met A.J., Lisa, and Bobby, as well as others who would go on to forge political careers on both sides of the aisle. His fervor, however, got him in the face of a touchy APD cop during the Norplant demonstration outside the campus clinic. Danny called the policeman an ignorant yokel, which earned him a trip downtown.

But Lisa sensed in Danny a certain savvy that the average protestor didn't have. He was tall, handsome, and telegenic, if a little rough around the edges. She went to the city jail and made Danny's bail out of her own pocket. She thought it would be cool to keep the incident among themselves, away from any misunderstanding with his parents. He had no idea who she was, and at first Danny wasn't so sure Lisa was as fully committed to life issues as he was. Still, he felt connected to her in the battle-veteran sense, for Danny never considered her as dating material.

Lisa made Danny her project. She thought all he really lacked was a little sophistication. She took Danny under her wing, getting him to sign up with her in a nineteenth-century literature class. Together, they took apart the classics of modernity: Zola, Nietzsche,

Dostoyevsky, and Dickens were just a few of the authors upon whom they nerded out. She would talk of the Texas political elite, inviting him one weekend to a family get-together where he met the ailing former Governor Dillon. Danny was always appreciative and cherished his experiences with Lisa, but soon after the literature class was over, Lisa had that fateful meeting with Bobby while walking across campus. And it wasn't so much what Bobby remarked on her striking eyes that captured Lisa's heart, as it was the warmth he had that Danny curiously lacked.

Danny seemed all ideas, all concepts. He had trouble loosening up. Lisa thought that maybe Danny's latent rigidity was due to the fact that he associated conviviality with his forsaken life of partying. To be sure, Danny was charming and full of sardonic jokes—he could entertain any size group—but he just seemed hardened. Lisa recognized her desire for him in spite of this, even if her class and manner wouldn't let her show it. She decided that allowing their hearts to share in politics would be the extent of their affair.

Shortly after her marriage, Lisa allowed her last act of care for Danny to be help in finding a job. Through a family connection, Lisa got Danny an interview in the Majority Whip's personal office where his quick mastery of any policy bailiwick thrown his way got him transferred to the Leadership Office. On the floor and in the cloakroom, Danny soon gained a reputation for being able to articulate core ideals in the heat of battle and to analyze how a given bill would or wouldn't uphold them. He was also tough. After the Election of 2000, he was part of an all-star team assembled for the White House's Legislative Affairs Office.

Then in 2001, right before 9/11, Danny made an unusual career move and asked the White House's Senior Advisor for a spot at the Republican National Committee, or RNC. Lisa couldn't really understand why Danny wanted to do this. The fraternal cadre of White House legislative staff wrote their own tickets when an administration ended, whereas the RNC track usually only yielded unstable consulting work out in the field. And even on a good year—

a busy election year—the RNC was little more than a racehorse pad-dock for the purely political junkies who hung around Washington, as opposed to those like Danny who could wade into the thick of a policy debate and protect core values.

Lisa began to lose track of Danny after he made the move to the RNC and was detailed to several high-profile races far from the Beltway during the next cycles. Much of this was due more to the all-consuming health issues of her mother than the later move back to Texas. The car accident that took the life of Danny's wife—a woman Lisa only met twice but never really liked—occurred in the year after the Jeffuses returned home. As a result, Lisa wasn't privy to the details. While Danny wasted no time making a golden name for himself back in Texas as a general consultant, she definitely noticed a change in him when they reconnected.

She came to the county line between Collin and Black where a left turn off Highway 78 led to a high school in the middle of a sorghum field. She knew that the school, while modern, served three long-ago consolidated farm-community school districts; her grandfather had attended one of them. She remembered how her grandfather had explained to her that when all the rural schools began consolidating back in the sixties, the students became the losers. Back then, consoli-dation was sold to the public as a way to improve a child's access to better facilities, better curriculum, and better teachers—in her grandfa-ther's words, an education economy of scale. But the true results were large class sizes that caused the weaker students to lose their sense of identity and slip in their studies. More sinister, it was a way for liberal educators from Austin to control what was taught in the classroom due to the financial system required to support large school districts.

Lisa pulled into a small quick stop across from the high school for a Dr. Pepper. She had been driving for a while and needed a break. She observed that her grandfather's complaints about school consolidation could now be seen as irrelevant what with all the sub-urban-style growth out into the country. It was the triumph of Rea-gan-revived capitalism and financial deregulation.

Lisa paid for her soda and got back in her Tahoe. Nate had called while she stepped inside. She felt a little better. Her head and emotions had cleared. She began her drive back toward Sachse, making plans to stop at a Sonic she knew of on the way to pick up lunch for Sharon and herself.

She liked Sharon, but it was the nurse's countrified Texanism that struck her wrong earlier in the morning. Lisa knew that people like her were solidly "our people"—Republicans, that is—and they needed to be kept in the square. The paranoia they seemed to latch on to bothered her; it was, after all, only government they were dealing with, but Lisa decided she'd cut Sharon some slack. She selected Nate's phone number and hit send.

"It's Lisa."

"Hey, it's me again. I am so sorry to disturb you."

"No, what's up? I'm just out running errands."

"Well, I figured I wouldn't be able to talk to anyone until Monday, but after going into page twenty of a Google search, I did find out that this Dr. Ranzim, the head of this biotech firm, was quoted in a BBC story as being aggressively in favor of embryonic-stem-cell research. This was back in 2001 when the President revised the existing regs."

"Hmm," Lisa surmised.

"I didn't think this could wait until Monday," said Nate. "But I'm sorry to bother you."

"No, no, I'm glad you called. I'll have the weekend to think about it. I wonder what I'll tell Paul. Don't say anything to him if you happen to talk to him before Monday, though."

"You mean … you mean we're going to proceed with the dinner?"

Lisa hadn't given the business side of the equation a second thought. Of course they'd hold the event. Besides the quick, hard work of the previous week, it was a fundraising faux pas to plan then cancel—almost as scandalous as cancelling a wedding! This didn't account for, of course, the thousands the Mockingbird Group would lose in commissions. Fortunately, she paused long enough in thought to remember where Nate was coming from.

"Well, yes, we probably will have something, but I'll talk to Paul about it.

"You haven't found out yet if they have anything going through Congress yet, have you? Like a simple grant or something?"

"No, not yet," answered Nate. "But what difference does that make? We now know where these guys are coming from. And besides being baby harvesters, it's just bad politically for Bailiff."

Lisa didn't like Nate's argumentativeness. He now seemed a little uppity.

"Listen, I'll make the call to Paul, and he and I'll talk about it. Don't worry about finding out any more." Then she patronized a little, like a good boss, "You've done a good job. I'm glad we know this now. I'll talk to Bailiff."

There was a pause over the cell waves.

"Okay?" insisted Lisa.

"You're the boss," replied Nate. Lisa didn't like his tone but decided it was time to end the call and not waste time trying to change any attitudes.

Lisa continued her drive and ordered two Sonic Burger Combos in spite of the fact that she had wolfed down a basket of grease just the evening before. She thought again of Danny, but this time his presence came over her in a sensual manner. She really wanted to help him. As she pulled back on to Highway 78, she thought it might be nice to invite him and his daughter for dinner, maybe even tonight. She had plenty of help with Sharon there. She could make a simple dinner with a quick Chicken Tetrazzini casserole she knew. Entertaining made Lisa feel better, which was all the more reason to invite over company. She dialed Danny's number from her recent calls list. She made a mental note to assign him a speed-dial number.

CHAPTER SEVENTEEN

After hanging up from Lisa, Nate regretted getting involved with the biotechies. Still, what kind of dilemma would he have in his job if his boss signed his check with blood money?

Nate became ill at ease. He wandered out into his garage where Stephanie and his older children were getting out gardening tools. The day finally became sunny, and Nate hoped the grass would dry so that he could eventually mow it later that evening.

Nate watched his youngest, a little girl, playing in a flowerbed they had been working on. She had insisted that she use a pair of work gloves she'd found. The old gloves were too big, but it didn't matter because soil was gluing itself everywhere over her three-year-old blond body in every place but her hands. Over the next few minutes, as his wife and older kids worked away, Nate watched his baby fill the gloves with dirt using a plastic shovel.

Nate went back inside and composed an email on his laptop to Lisa. It was an explanation that he wanted to be removed from the finance effort with the biotech group. It didn't solve the blood-money issue, but he thought it would be an appropriate shot across the bow. He always had as an excuse that he wasn't a fundraiser; he was just the reporter. The bigger problem would be explaining his withdrawal to Paul. Nate's conscientious objections might trigger Bailiff's own political insecurities at best or set off a temper tantrum at worst.

He, of course, didn't send the email. He saved it in his drafts. Once written, the request seemed small-minded, which he feared it would. He went back to surfing for news, his opiate, starting with a visit to CNN.com. On the nearby kitchen counter, his cell phone rang.

"Yes?"

"Nate, it's Paul."

"Yes, sir, Congressman."

"Hey, what did you find about that thing Masters was worked up about last night? He said someone told him they were doing stem-cell research at Metroplex Children's?"

"Well, I did do some legwork," Nate said. He assumed that Masters found out about the project from the pediatrician or someone Joan told him about. He didn't want to admit that his inquiry might have let the cat out of the bag. But instead of being dishonest, maybe this was God's providence to alert Bailiff using the information Nate found out about Ranzim. That was the bigger issue, anyway.

But blackballing the biotechies was not his job. Lisa, the boss, said she would handle that. Would she even do it? Nate decided to play it dumb. He was having trouble discerning truth from specula-tion, anyway. "I don't know what Masters heard"—which was tech-nically still true—"but hopefully I can find out more on Monday," Nate said in the hope that Bailiff would accept delay.

"Well, let me know what you find out," Bailiff said. "By the way, I talked again with Dr. Ranzim, and he assures me the program only uses adult-stem cells, not the ones where you kill the baby and take the cells."

This was unexpectedly joyous news. Nate felt a wave of relief come over him. In fact, his soul was lifted up to the highest heaven. But what about Ranzim's published statements he found on the Internet? Maybe he read it wrong.

"And remember, the First Lady is behind this deal. I'm just the clerk on it. So, what we can do is tell Masters or whomever that she's in support of it, so how can it be something evil?"

"Yes, sir. That makes sense. Wow." Nate again felt a wave of comfort. "I have to tell you, Paul, I was a little nervous there for a second. This is complicated stuff."

"It is, Nate, it is. We have to be extra careful, but it's a brave new world; and we can't miss any opportunities."

"Did you want me to get in touch with Masters?"

"Oh, no, I'll call him.

"How's Lisa?" Paul asked, changing the subject. "How's it going with Bobby being at home? Do you know?"

"I haven't been by there yet, but Lisa seems to be managing it okay."

"Good, good. It'll be good to get her back moving the rock."

"Yes, sir. Actually, Paul, I have one question for you."

"Shoot."

"Who was that guy out at Black County GOP who was all over you about stem cells?"

"That man in the crowd?"

"Yes. Not Masters but the guy who asked the follow-up? He seemed kind of radical."

Bailiff snorted on the other end of the line. "They're all radical," he let loose, "but I think you're talking about Jim Geister."

"That was him?"

"Yeah. You know his son … or Lisa knows him, I know," explained Bailiff.

"Danny Geister?"

"Yeah. Big time consultant. Never loses. I think it's 'cause God's on his side. But yeah, that's his dad. Pretty hardcore folks."

"A nut?"

"No, no. Just committed," chortled Bailiff. "His dad is actually well-respected out at that aerospace plant, knows everything about aircraft. Danny used to fly, too. He flew us around several years ago, back when I was first running and before he moved up to DC."

"I didn't know any of that," said Nate. "Makes sense. He and Lisa are working on another race together, one in East Texas."

"Oh really?" said Bailiff. "I didn't know he was in her orbit anymore."

Nate thought that last statement from Bailiff sounded a bit loaded, and he decided that ignorance was bliss. He also became concerned that he might have revealed something he shouldn't have. Danny was a proprietary client. Nate wanted to end the call. "Well, Congressman, let me know what else we need to do. I'll let you know about anything Masters heard whenever I hear it."

"Thank you, Nate. You have a true servant's heart," Bailiff said.

Lisa carried in the Sonic combo to Sharon, only to hear from her that she had brought her lunch and had already eaten. Lisa thought she remembered that Sharon always showed up in the morning with a lunchbox, so she wasn't upset about the refusal.

Lisa sat down to eat her bag of grease. She was mulling whether or not to call Danny and invite him over for a bite of supper. She decided it would just be wrong if he came alone, so she wanted to insist his daughter accompany him. If it got out that Danny was there, feeding the single dad would be her cover. Without Angelina, it was no date. As Lisa dipped her tater tots into the ketchup, she thought about the exact nature of her attraction to Danny. He was her type physically, no doubt. He was a true politico—the kind who had the virus of winning elections in his blood. She concluded that whatever her thoughts were, they may have been rooted in a hidden, unrequited desire for him. She considered what it might be like to be close to him and then realized there was nothing. He was just too aloof. He couldn't be gotten close to. She decided it was perfectly fine to extend the invitation but that she needed to run it past the proper regulatory body.

"Hey, girl," Lisa said into her phone as she tossed out her Sonic trash. "I got your text about your friend—is he a masseuse?"

"Yes ... well, he calls himself a therapist. Great!"

"Can I call him today? I haven't talked to the nurse yet, but I think it would be good to have him come in as soon as possible."

"He does 24/7. He's really one of your kind … a small business-man. But I'm pretty sure he'll be voting for Oltan next year."

"Well, I'll give him a call. Hey, I wanted to talk with you about something that's been on my mind. I already know mostly what you're going to say, but I just want you to hear me out."

"Go ahead," A.J. said.

"I know how you feel about Danny Geister, but he's back around because of a client he asked me to help him with."

"Okay." A.J. listened. She had a sense of what her best friend thought of Danny those years ago and knew that Lisa held back some of her feelings about him with her. But A.J. also knew that business was business and that she shouldn't allow her partisan opin-ions about an RNC operative to cloud the possible needs of her friend.

"He's not doing well, between you and me," Lisa said. "I know you remember about that car wreck those years ago that killed his wife. I am really concerned about him."

"All right." A.J. sounded skeptical but allowed Lisa to continue speaking.

"Because we're already working with the same client right now, and because he's an old friend, would having a casual supper with his daughter and him violate the A.J. Manual of Propriety?"

"At the house?" A.J. asked.

"Yes, I can't leave here after the nurses leave on the weekends. That's our current setup."

"I don't know, Lise. I guess he is an old friend. He knows Bobby too, right?"

"Oh, yes. He really admires Bobby and is respectful of him, and even you have to admit that Danny has his own propriety there, too."

"Right, right. You have to be careful of that little girl, though. It's bad if she gets attached to you then you don't see her—"

"That's what I mean. I'm just a friend to her as well and will be over time. Danny's just not a problem, a temptation I mean. I don't see a problem with it, but I value your opinion.

"Who else better for a Republican to ask about propriety than a Democrat?" she added jokingly.

Andrea laughed through the receiver. "It's probably okay. I just have my problems with him, you know. I've always heard about the questionable tactics he used at the RNC—not that it doesn't go on among Democrats too—Danny just always seemed a little too aggressive."

"I know, friend. It may be short notice anyway, but I just sense that he is isolated and that is causing him so much pain."

"Well, as long as your motives are pure. Don't you be rationalizing anything. If it were some other guy, I'd veto the arrangement."

"Thanks. You're a big help." The call ended. Lisa found a spring in her step now that she might have something to look forward to. She strode into Bobby's room where Sharon was sponging his arms. "Say, Sharon?"

"Yes darlin'?"

"What has been your experience with medical massage? Can that help someone like Bobby?"

"Well, I haven't cared for someone quite in this condition, but I know several of our patients get massages regularly. It's a good thing. Still, I'd check with his doctor first. I know of a couple I could refer to you."

"Thanks, that's all right. A friend recommended someone to me." Lisa still wasn't fired up about engaging Sharon in a down-home discussion of anything and stepped back out into the hall, dialing the number A.J. had texted her earlier. She thought it was bureaucratic to try and call Asitajee for approval. She first wanted just to see what kind of person A.J.'s friend was.

"Potter's Hands Massage Therapy," answered a voice that was distinctly African-American. "Mundy Lewis speaking."

"Hi, my name is Lisa Jeffus, a friend of Curtiss Small's. His girlfriend gave me your number."

"A.J., yes! You're the Republican friend! Thanks for calling."

"I guess she mentioned my husband and me to you."

"Yes," said Mundy with sincere compassion. "I am so sorry to hear of your trouble. Is he home with you?"

"Yes, he is, and I wanted to see about scheduling a massage sometime. We're up in Sachse—I don't know if that's too far for you."

"No, no. The Potter's Hands reach into all the world! When did you want to schedule an appointment?"

CHAPTER EIGHTEEN

3:00 p.m.

Dear God–

Please let your will be done as I reach out to Danny. I want to help him, but I want you to be the one to bring him to the place where he knows you in a greater way, according to your grace.

    Amen.

After lunch, Lisa was hit with midday weariness and laid down for a nap. She thought it was not time to try Danny. After she'd slept on the idea, Lisa dialed her BlackBerry from the privacy of her bedroom.

Danny answered after a few rings, "Yes, ma'am?"

"Hey. I'm kinda homebound this weekend, and so I was wondering if you and Angelina maybe wanted to swing down for supper tonight. Nothing fancy. But I thought it would be good for y'all to get out."

"Why is Angelina invited? She'd be bored with all our talk."

Lisa wasn't prepared for that reaction. "Well, I know you have limited time with her when you're in Yale, so I was going to get you to bring her. I insist on it, in fact." She made the last statement with a hospitable tone.

Danny paused on the other end of the line. "Well, I appreciate the offer, but I'm not sure we can get over there tonight."

Lisa was also unprepared for a rejection, in spite of attempting to lower expectations during her conversation with A.J. Her mind began to race, feeling the contributor was getting away from her. Thinking Angelina was Danny's another thing was a mistake. How could she recover?

"Angie has some church party she wants to go to, and I was going to have to hang around for that. I'm trying to take your advice from yesterday."

Lisa actually heard some mirth in Danny's reply, but this made her angry. She became upset but kept her front up. "That's all fine. I hope you both have fun. We'll do it again another time."

"Sure, you bet. I would like that," said Danny. "Gimme a call on another Saturday."

Lisa swung from simmering rage to blinding hope. "Okay. I'll talk to you later. Bye."

"Bye," said Danny.

Sharon quietly knocked on the master bedroom door. "Lisa?"

"Yes? What is it, Sharon?"

"I'm sorry, honey, I wasn't sure if you were resting. But I've gotten Bobby cleaned up for the day. Is there something else you need?"

"No," replied Lisa. "And you have been a huge help today. Why don't you go ahead and head home. All that's left is the evening feeding, right?"

"Yes, ma'am. Are you sure it's all right for me to leave?"

"If you're done, it doesn't make any sense to stay," said Lisa, walking out into the hall and into Bobby's room. The college fight music Danny had brought over played at a low volume on the CD player.

"Thank you, Lisa. I have a few things to do before I get home. A different nurse is supposed to be here tomorrow. Just tell her what to do, and let me know if you need anything."

"Thanks again, Sharon."

McAnnas exited the house, lunch bag slung over her shoulder. Lisa watched her load up into her older model Caprice and drive away. The sun had stayed out in the afternoon, and the sky became hot and slightly sticky.

Lisa closed the front door. She walked back into the house. The music coming from Bobby's room had returned to Texas Fight. Lisa followed it to the doorframe, entered, and leaned against the bed.

Bobby's face still had a living, vital color. But even though his linens and sleepwear had been changed multiple times over the past few days, it looked like he had not moved one millimeter in the bed.

Here in the house, away from the beeping and simmering hustle of medical facilities, Bobby seemed, well—dead. Lisa felt a shudder that he might be brain dead, though Asitajee had said nothing at all of such a possibility. Bobby's coma was surreal to look at … like a living sculpture. His skin was warm, just like he was in a heavy slumber, but otherwise Bobby had as much potential energy as a lump of clay. Lisa saw that her husband's body was becoming lax. Contrary to what Asitajee had said about him losing weight, Bobby seemed as large as ever, his mass melting into the bed. Lisa became concerned about the physical impact of the coma. What if he were starting to wake up—gradually, as Asitajee had described—but his body was so atrophied he wouldn't be able to properly recover? Would overweight, wasting limbs inhibit Bobby's return to health?

The music ended, and a truly morbid stillness filled the room. Lisa touched Bobby's unresponsive hand and then drew it up to her face, resting her chin in it. She realized what was needed, but she might have to be a little crafty to get it done. After a moment, she set his limp arm back along his side. Lisa crossed over to the feeding chart and checked off the afternoon box on the schedule. She looked at her watch and recorded the time as 5:53 p.m., exactly two hours in the future. She then stepped next to the feeding table, where another half-opened can of Milksure awaited the syringe and PEG.

Lisa drew the Milksure up into the syringe. She tossed the empty can into the wastebasket Bobby's father had placed in the room. She then walked out into the guest bath and injected the nutrition liquid down the very same toilet where she'd had her morning sickness a month earlier.

Southfork Church had originally been a small, garden-variety Baptist congregation like many others rooted in the Blackland Prairie of North Texas. In 1981, the calling of a studious but avuncular Southwestern-seminary grad with a crisply parted hairdo named Keith Kenner transformed the small church bound by red bricks into a nationally famous mega congregation shimmering with glass architecture.

The change, however, happened over time. Kenner, well in touch with contemporary evangelical styles and the concept of a community church, put his entire career on the line in 1989 by persuading the congregation to drop "Baptist" from its name when it built its first new worship center. When the saints didn't come marching in as hoped, Kenner endured some cold years.

But by the mid-nineties, something different began to happen. While the average Boomer turned forty-two, his and her kids turned nine and could dress themselves on Sunday morning. Moreover, they only had to put on nice jeans if they came to Southfork Church's more casual atmosphere. In addition, many of the Bible churches created in North Texas towns in the sixties and seventies began to age out, and the children of these congregations began to seek a nondenominational congregation where "in Spirit and truth"—truth not wedded to tested doctrinal traditions, but truth derived from an articulate speaker's own study—was felt. Add to that new, young-adult Christians who had forsaken the organized religion of their childhood, and the megachurch was born.

Kenner was just such an articulator, but his administrative skills perhaps served the super growth of Southfork even better. His parents had owned a farm supply store in San Angelo, Texas, where Kenner had worked since childhood. He knew organization, inventory, and how to control costs. He was as much a CEO as he was a pastor.

He also knew style. By 1996, Kenner was never again seen wearing a tie on the stage of Southfork. Lisa appreciated what Kenner was trying to do. From a political standpoint, she saw him as fostering a mainstream approach to Christian faith. Kenner had left behind the lapelled formality of the denominations, and his earthtone shirts belied the extremism of homeschoolers and those believers Lisa identified as fundamentalist. On top of all of this, he was so deferential and sincere. Kenner was a true servant of the Lord and his flock.

This Sunday morning, Lisa felt more like a black sheep. She fed Bobby that morning, opening a new can of Milksure and leaving the unused portion for the nurse later, in case Lisa didn't make it home in time after church. There was no reason to feed Bobby every single scheduled time, she had decided. He would only get heavy, lying as he was, utterly motionless in the bed. There was plenty of nutrition and vitamins in his Milksure to keep him from developing sores. But Lisa's feeling of isolation, so powerful even as Kenner's reassuring voice gave a lesson on Psalm 35—something about life's trials, as those words were on the jumbo screen toward the front of the auditorium—was due to the fact that she felt she was utterly alone in making right decisions. She felt she carried the burdens of everyone, not just her husband's.

She remembered how Sharon's rambling the day before irritated her. She thought of all the harangues about another thing she heard in the course of a day. In a way, Lisa was tired of politics inasmuch as people expected her to influence change. The truth was, she knew, that those expectations may have been her imagination, but she still felt responsible. The new trial of caring for Bobby was really no different; the challenge was in executing her duty in a way that didn't upset those expectations. Withholding nutrition from Bobby and doctoring the chart may have been sneaky, but it was best for her husband.

Although she skipped small group at 9:30 a.m., Lisa had still been accosted by many members as she came in and out of morning service. They were all very concerned but happy to see her. Many who were from her small group approached her with congratulations on her new baby, as they had no doubt been informed by Stephanie Knight, the shower planner. She heard herself giving a concise update to each acquaintance not unlike a politician working a room. She was relieved to leave the church and felt tired again.

As she drove down the George Bush Turnpike toward home, Asitajee lit up her BlackBerry. "Hello?"

"Hi, Lisa, this is Dr. Asitajee."

"Hello! How are you? Wow, weekend check-ups."

"I know. But I really wanted to see how everyone was making it, being home these first days."

"We're doing great. You were right, Masters is an exceptional group. Did you know I already knew him through work?"

"No, I didn't. That's great. I'm glad they are working out. So how is Bobby?"

"I think, I mean he's the same. Normal—"

"Stable?"

"Yes." Lisa wanted to head off any questions about feeding. "Doctor, I wanted to ask you about therapeutic massage. Would that be good for Bobby?"

"Sure. It may even provide some stimuli for him. Make sure you have help, as Bobby's obviously a big guy. Depending on who you get, they may just work his limbs, though, without turning him."

"Sure. A friend recommended someone from her church."

"That sounds great. Anything else?"

Lisa felt she had dodged a bullet. She wouldn't have to fib about something she knew in her heart was the right thing to do for Bobby.

"I think we're getting our sea legs. Thanks so much for calling."

"You bet. I'm going to order some labs in the next week or two," said Asitajee. "The nurses will draw his blood and check his urine. They'll also bring in a scale, which is a swinglike device they'll put Bobby in."

"Okay."

"How are you doing?" asked Asitajee. "The pregnancy going well?"

"Yeah, I think so. I'm coming up on another appointment. I get tired, but that's normal. I'm not near as sick feeling."

"Great. Stay off your feet if you need to. Take it easy. I know your job must be demanding, but take care of yourself," said Asitajee.

"Thanks, Doctor." The call ended. A voicemail message became visible on her BlackBerry. The message Lisa retrieved was from the afternoon nurse stating that she would not be able to make it. She apologized, but she couldn't find a replacement from the agency. Lisa was surprised that Masters Home Health seemed a little unprepared, but she didn't mind not having a nurse come this afternoon. She wanted to go home and get into bed without a stranger wandering around her house. As Lisa exited the turnpike for the final short leg into her neighborhood, she noticed the southern sky clouding up for another rain front. The sharp contrast between the sunshine and the black-blue sky struck Lisa with a sense of majesty. She picked up her phone.

A.J.'s iPhone went off as she visited with fellow churchgoers in the malllike corridor of her boyfriend's church. She stepped down away from the exiting crowds while she watched Curtiss standing next to his boss, greeting their flock. "Hey, love. How'd it go last night?"

"He was busy," reported Lisa.

"That was God talkin,' girl!" A.J. had a filling of the Spirit right after service. "The more I thought about what I said, the more I wished I hadn't said it. You need to keep it business only with him. Meet only at the office with other staff present. You're on thin ice in your heart."

"I know, I know. You are right. I think I'll also add a rule that I'll never call him, even on business. Email only if I need something."

"Now that's my steel magnolia!"

"I'm from Texas not the Deep South."

"My steel bluebonnet! I've been so worried about you, Lise," said A.J. "You are just in a very, very vulnerable state right now, and you got to hang tough. I've been praying for you, and I am going to keep praying for you."

"Thank you. I love you. Say, my first ultrasound is scheduled for Friday. Can you get time off to come with me?"

"I would love to! That is the happiest thing you could ask me to do."

"Fabulous. It's scheduled at Presbyterian for 10:00 a.m. Do you mind meeting me for breakfast maybe at Café Brazil, and then we can go?"

"Sounds perfect." A.J. saw the line thinning in front of Curtiss and his boss. They turned to come back in the church. "Speaking of big meals, I'm supposed to go with Curtiss and have dinner at the big pastor's house."

"Sounds like that's getting more serious."

"I hope. He's a good man. Get some rest this afternoon," A.J. admonished.

Lisa turned into her driveway as the deep, dark clouds arrived overhead the Jeffus home.

CHAPTER NINETEEN

Nate finished combing Politico.com for his morning fix and looked at the time on his computer screen: 8:34 a.m. He dialed Cara's extension on his phone. "Has Lisa called in? Is she going to be late?"

"No, sir," answered Cara. "Should I call her?"

"No. It's okay. I'll try to get in touch with her." Nate hung up and dialed Lisa's number. He let it ring into voicemail. As he was leaving a short message inquiring as to her whereabouts, Cara's extension lit up his phone with an incoming call. He quickly finished, urging Lisa to call in.

"Mr. Knight, it's an Asian-sounding man, but I didn't get his name—Wen or Wan?"

"Put him through."

"This is Nate Knight, can I help you?"

"I am looking for Leeesa Jeffe-son," said a man in broken English.

"Yes, sir. What was your name again?"

"Carl Wang." Mr. Wang stammered through his English but managed to express to Nate something about having an immigration problem and that he needed to talk to Leeesa Jeffe-son, girlfriend of Paul Bailiff, about it.

"Well, I'm glad to help, Mr. Wang, but you really need to call Congressman Bailiff's district office with your immigration problem. Their case workers are just down the hall from us, and I'd be glad to give you their number." Nate quickly assessed what had happened. In all likelihood, some prominent member of the Metroplex Asian community told this gentleman to get in touch with his congressman about his immigration issue. They probably gave Lisa as the contact, as she often interfaced with those leaders when Bailiff held his modest fundraisers with them. Having gone ahead and called the Mockingbird Group, Nate knew the simple solution was to refer Mr. Wang to the district office, which was set up to assist with just such a constituent concern.

"No, no-no!" shouted Mr. Wang on the other end of the line. "I need Leeesa Jeffe-son … not talk Cong-man Bailiff."

Nate smiled in spite of some mounting frustration. As a hold-over from his own Hill days, he knew he had done all he could and had to end the call.

"Yes sir, but you really need to call Congressman Bailiff's district office. But I will have someone call you back; is that all right?"

Suddenly Mr. Wang relented with a demur—"Yeh, yeh"—and Nate successfully ended the call. In the event a VIP had referred Mr. Wang to Lisa, Nate knew he should touch base with her about this—as soon as he figured out where she was. He cut her some slack given the situation with Bobby, but he was surprised he hadn't heard anything.

Lisa only awoke Sunday evening for a light snack. With the nurse not reporting, she skipped the remainder of Bobby's feedings for the day. She was doing the right thing. She didn't want Bobby to wake up and be so flabby that he might not be able to respond properly to stimuli.

Lisa got up early on Monday for the start of the new week. Sharon called at 7:45 a.m. to say she was caught in traffic but was on her way.

At eight o'clock, the doorbell rang and a tall, slender man wearing khakis and a red Polo shirt and holding a walking cane stood outside in the morning sun. A.J. had been right; Mundy Lewis was 100 percent visually disabled. Across his face he wore the blackest horn-rimmed sunglasses she had ever seen.

He gave an endearing smile. "I'm Mundy."

Lisa smiled. Something between the glorious morning after the constant storms and Mundy's gracious presence reignited inside her that ebullience that had been so heavily taxed over the past few weeks. "I'm Lisa," she said perkily, offering her hand in classic, political fashion. She quickly retracted her hand when Mundy did not return his, as Lisa realized he couldn't see it. She liked him but knew this would take a little getting used to.

Mundy snapped his cane around to find the door threshold.

"Watch your step," said Lisa. "We're down here to your left."

Mundy carefully entered and felt his way inside the Jeffuses' home.

"The nurse is running late. I wanted you here so that she could meet you."

"That's a good idea. We'll need help to turn the patient."

"Yes, she should be here shortly. Is anyone with you?" Lisa asked, looking outside before shutting the front door.

"I have a driver, but she dropped me off and went to run some errands. She'll be back in an hour, when we're done. What is your husband's name again?"

"Bobby. This way," Lisa directed.

"Bobby. My daddy's name was Bobby. That's a good name. You have a nice house. I can tell by its clean scent."

"Thank you. You are so kind."

"I try."

The two found their way into Bobby's room. "I don't know how you want to do this…" said Lisa.

Unhearing, Mundy immediately found the bed with his cane, reached down to feel the hospital rails, and stretched his hand to feel Bobby's leg.

"There he is. Can you drop the bed rails for me?"

"Sure, sure," said Lisa, quickly doing so. Once the rail on his side was dropped, Mundy wasted no time feeling the length and breadth of Bobby's lower limbs. He set his cane against the close-by wall. With all rails lowered and Mundy in possession of his bearings, he went to work massaging Bobby as if he weren't impaired at all. He was clearly in his element.

"Bobby, you're strong. A big fella. Did he play football?"

Lisa replied, "He did in high school."

"Strong fella. Big fella. You said he was in a construction accident?"

"Yes."

"Is he a carpenter?"

"No, he's an engineer/manager. It was just bad luck."

Mundy was silent for a moment. "What work do you do?" he finally asked after moving around to the other leg.

"I'm a political fundraiser."

"Oh, so that's how you're a Republican. I assumed you were like a representative or something."

"No, no, I don't hold office. I can't afford it."

Mundy laughed. "I guess the Republicans have fallen on hard times."

There was something good natured in Mundy's observations, and unlike Sharon, Lisa wanted to engage him in a political conversation. Because he was African-American, Lisa planned for a lively back and forth.

"Yes. I'm afraid we've had a few problems lately. And unfortunately, they all seem to start with the White House."

"You don't like the President?" asked Mundy, not breaking his therapy.

"Oh, no. I love him—"

"He's a strong man of integrity," Mundy said to Lisa's shock. "It's just that he's had bad advice. If he has any fault, it's that he's hardheaded."

Lisa somewhat agreed with Mundy's gentle assessment.

"I think the problem with our country," Mundy continued, "is that we've lost a sense of what we expect of the government. We all seem to want more—thinking it will make things better or safer—but I think we don't know any more what's realistic."

Lisa listened to a clear voice of wisdom coming from this humble man who took seriously his role of healer. Mundy would lift Bobby's legs up at the knee and massage his hamstring. She watched his massive ebony hands work Bobby's stationary limbs in a way that proved energy could return to them. For a fleeting moment, it appeared as though Bobby had bent up his knee himself.

"In my case, I wouldn't be anywhere without the state of Texas. The state school for the blind paid for me to take massage therapy classes. And even though I'm entitled to disability under Social Security, I don't take it. When I heard of that program, I thought that was for cripples."

"May I ask how you lost your sight?" said Lisa.

"Born this way, but Daddy never let me get down. He said it was God's will."

"He said that to you as a kid?" asked Lisa.

"No. He said Jesus said that. Daddy told me he was mad as hell," said Mundy with a grin. "Yes, I was a kid when he swore like that."

Lisa heard Sharon coming in through the front door. She had given Masters a house key for emergencies. Lisa thought Sharon may have assumed she left and so let herself in. "We're down here, Sharon!" called Lisa. "The masseuse came."

"Wonderful," said Sharon, making her way to Bobby's room, lunch bag over her shoulder.

"She's just in time to help us turn the patient. Big boy," said Mundy.

After introducing the two, all three carefully turned Bobby onto his stomach, making sure his head stayed elevated on a pillow. Sharon had adjusted the bed so that it was level. Lisa heard her phone ring in the other room but ignored it. Asking her for a towel, Mundy opened the rear of Bobby's gown and draped the cloth over his buttocks without a hint of blindness. He was so deft, so skilled.

Sharon noticed some red, inflamed areas on the buttocks before the towel fell over them. They last changed Bobby's bedding on Friday, and she hadn't noticed the inflamed areas when she changed his diaper on Saturday. She made a note to apply some ointment to the areas. Sharon feared the gown was bunching up and causing the inflammation. She would wait to dress Bobby after the massage. The therapist had arrived at a perfect time.

"That's it," declared Mundy after about forty minutes. "Did you want to make it this time each Monday? It's a good way for him to start the week."

"I think with your name, that's a good way for us to remember it," said Lisa, joking with her new friend. "Mundy on Monday."

Mundy smiled while Sharon busied herself by fetching the ointment from a plastic set of drawers. "Are you ready to turn him back?"

"Let me get this," Sharon said, removing the towel and squeezing some of the ointment onto Bobby's buttocks. "We don't want this to get anywhere," she said, applying the thick substance. Sharon affixed an adult diaper onto Bobby. She and Lisa then turned him back around. Sharon also put on a clean gown, allowing Bobby to fall forward into her arms as she reached around and tied the top string.

Lisa hadn't witnessed an actual gown-changing since Bobby went to the Rehab Hospital. Without a garment covering him, Bobby was unquestioningly without weight loss since coming home. He was becoming flabby. She unconsciously placed her hands over her belly. She would have to keep shorting those feedings if Bobby were to recover properly. He would turn into a big, starchy vegetable if she didn't. He would have no chance to interact with his child at all if she didn't.

"Do y'all mind if I get your help really quick changing the bedding?" Sharon said, pulling the sheet and mattress pad in one grab off one side of the bed corners. Lisa and Mundy lifted Bobby onto his side, while Sharon switched over and pulled the bedding from under the patient. Lisa and Mundy then let Bobby fall onto his back while Sharon prepared the clean linens.

Dear God–

Is this what the future holds?

"Thank you so much. I'll do the rest if you need to go, Lisa," said Sharon.

Mundy felt his way around the bed to retrieve his cane. "Let me show Mundy out," she said.

"Nice to meetchew," gushed Sharon at Mundy.

"Yes, ma'am," answered Mundy, making his way back down the hall.

Back at the front door, Lisa wrote Mundy a check. She was so taken with Mundy that she wanted to express how impressed she was with him. This time, she reached out and took his hand. "Everything A.J. said about you was true. You are so gracious. Thank you for coming all the way up here to Sachse."

"Yes, ma'am. You have a strong man in there. I know you're doing right by him."

Lisa now felt a little concerned and guilty about withholding the feedings. But she knew what was best. She changed the subject. "Do you go to Curtiss's church also?"

"No, no, I actually come to church up over here on the north side. A little church. So, it's nuthin' for me to get around town." Mundy turned and found the front door, opening it.

"It looks like your ride is here. A red Mercury?" asked Lisa, seeing an unknown vehicle parked out front.

"That's her. It's my sister. She goes to Curtiss's church. Curtiss's church is just too big for me. It makes me suspicious when a child of God wants to hide among other Christians. I guess I'm kind of a black sheep. So what. Black is beautiful! Anyway, you take of yourself. I'll see you next week."

"Sure thing," Lisa said, not relaxing a smile that Mundy had brought to her face. Watching Mundy walk up to the Mercury and get in, she returned to Bobby's room.

"I guess they told you Jenny didn't make it yesterday?"

"Yes, Lisa, I'm so sorry," said Sharon. "She's a good caregiver, but Jenny has so many kids and thangs that come up."

"No, it's fine. It was pretty quiet over here."

Sharon walked over to the chart. "I see you kept up with all the feedings yesterday. Good."

Lisa gave no response. Back in the confined guest room with her motionless husband, all concerns about what she planned for Bobby vanished. She didn't care about the chart. With all those calories, Bobby would just turn into a blob.

"I'm going to finish getting ready and head into work," said Lisa.

"We'll be fine. Thanks for staying with the masseuse. He seems like such a nice man."

"Yes, I think so—a real gift from God."

Getting back down Highway 78 for the commute, Lisa returned Nate's phone call. "I'm sorry I didn't call. Things got busy when our new massage therapist arrived for the first time today."

"She's not too good looking, is she?" teased Nate.

"No, no. He's a blind man, trained by the state. There is something good government does after all," said Lisa.

"Huh," answered Nate. "Well, thanks for calling. I guess I'll see you shortly, but we had some Asian—I'm not sure what nationality—fellow call and ask for your help with an immigration problem. I told him to call Bailiff's district office."

"What was his name?"

"Wang, Carl Wang."

"That's Chinese. You know what, I'll bet he's a friend of Charlie Lin's."

"The big restaurant guy up in Plano!" said Nate. "Of course, I should have known that."

"Did you tell him I'd call him back?"

"I said someone would."

"Lemme call Charlie and see what he wants. I should have his cell number saved here. I'll be in the office in a few minutes."

Lisa hung up and found Charlie's number in her address book.

Lin was the Metroplex's most-successful Asian restaurateur and a close confidant of Bailiff. If anyone was a grassroots VIP, it was Charlie, no question.

"This is Charlie," he answered from his flagship, the upscale Zhang Wo off of Spring Valley Road. A porcelain Budda—its eyes shut against the world's evil—stood over the empty bar where Charlie was reading the paper. Charlie had been born in Texas, but his parents immigrated straight from the mainland in the late '40s after Mao's takeover. Charlie's first language was English, and he even spoke with a slight Texan lilt. He also had a slight crush on Lisa.

"Hey Charlie, it's Lisa Jeffus."

"Yes, ma'am. How is the crown princess of the great state of Texas?"

"You're so funny. Hey, we had a gentleman call in this morning and ask specifically for me, a Mr. Wang? I know it's a little presumptuous, but do you know who that is?"

"Great. Yes, I told him to call. And it's not presumptuous."

"Awesome. He told my staff something about an immigration problem? We told him he should call one of Paul's caseworkers."

"Yes, he already did, and Paul's people opened up a case on him. I think it went stale over at ICE. So many times," Lin explained, "folks from the old country get in their heads that they have to bribe the government over here too, to get what they need. Carl's case is kind of complicated, but he actually came here from Korea. He is ethnically Chinese, but his citizenship was Korean.

"He's already naturalized, but to make a long story short, he wants to sponsor someone for citizenship who is from Korea. And I think because of some confusion over his nationality, Homeland Security is holding up the processing of this person he's trying to sponsor."

"Wow. What a mess! Tell him to take a number."

"I know, I know. But his English is so bad. I really think that is one of the main problems. Yet he's fluent in both Chinese and Korean. Paul said you knew someone who might be able to help—some consultant you knew?"

Lisa immediately thought of Danny at the start of Charlie's story, but how did Bailiff know Danny spoke Korean? Even then, she wasn't sure how well he spoke it. Danny was only over there in high school, and that was years ago. "I guess there's someone I can call. I think he knows the language at least. I'll see what he can do, but I can't make any promises."

"That's no problem. Anything you can do would help. You don't have to call me back, even."

"I'll do what I can. How's everything else going?"

"Great. When are you and your husband going to come by again?"

"Well, actually, Bobby's been in a serious accident, and he's in a coma."

"Oh, Lisa! I'm so sorry. What can I do?"

"Thanks, Charlie. We're making it, but it's not easy." After some chit-chat, Lisa ended the call. She immediately dialed Danny's number.

CHAPTER TWENTY

Nate had finished his donor list, and it was time for Lisa's Midas touch. Beside each name, he provided an annotation of the essential professional facts he had discovered, such as where each prospect went to college, any postgraduate education, and whether they had contributed to a federal candidate before. He handed to Lisa some interesting results.

Nate had compiled ten other figures in the DFW medical community. Besides the possible leak out to Masters via the pediatrician, Nate was pleased with his work. The list was exactly the type of thing Lisa wanted: a kind of cross-section of players in a given field who could sit down and examine each other's egos, while forgetting that within a few short weeks of consuming Bailiff's prime rib they'd receive a hand-signed request letter with an enclosed envelope.

Once Lisa had the list—around seventeen possible attendees—she could make a simple call on behalf of Congressman Paul Bailiff and ask them to a dinner, welcoming them to Dallas. The event was not a fundraiser, she would clarify, just a get-together. She would attend and make personal connections with each attendee, which would make the true "ask" later on that much easier.

Lisa began her calls down the list with the biotechies, as they were an unknown quantity and would require the most of her game. She started with the principal, Dr. Joseph Ranzim. She called the number provided by Paul via Nate. As expected, an assistant answered. Introducing herself, Lisa was put straight through to Ranzim. She was pleased with her first catch of the day.

"Dr. Ranzim, my name is Lisa Jeffus. I work for Congressman Paul Bailiff. How are you?" she said with her peppy charm.

"I'm fine," said the reserved voice on the other end.

Lisa decided not to lay it on to thick. "Doctor, the congressman wanted to invite you and your associates to dinner when you come to Dallas on the twenty-ninth."

"Yes, he and I had talked about that. We look forward to it. Do you have the names of everyone attending?" Ranzim seemed meticulous over the phone, something Lisa appreciated. "My assistant can help you."

"Thank you very much, Doctor. I'll definitely check with her once we've ended our call."

"Wonderful. I was wondering, though, what are the congressman's personal interests or hobbies? I understand he is a gun enthusiast?"

"Yes, sir. He is. In fact, he got a new sporting shotgun for his birthday a few months ago." Lisa hoped Ranzim wasn't going to ask about bringing a gift. The rules of the House of Representatives prevented a member of Congress from receiving any gift over fifty dollars, unless it was from a personal friend. And the definition of personal friend was a pathetically gray area that Lisa hated defining, let alone losing sleep over. Moreover, this was an event where she wanted them to be obliged to Bailiff, not the other way around.

"I see. I understand there are limits to the types of things a federal official can receive," Ranzim said, much to Lisa's relief. "But we wanted to give him a token of our appreciation for reaching out to our vision of advancing medical treatments."

"I'm sure anything would be well received, as long as it's within House rules." She felt that to specify fifty dollars showed no class.

"Thank you. We'll check into that. Let me return you to my assistant."

"Thanks so much. We'll see you in Dallas in a couple weeks."

Lisa conferred with Ranzim's assistant about the other attendees. Six of the eight board members Nate had identified would be coming with Ranzim plus three researchers who were senior in the firm. Lisa persuaded the assistant to email her a list of the attendees with their office phone numbers, and once she received it in her inbox, she proceeded to call each one, only leaving messages with either assistants or in voicemail that Congressman Bailiff was looking forward to their visit.

Less than two hours later, she then went to work on the local list. She vaguely recognized one or two names from her mother's days of involvement with the DFW-medical community. Halfway through the second call, Cara interrupted Lisa by entering her office.

"Lisa, that consultant is here to see you."

Lisa was surprised but shouldn't have been. All she got Monday after talking to Charlie was Danny's voicemail. She left a message stating only that she needed his help with one of Bailiff's donors. She followed Cara out to the reception area.

"I told you to quit sneaking around—" Lisa said, smiling, but she dropped the banter when she saw that Danny was very agitated.

"I need to talk to you outside," demanded Danny.

"Uh, okay," said Lisa, puzzled. "I'll be back in a minute, Cara. We're just going down and outside the lobby."

"Yes, ma'am."

"What?" asked Lisa sharply as they boarded the elevator down alone.

"We'll talk outside." Danny had that dark mood but was a bit more tumultuous under the surface. They passed through her office building lobby, out the glass double doors and around the corner into one of the building's exterior nooks. The afternoon produced a hot, muggy day. Lisa felt her blouse lose its crinkle. "Who called you, Charlie or Bailiff?" he demanded.

"Whoa, wait! How did you know Charlie was involved?"

"Tell me!" shouted Danny.

Lisa was alarmed and confused. "Neither," she asserted, meeting

Danny's aggression. "This Wang guy called Nate, and I decided to check with Charlie. Charlie said he told Wang to call us. He also said Paul thought I could get you to help."

"Why did he involve you?" Danny asked, but he was being rhetorical. He was also angry under his breath. He began pacing about.

"What are you talking about? Tell me now! I am not going to put up with all this shady runaround!" she said, grabbing Danny's arms.

Nate had briefly looked up from his news screen to see Cara get Lisa. After a moment, he inquired of Cara what was going on only to see Danny follow his boss onto the elevator. The moment Nate hustled into the lobby off a separate elevator, he saw Lisa holding Danny's arms through one of the tinted lobby windows.

"I want all this crap inside you to come out and stop whatever it's doing!" Lisa insisted, shaking Danny's arms, which he could not remove from her grasp.

Danny looked Lisa square in the face. She realized it was his carnal power that had to be resisted at all costs. But that was the one thing she needed most. "There is nothing you can do now. I can't save you, and you can't save me," he said.

"Tell me what is going on. Please," she begged as the hot sun baked the pair against the building.

Danny jolted her aside yet again, making one of his typically abrupt departures.

Lisa was furious. A sudden letdown hit her. She dragged herself into the lobby.

Nate did the church mouse thing and hid, watching Lisa stagger into an elevator and back upstairs.

Lisa walked slowly past Cara's desk then back around to her office.

"Lisa?" Cara asked.

"One minute," Lisa said, not stopping. In a few seconds, she had gathered her purse and BlackBerry and was back out front. "I'm heading home for the day, Cara. Just take a message if someone calls."

"I hope you feel better."

Danny's Durango turned right onto Northwest Highway and headed west. Over and over in his head, his rage brewed over Bailiff's entanglement of Lisa into his crooked racket.

After several minutes, the Durango crossed through some of North Dallas's seediest sections. He passed through Bachman Lake, now a Little Mexico all its own with Southwest jets roaring overhead. He approached the Stemmons interchange, just north of Texas Stadium. This section of Northwest Highway had become the unofficial red light district of Dallas, the city's most upscale strip bars serving as anchors to a myriad of heterosexual services. Danny turned right onto Shady Trail Lane, past the U.S. Post Office, and up into an industrial warehouse area.

After making several blocks, Danny pulled into a parking lot bordered with lush Saint Augustine grass and live oaks. The Durango pulled up to a low, brown-brick office-type building. On the black-tinted door, white vinyl letters formed characters that read Medical Services in Chinese and Korean, each from top to bottom. In English, the words Carl Wang, Acupuncture were carefully laid out beneath the Asian symbols.

Danny stormed in and down the hall to Wang's office in spite of the shrieks of the middle-aged Korean receptionist. As he marched down a hallway lined with exam room doors, Danny could hear the T-Mobile squeaks of the receptionist's phone. He sat down in the back office, across from Wang, who was wearing a white coat.

"Price has doubled," growled Danny in perfect Korean.

Wang stayed seated, intimidated, but nodded. In Korean, Wang told Danny he would meet the offer but that he would have to come back Friday night at 8:00 p.m.

"Only you, understand?" continued Danny in Korean. "The Statue of Liberty carries a hot torch."

Mr. Wang nodded. Danny left, bumping the receptionist on his way out, who had relented after a bit not daring to approach the back office.

A woman in her early forties holding another T-Mobile phone came through a door that connected another suite with Wang's. "Did he want more money?" she asked in Chinese.

"Yes. Not much longer and you will have your citizenship in this great country."

Once she arrived in Sachse around 4:00 p.m., Lisa dismissed Jenny, who was all too eager to quit early. Lisa sank onto the sofa and stared at a renewed-storm warning on WFAA. By the time she could collect a thought, it was that she couldn't believe all the nonstop rain.

Kicking off her shoes, she walked down the hall and looked in on Bobby, stopping at the door. There would be no feeding.

She decided that Danny would never respond to her overtures of help as long as she was married. She knew his rigid scruples on morality wouldn't permit it, even though she had convinced herself she didn't feel anything for him.

Would Bobby ever get pneumonia? she asked herself.

She vainly shook her head, attempting to physically disrupt the dark circuit her mind was following.

She crossed back around the chest of drawers and hit play on the CD player. The University of Texas band music started. She left the room and prepared a hot bath.

CHAPTER TWENTY-ONE

Thursday was nothing more than a new day. What got Lisa through it was the upcoming ultrasound, an event she had managed in her mind to completely separate from everything else going on. She completed some follow ups on the call list for the biotech event the next Friday, going through the motions during much of it.

Lisa found that she had a role—an act—she could step into in order to complete the calls in spite of her emotional emptiness. She felt fake as she feigned vivaciousness, but at this point, she just wanted to get the job done. Most of the calls were voicemail anyway. Maybe by the time anyone called back, if at all, she'd be feeling better.

Cara had stepped up to the plate as an intern. She felt a little lost at first, but when calls began pouring into the Mockingbird Group within hours after Bobby's accident, Cara quickly devised a record-keeping system of everyone who called. Once Nate first returned from Parkland, she cross-checked each name with him, wisely thinking many were VIPs of some sort.

Nate was impressed with how carefully Cara went about this unexpected job assignment. He had initially been unimpressed with her, thinking she was just another offspring of Lisa's pretty-faced aristocracy, but after seeing what she was trying to do, Nate obliged her and gave her limited permissions to use the database and see who was who. Cara's system of keeping track of who called and who would get a call back also impressed Lisa, and although the pair lacked the time to really bond, Cara took a personal interest in Lisa's well-being. Cara had come to feel a part of the Mockingbird Group, if not fully connected with its owner.

Lisa informed the staff of the pregnancy via email after the blood test. There were only two other full-time workers: Marcia, who did the event planning; and Vicki, who kept the books—a significant job given all the complicated financial information required for the group's operations. Nate served as a de facto IT director, but most of the technology services were outsourced.

Though she felt she didn't know her that well, Cara watched firsthand Lisa's emotional ups and downs from the front desk. For the most part, the boss was up when she came bounding in. By contrast, mornings when Lisa seemed more demure or even spacey were kind of dramatic. Cara figured they were due to the challenges of early pregnancy. Not wanting to overstep her bounds, Cara approached the other staff about some kind of cheerful breakfast or lunch for the boss. The suggestion was well received, and once Nate was clued in, Cara planned a simple recipe called "Bailin' Billy" for lunch the next day. Everyone would bring an ingredient that could be dropped in a portable fryer, using a tasty batter Cara would prepare. The modest but festive lunch would be a good way to celebrate the ultrasound that morning and recharge for the busy week that would follow.

Lisa ended the day early again. Cara noticed a natural smile returning to the boss's face, if only due to the fact that she was going home.

"See you tomorrow," said Cara.

"Yes, I should be here before one."

"Yes, ma'am. I think we may have something planned around here, then. So, do you think you could skip lunch until you get back?" Cara asked shrewdly, making sure her plans were not spoiled by another appointment.

Lisa was caught off guard a bit but smiled bigger. "Sure. I'll call when I'm on my way back."

Home once more, Lisa dismissed Jenny early again. She wanted those extra feedings to be avoided, and she didn't want to have to explain herself. Once she got through next week, she decided she would call the doctor and Masters and cut back the nurses' hours. Bobby was low-maintenance and didn't need the constant care Asitajee had prescribed.

Lisa was spending less and less time in the room with Bobby. For the most part, she was only in there to check the odor, making sure Bobby's diaper didn't become too pungent. She also continued her updates to the feeding chart.

Lisa was tired, but the weariness was chronic now and didn't necessarily mean she wanted to go to bed. She decided to catch up on some reading in the hopes that it would hasten sleep. By her bedside she found a book she hadn't picked up in a while: a copy of Keith Kenner's *Marriage Manual*. The book had an extra small printing, but it had become required reading for couples at South-fork. It had even spawned its own jargon among the church's small groups. For example, "C2" was often used to refer to a couple's quality time together.

Lisa had stopped reading at chapter five, the bulk of the text being regular fare about God's institution of marriage and what his standards of a man-woman relationship should be. Mixed in were the only slightly humorous anecdotes from Kenner's own marriage of thirty years—all pretty basic information, the kind of marriage advice one would expect from a pastor who never preached more than twenty minutes.

Picking up where she left off more than four months ago, Lisa noticed the chapter heading, "In Sickness." She began reading. The chapter was about when a spouse becomes ill, with Kenner using as his example one of many anonymous couples he knew. The wife had developed breast cancer, and Kenner uncharacteristically went into detail about what happened.

Lisa was all too familiar with what happens when a mastectomy occurs. In the case of Kenner's friends, the procedure on the wife was radical for both breasts, and after standard treatment, the cancer went well into remission. What was different about Kenner's friends was that the husband insisted there be no reconstructive surgery. Insurance coverage was not an issue, but he was so conservative in his thinking that he felt implants would have been a vain, lurid indulgence. Trying to be what she thought was a Christlike spouse, the wife submitted to her husband's wishes. There was no "happy ending" to the story other than a vague observation by Kenner that the couple's devotion inspired others in the church.

Kenner seemed to draw from the couple's demonstration of faith that if God's model were followed—that of a believing wife obeying a believing husband's wishes—a climate of faithfulness enveloped the believer. Those were his own words: "climate of faithfulness." Lisa tried to reflect on what this meant.

After a moment, she could only understand that submission to one man's preference was sad humiliation, not faithfulness. The morality of breast implants was nowhere in the Bible, as far as she knew. Kenner's friends may have been a model of female deference, but that was it. Lisa thought the "climate of faithfulness" was really more of an air of chauvinism.

She thought again of what Bobby had told her those years ago about being a stroke victim like his uncle. In fact, the discussion had occurred right when they heard about Danny's wife's car accident, as she had been declared brain dead on top of her massive injuries. She recalled that Bobby had remarked that he just would not want any life support, which would cause him to linger.

Lisa began to think more about approaching Asitajee, not just about discontinuing the nursing program but of withholding nutrition completely. It was time to discuss the living will again, she believed. Having been reading while in her bed, Lisa got up and booted up her laptop. Back in bed, she did a search on long-term vegetative state. She was looking for statistics on the average lifespan of someone with PVS or SPVS. After a few minutes, the average date of mortality for victims in PVS was around six months the best she could tell.

This meant Bobby might wake up just in time to hold his newborn child. Or he might die on the infant's birthday. Lisa felt a certain fatalism at the notion. She felt she had confronted the worst that could happen.

But then she went a step further, wondering if she would survive emotionally over the next six months with the hope that Bobby would wake up, only to watch him decline and pass away right as she was ready to deliver. She fell back into her pillow, letting the computer fall off her lap onto the bed. Finally, the full weariness of the day overcame her, and she fell asleep.

CHAPTER TWENTY-TWO

Lisa wore a white silk blouse for the ultrasound. The navy skirt she put on with it had always fit loosely, but now its waistband was perfectly snug. By 9:00 a.m., she was down at Café Brazil on Central for a late breakfast with A.J., who arrived a few minutes after her.

"Appropriate, isn't it?" asked Lisa, still feeling flat from the emotional rollercoaster of the evening before.

"Appropriate, meaning that I'm with you for the ultrasound?"

"Yes, we met while crusading for women's health. Here we are going to that ultimate confirmation of womanhood: life growing inside."

"I'll tell you a story," began A.J. "When I was working for Steiner on the Hill, y'all set up the first vote to ban partial-birth abortion. I told him to vote for it—Steiner wasn't 100 percent choice anyway—gave him good reasons to end the procedure, and sketched out his cover, as more than one hundred Democrats were already going to vote for the ban. Do you know what Steiner told me?"

Lisa shrugged. "No telling..."

"He said it didn't matter how few voted against it, he didn't want to be in the win column on an issue so linked with intolerance."

"So what you're saying is that while your people affirm life, the motivation for their opposition is simply for the sake of opposition? That doesn't sound very

160

tolerant," Lisa said, smiling even bigger. The omelet she had eaten gave her the strength to be facetious.

"I'll never forget what he told me," continued A.J. "He said his mother, who was a Holocaust survivor, told him that pro-life Christians reminded her of the Nazis and that he must vote against them every time."

Lisa groaned as loud as she could, but she knew A.J. didn't really take such talk seriously. "A.J., that is so unfair and ignorant." Since her emotions were back up, Lisa was enjoying the political back and forth.

"You're missing my point," said A.J. "Steiner was influenced by someone who simply saw things differently and could control him emotionally. And evangelical Christians—you know who, I mean, the white ones—continue to fail to grasp that they are but one of many groups in our type of democracy. They just can't believe that someone may see something differently, and that if they do, they are somehow sinners. And that perspective gets worse when they believe that God put them in charge of various pieces of your party, not to mention Congress and the White House."

"Check, please," Lisa told the waitress.

"Do you know what y'all's problem is?" A.J. was on a roll even as the pair loaded up in Lisa's Tahoe and headed back up 75 to Walnut Hill Lane and the exit for the Presbyterian Hospital campus.

"Let me guess, we're hypocrites?" answered Lisa, cranking up her vehicle and donning her sunglasses.

"No, no. Not that. Y'all are afraid to call a lion, a lion."

"I'm surprised you didn't say 'a wolf, a wolf,'" Lisa said.

"Republicans want power. Democrats know that controlling government and the Treasury is all we have—that's why winning is everything. But we know that win or lose, God still loves us. The Republicans—evangelicals at least—have not only bought the lie that you can't make a difference outside of politics; they've been deceived into thinking God doesn't love you unless you protect babies with the ballot box.

"Democrats need government. Republicans—Christian Republicans—want government. There's a big difference, and among yourselves, that want has changed all you as voters into thinking first about how government can do this or that. That's a far cry from the Libertarianism that once dominated the GOP.

"We naturally start with the government solution. Democrats know the lion is the king of the jungle and should even be feared. Republicans don't want to admit the lion is king, yet you have now come to depend on him."

Lisa thought of George Masters and his activism on Medicare provider payments. Here was a small businessman who behaved in a way that suggested he couldn't operate without taking assignment from the federal government. She conceded internally that A.J. had a point. But here she was yet again, listening to a rant. At least A.J. was a little more interesting than average. But Lisa was grateful she could keep her eyes on the road, shuttered with her sunglasses.

A.J. continued her polemic, "Because they hoped to be raptured into the kingdom, Christian conservatives were never serious about establishing it down here. Yet, in a moment of schizophrenia, they wanted the power to try. And getting the power, but then losing it—either literally or via bad leadership—has created a crisis of faith among evangelicals, at least those who thought God gave them government and commanded them to do good with it."

"I don't know if there's any 'thought'—past tense—to it," said Lisa, yawning.

"And that has fostered greater concern in churches, to the point where many are flirting with apostasy over worn-out teachings about the apocalypse," said A.J. "Your people take a perverse comfort in thinking that if they no longer control the U.S. Government, a new Democrat President will be the anti-Christ or will sell us out to him."

"Ouch," Lisa said, pulling into the parking garage for her doctor's office.

"That was a good breakfast, wasn't it?" said A.J.

"Everything looks great, Mrs. Jeffus," said the technician as the scanner worked its way over the gel she had smeared on Lisa's abdomen, her blouse being opened for the exam.

"Yay," said A.J., taking Lisa's hand.

"You said you were at ten weeks, right? I'll get these to your doctor."

The technician gave Lisa some moist wipes and told her she could get redressed. After finishing with her blouse, she sent Cara an email with her BlackBerry, letting the staff know that everything was fine and that she'd be in within the half hour.

"Our intern released a controlled leak yesterday that the office was cooking some lunch," Lisa said to A.J. as the pair walked out to her SUV after the scan. "You should come by."

"Executive Director for the local Democrats in Bailiff's money vault—I hope the *Dallas Morning News* isn't there," said A.J.

Lisa laughed. Her soul had been restored by the sonogramic vision of the peanut with the rapid-fire heartbeat. Completely gone were the dark thoughts of the evening before. She felt full. Her energy level rose. She felt a return to the confidence she had about life before all the problems with Bobby. She was going to have a child, for sure, without a doubt. God would help her make the right decision about Bobby.

She and A.J. strode into the Mockingbird Group. A small reception display had been set out in the center of the suite on a card table draped with a blue bonnet themed table cloth, and the staff let out a warm cheer. A.J. paused at the big portrait of Governor Dillon. She suddenly felt the old man reminded her of someone.

"Fraternization with the enemy?" asked Nate.

"Yes. Everyone, this is A.J. Be advised: she is a D among Ds."

"And the D doubles as short for E.D.," Nate said.

The staff greeted A.J., and the group seated themselves around the card table in an assortment of ergonomic chairs. They then helped themselves to small bowls of slawlike, batter-fried squash, zucchini, red peppers, steak, and chicken strips covered in seasoned salt. Cara also provided plenty of iced tea to wash it all down. After a few minutes of light gluttony, Lisa thanked everyone for hanging in there over the past several weeks. She explained that things were stable but still needed a lot of prayer.

Close to 1:30 p.m., Bailiff unexpectedly entered the suite to find the impromptu feast. The scent of fried everything hung in the air. Only Lisa was sitting at an angle by which to see the congressman walk in.

"Any left for me?" Bailiff bellowed.

Immediately, the group rose to its feet, with the exception of Lisa, who acted like a familiar uncle had just walked in. Even A.J. stood, but only after a second.

"Please, no, everyone." Bailiff moved straight to Lisa. "I heard the good news," he said to her, giving her one arm.

"Guilty," confessed Nate to Lisa.

"Everyone, this incredible woman—no, Texan—has been to hell and back but has proven that God is good." Bailiff was making a speech, and the dialect dial was turned up to the max.

"We know that sometimes life hits us with impossible things, but I think we know that Lisa can not only survive the impossible but can overcome it." He took her hand, holding it up. "I love you, Lisa. Please know that we all love you."

Lisa teared up. She felt guilty over the fact that she allowed herself to feel isolated. She stood up and embraced Bailiff around his neck. "I love you too, Congressman."

Bailiff proceeded to exit, but not without glad-handing everyone. A.J. was first. "How's Ms. Evans?" he asked of his colleague and fellow Appropriations Committee member, A.J.'s old boss.

"She's good. I haven't talked to her in a while."

"Tell me again, what it is I can do to persuade you to come work for us?"

A.J. laughed, as much at as with Bailiff.

"Take care of our girl," he said.

"Yes, sir."

"You've become quite the consigliore," Lisa said softly to Nate as Bailiff worked the room on his way out. "Good to know I can retire soon."

"It's no different than the Hill days. There's no real secrets between us, anyway."

"That actually brings up a good point," Lisa said. "To the extent our work with Danny and his client is tossed in the air around here, we may want to not mention it to Paul."

Nate felt his heart pick up and his kidneys spill their adrenaline.

"There's something going on between those two," said Lisa.

"Between whom?" asked Nate, desperately hoping Lisa was talking about Bailiff and A.J.

"Paul and Danny. It was really pulling me down Wednesday. But, thank the Lord, I think I'm over it. They actually go way back. I think Paul tried to get Danny to do something he didn't want to or something—I don't really know. It was weird, and it was a long time ago. So just don't mention to Bailiff that we're doing anything with Danny."

"Sure thing." Nate tried not to skulk on his way back to his office. "Time for the NationalJournal.com update," he said to Lisa. He wished for once he didn't have a Southern Baptist's nose—or tongue—for news.

Danny finished eating a dry Whopper that constituted supper and crumpled its wrapper back into its sack. He tossed the waste into the passenger floorboard of the Durango, where other refuse had collected.

As dusk fell, he had parked across from Wang's clinic underneath one of the mature live oak trees. It was officially summer, and the rain had stopped for a couple of days, allowing North Texas's trademark blistering, humid heat to congeal in its place. He wore a dark but wrinkled suit as he observed the evening car traffic thin out from in front of the low, brick office units. By dark, only Wang's older model Mercedes remained.

Still, a vehicle or two would pull in and park a few meters down from Wang's office. Danny knew why the johns came and were inside absolutely no longer than thirty minutes at a time. He had already told Bailiff he wouldn't be the bag man for Wang upon finding out the person having problems down at Homeland Security was his mistress, and a madam at that. The dark side of Danny's moon made exceptions for those who were up against the notorious agency and its bureaucratic inertia, but what Bailiff and Lin wanted went too far. He decided to make the most of it if Bailiff was going to send him a message by making Lisa the fall girl.

Danny was about to exit his vehicle into the darkness when another car pulled in and parked in front of the next door unit. The vehicle was a BMW, which he thought looked familiar, and when its driver stepped out and toward the door, his large silhouette reminded Danny of someone. After the man was inside, Danny made his move to Wang's office but not without taking out his phone and snapping a quick photo of the BMW's rear. Before doing so, he turned off the flash. The halogen lamps covering the lot illuminated the back of the car just enough.

Safely inside Wang's empty office, the image on the phone triggered Danny's memory. The dim license plate read WWBOD. The shot angle Danny used captured the brick building in the background, although no signage indicating its illicit tenant was visible. Still, the jaded hack thought the info might come in handy.

Danny was expected, which was why the door was open. He marched back down the corridor of exam rooms to Wang's office. The acupuncturist was alone, as Danny had demanded. Wang placed a small Gortex bag—like a lunch bag—on his desk. Danny checked inside, and a spot count led him to believe the entire twenty-thousand dollars were there. Danny zipped the bag shut and made a deliberate exit.

CHAPTER TWENTY-THREE

Lisa spent the weekend driving back and forth between Home Depot and Lowe's, trying to decide on colors for the nursery. Brenda and Ron came by for much of the morning Saturday. Lisa praised her merciful Lord for enabling the elder Jeffuses to respect her privacy and the need for adjustment to the early days of Bobby being home. Lisa couldn't allow her husband's mother not to be there, however, and after the first week was done, she made sure Brenda and Ron knew they had full privileges. The Jeffuses' visit on Saturday was tempered by the anticipation of the Baby Expo a week hence. Stephanie Knight had come by to go with Lisa to look at paint colors, knowing she'd eventually be planning a shower later on.

The elder Jeffuses had been at Lisa's house for about an hour when Stephanie swung by. Soon after, a different nurse from Master's Home Health arrived, named Tami. In spite of asking her to write her name down, Lisa still called the new nurse Jenny.

And Jenny came back on Sunday for a few hours. Lisa and Sharon had decided to wait and change Bobby's linens Monday morning, as Mundy the therapist's visit had coincided well with changing out the bed. Lisa still updated the chart, allowing Jenny to do the only feeding for that day. Lisa did go to church and actually talked briefly with Pastor Keith, who apologized for just now checking in with her. Lisa told Kenner that all was well, including with her new baby, and she said to him how much she appreciated his prayers.

On Monday morning, Lisa felt rested but was planning for the week, not just the day. She wouldn't feel any job was done until Friday night after the biotech event. Then Saturday, during the baby expo, she could take in some satisfaction. On the tick, the doorbell was rung by Mundy. Sharon was nowhere yet to be seen.

"Good morning," Mundy said, cane in hand.

"Good morning, Mr. Lewis," said Lisa. That cheerful business aplomb was back.

Mundy followed Lisa back down the hallway, letting his cane follow the floor molding. Once he was back in Bobby's room, it did not take him long to regain his bearings and get to work.

"Skin feels dry," he said, working Bobby's legs. "Any oil over there?"

"Sure," Lisa said, retrieving some generic body oil with a medical-looking label.

After applying it, Mundy resumed working down one leg and back up the other. "Is the nurse coming?" he asked in anticipation of turning the patient.

"Should be here soon," Lisa said, exiting to use her BlackBerry. She thought it was in her room, but instead she had to search for it a minute. Finally, she found it in her purse. She picked it up and dialed Sharon's number. As it rang, she noticed her prayer journal was forced into the bottom of her purse and underneath her sunglasses case. Lisa remembered she hadn't been writing in it for over a week. She left a voicemail for Sharon. After no one answered, she returned to Bobby's room.

"His skin feels loose, not going back to its shape after I work it," said Mundy. "Is he getting enough liquid?"

Lisa felt a slight pit in her stomach. "I think so," she heard herself say.

"Usually, if they ain't getting enough to eat or drink, their skin gets pasty and loose. See here?" Mundy pinched Bobby's leg, but the skin did not return to its normal shape immediately after he released his fingers. Mundy's black-glasses-covered brow only faced the wall, knowing the condition by touch. "You ought to maybe check with the nurse and make sure our man is getting enough to eat. Are you feeding him Milksure or something?"

"Yes. He is scheduled to be fed about a liter a day," Lisa said carefully. It would have been a lie to say, "He is fed about a liter a day.

"And the doctor said he would lose weight," she added quickly.

"Maybe. You don't want him losing weight, though, 'cause of not enough nutrition," Mundy warned. He and Lisa both heard a large vehicle pull up out front.

"Just a minute. Maybe that's the nurse," she said, eagerly leaving the conversation.

She opened the front door to see a full-sized Dodge van park along the curb with its back to the driveway. Sharon and a large man climbed out. As Sharon walked to the house, the man opened the back of the van and pulled out a swing-looking contraption on wheels.

"Sorry I'm late. We brought the scale for Bobby, doctor's orders."

Lisa felt a panic rush over her. She had forgotten that Asitajee said he was going to order a weight test. She was unsettled by whatever Bobby's skin condition was and by Mundy's linking of it to nutrition. She wondered if Sharon—then the doctor—would deduce a link between the two. What if they confronted her about the feedings and the chart? What would she say? What if Masters found out? Would he go so far as to accuse her of euthanasia?

She decided to play it cool. But what if Sharon said something about the skin—or Mundy told her. Would that begin the great unraveling of her unilateral, secret plan? Who cared what they thought; she new best! She hurried back down the hall, leaving Sharon to enter on her own.

"Mundy, I'll ask Asitajee about the skin—," Lisa started to say as she reapproached Bobby's room.

Mundy was talking to himself and didn't hear her. In fact, he was carrying on a one-sided conversation with his patient. "Yes, sir. You are strong. You remind me of my older brother. He played football for TCU. He had a hard time after college, though. Started smoking crack. One day, he passed the pipe to me. I almost took it, but God kept me from—"

"Hi, Mr. Lewis!" interrupted Sharon. Lisa jumped. "Oh, I'm sorry. I didn't mean to scare you," she said to Lisa, putting her arm on her sleeve and laughing. Lisa chuckled nervously.

"Oh, hi!" Mundy said. "You just in time to help me turn the patient over."

"I had hoped we timed it right. After you're done, we need to put him in the scale and weigh him."

"Okay," Mundy said as Sharon moved to help him rotate Bobby. Lisa hovered nervously around the bed, anxious for something to be said about Bobby's skin.

"If you need to go, Lisa, we're all right, I think," said Sharon.

"No, that's all right," she said quickly, rushing to assist with turning Bobby's lower legs. "I want to see how that funny-looking scale works."

"Oh, it's like a swing," Sharon said.

Lisa was eager to talk about anything other than skin/food. "I see, he sits in it, and it weighs him."

"Yes," Sharon said. The agency orderly arrived with the device in the room.

Mundy began speaking again. "Y'all are changing the sheets today, right? I had to use some oil for—"

"I really wish more people knew how much care goes into someone like Bobby," Lisa blurted out. "I mean, there's pro-life, then there's pro-life, huh?" she said with a goofy grin.

"Oh yes, honey," Sharon said. It was the chain reaction Lisa desperately hoped would occur. "Lots of people think that being pro-life is only for babies, but really it's for all people who can't decide for themselves.

"Look at how defenseless poor Mr. Bobby is. I just don't know what he'd do without you, Lisa. I know you do a lot of that political stuff, and that you are pro-life; but until you have to deal with it, only then do we really have a chance to practice our beliefs."

"Medicare and Medicaid, too, are really pro-life programs," said Mundy. Lisa could not have asked for a better course of conversation. "Lots of Republican people want to cut Medicare 'cuz of the budget, but really it's what keeps people alive, especially poor folk."

"You know what? You're right," Sharon said. Lisa was giddy that the pair of caregivers became joined in conversation. "I never thought of that. That is a good reason why we need Medicare. We need to make sure everybody gets paid under Medicare. That is all Mr. Masters complains about, and I never realized that that was why a godly man like him supports Medicare. Are you ready?" Sharon asked Mundy as she and the orderly moved the scale into position.

"Here, let me get out of the way," Mundy said, moving around from the bed.

Sharon removed Bobby's arms from his gown so that it wouldn't get tangled in the scale. In a giant grab, the orderly wrapped his long arms around Bobby's back and chest, then pivotlike lifted him off the bed and into the scale in one breath-taking move.

"Let's see," Sharon said, looking intently at the reader. At the same time, she took Bobby's wrist to read his pulse. "Wow, that skin is dry!"

Lisa's eyes flared.

"Feels dry to me, too," said the orderly.

"202," Sharon read. "Let me write that on the chart over there. 202."

"Let me help!" Lisa grabbed the chart off one of the tables before Sharon could move over to get it. She searched for the place to record the weight.

"It's up on the left side," Sharon side, moving around the scale, which had blocked her from the rest of the room.

"I don't know if he's getting enough food and water," said Mundy aloud to the others. "But I'm no expert."

Lisa still couldn't find where to write the weight. Sharon could tell she was still searching. Lisa became flustered as Sharon got closer. The blood rushed up to Lisa's head.

"Here, sweetie," Sharon said, taking the clipboard from Lisa. "Oh," Sharon let out with a laugh. "This is the wrong page." She flipped over a couple of pages to the vitals sheet. "Mr. Bobby, you've lost weight since we moved you in here."

Lisa broke out in a sweat.

Sharon flipped back to the feeding chart. "It says you haven't missed any feedings." She turned to Lisa. "You haven't missed any feedings when you were by yourself and then maybe forgot and marked this anyway, have you?"

Sharon gave Lisa her out, but she did not take it. "No," Lisa said, the lie blocking most of the sound of the reply.

"Well, maybe we should up your intake, Bobby," Sharon said.

The orderly lifted Bobby once again, this time setting him on the bed. He then carefully spun and laid him down in one motion. "Were his eyes open when we came in?" asked the orderly.

Sharon and Lisa leapt to the bedside to see Bobby's eyes wide open. "Praise Jesus!" shouted Sharon at the top of her lungs.

"Bobby…Bobby!" said Lisa, grabbing her husband's hand and shaking his arm. "Are you awake? Can you hear me?"

Bobby only stared. No lucidity was discernable.

"I have to call the doctor," said Sharon. "Praise his holy and omnipotent name! Glory!"

Lisa watched Mundy leave. She chased him back down the hallway. "Thanks for coming again. Thanks for alerting us to the feeding problem," she said, guiding him back to the front door.

"You lied about the nutrition," Mundy said, Lisa seeing a distorted reflection of herself in his ultra-dark horn rims. "I could tell it in your voice."

Lisa exhaled rapidly at a loss for spin. "You're no mind-reader!" she finally shot out.

"Call me, and let me know how he does," Mundy said, turning to leave upon hearing his sister's car drive up.

Danny pulled into the Taco Bell off Stemmons and Regal Row and went inside to order a plain bean burrito and water. He sat in one of the two-seater tables overlooking the southbound freeway and a side road. Danny's appointment would be coming down the latter before turning into the parking lot. The summer sun had returned with a vengeance, but Danny stared outside without any shades.

Gene Shin pulled in right on time, during what was normally his afternoon break from over at DHS. He would smoke just for the odor whenever he had meetings like this, making his supervisors think he had indeed wandered off for a cigarette. There were still a few smokers at the old INS processing facility down the road, but a ban on smoking anywhere on federal property required that they go well off campus. In typical, bureaucratic fashion, ten minutes was added to the afternoon break to accommodate the off-campus smokers, as if productivity weren't already a problem.

Shin sat across from Danny and said hello in Korean.

"Howdy," Danny said in English in between bites from his unwrapped burrito.

Shin hadn't ordered anything, but he looked down on Danny's tray and saw an overstuffed envelope now covered in the burrito wrapper. "Would you like a Mexican treat?" Danny said, using his Korean. "You know, I'm really glad for their contributions to our country."

Shin took the ersatz burrito. "It should be Thursday when it's processed. The standard notice will go to the district office." Shin did not continue the conversation in Korean. He thought it looked suspicious for a redneck in snakeskin boots to be using the language. Plus, to hear some political bum speak his native tongue dishonored it. "I think there's a ceremony scheduled for Friday. If the alien want—"

"District office will handle it," said Danny, still using Korean.

Shin wasted no more time getting up and leaving.

Danny finished his food, staring with an angry squint out at the sun melting the distant freeway.

June 25

Dear God–

I am a sinner. Please forgive me. My heart is crushed with guilt. Please save me.

At her office desk, Lisa reviewed Marcia's confirmed guest list for Friday night at half-speed. There were still seven of the DFW-based invitees who had not responded, and the short notice required a phone call, anyway. The only thing that motivated Lisa was that by busying herself on the phone and calling every conceivable number possible for a given invitee, she would have a second to dodge that inevitable call from Asitajee about what happened this morning. The thought of being potentially interrogated over the feedings made Lisa want to curl up with paranoia. She decided that the overwhelming guilt came from remorse mixed with her dishonesty. But she knew what was right for her husband and would figure out the best for him. She found a touch of relief at the thought of using any call with Asitajee to bring up Bobby's true prognosis, open or closed eyes.

Eventually, her phone did ring. It was Brenda. She just had to take it. "This is Lisa."

"Have you talked with the doctor? What does he say this means?" Brenda fired off. Brenda and Ron had rushed over to her son's bedside as soon as Lisa gave her the obliging call. The blithe distance Lisa had been granted by Brenda in recent days was quickly closed with her mother-in-law's anxiety.

"I don't know, Brenda. I haven't talked to him yet. It's encouraging, but that's why I'm at work. It could just be a neural reaction of some kind."

"You should be at home!"

"Trust me, he is not lucid. He does not register that I am there that I can tell," Lisa said, ignoring Brenda.

"Well, I can tell! I know he knows it's me!" Brenda declared.

"I'll be home later. Life has to go on, Brenda. Bye," Lisa said as she hung up. She was in stiff-arm mode. She knew she was right about the feeding, but she had no idea it would mess with Bobby's skin like that. And so what if Mundy decided she was lying. He had no proof.

Nate came in from a late lunch with one of his reporter friends. He had not seen Lisa yet, but she had emailed him about Bobby, also telling him no one else on the staff had yet been told. She needed everyone to stay focused on Friday. Hosting the biotech group for dinner was a small event, but she wanted the details perfect; and they had never worked with the Palomar before.

"Any more news?" Nate asked his boss. He was still sheepish from his white lie of the previous Friday. He should have told Lisa right then that he had told Bailiff they were working with Danny.

"Not from the doctor. It's stirring to see his eyes, but they are just a glassy reflection. The brain is just not back on line," Lisa explained. "My question for the doctor is: is the opening of the lids a sign that the brain is healing?"

"Why don't you think he's called?"

"Busy, I guess. So, are you done for Friday?" Lisa signaled impatience.

"Yes, ma'am. Can I call any of these people?" Nate asked, pointing to Lisa's call list.

"No, I'm almost done. Have you talked to Paul today?"

"Not yet." There was a pause, and then Nate sat down. "Listen. I'm really sorry, but I accidentally let out to Paul that Danny had steered Brookshire our way."

Lisa furrowed her brow at Nate.

"Well, I mean, I didn't tell him it was Brookshire specifically. Just that we were working with Danny. I forget that we are a proprietary organization and that I'm not working for the congressman anymore. I am sorry."

"Is that all you said?"

"Yes, yes, that was all I said. I'm sorry for doing it, and I'm sorry for not 'fessing up to it Friday when the subject came up."

"You're so conscientious," Lisa said with a smile. She felt gracious given the fact that she had been accused of lying that morning. She was comforted to know she and Nate were siblings of dishonesty. She knew it came with the territory. She leaned back in her chair, the way a big-business baroness might process a tidbit of insider knowledge. She wondered why Danny said and behaved the way he did. What did it mean? "You can't save me, and I can't save you?" were Danny's cryptic words. "Tell me again what that Wang guy said to you," Lisa said.

"I honestly could not understand, but even then he just insisted on speaking to you. Leesa Jeffe-son, he kept saying. I assumed it was a simple case of Charlie Lin giving him your name, because he doesn't know anyone in the district office. Lin would've known that you would have steered the guy right, getting him touch with the girls down the hall."

What Nate was saying would have made perfect sense to Lisa had Danny not freaked out over it. And of course, Lin had told her of Bailiff's suggestion for Danny's help. What could have possibly bugged him so much about an immigration case? Lisa's BlackBerry buzzed on her desk. State of Texas came across on the screen. Lisa knew it wasn't a VIP, as they should have the sense not to call a political fundraising entity using a government line.

"This is Lisa Jeffus."

"Ms. Jeffus,"—Lisa knew better when someone who used "Mz" in their greeting—"my name is Anita Velasquez with Dallas County Adult Protective Services. I am hereby notifying you that a case has been opened on your husband, Robert T. Jeffus."

In an instant, she put up her defenses. She instinctively felt that if she were in trouble, there would be no call like this—only the cops. She would both fish for a cause and release a red herring if needed. "Please don't tell me my home health agency has been hurting my husband," said Lisa.

"We don't have any evidence of that being the case yet, Ms. Jeffus. But we would like to ask you some routine questions."

CHAPTER TWENTY-FOUR

Lisa sat outside the social worker's office downtown for twenty minutes, waiting to be interviewed, as they called it. Finally, Ms. Velasquez came out from her dingy office festooned with papers of all sorts. The woman was unpleasant to look at but unintimidating. She reminded Lisa of Exidor from TV's *Mork and Mindy*.

Lisa decided to play it safe and was accompanied by an attorney, an old college friend named Cindy Watkins. Cindy was definitely of the pragmatic school of politics. While she was a Republican at heart, she was definitely pro-choice and never met a plaintiff's lawyer she didn't like. She explained to Lisa that she buttered up Dallas trial lawyers, because you never knew who would be sitting over you on the bench one day, given the current trends in the county.

But even with counsel present, Lisa knew she was not being investigated. While the feedings may be an issue, she knew what she wanted to do. She was still restless about the lying, but she wasn't going to discuss that with Exidor. Lisa felt that she was the only true advocate of Bobby's care, fulfilling what he needed and wanted.

"I hope you know, Mz. Jeffus, that this interview is only a matter of routine," said Ms. Velasquez. While she was trying to be reassuring, Lisa sensed that Ms. Velasquez was only rattling off the required disclaimer, "Neither the State of Texas nor the petitioner nor I are accusing you of anything. Have a seat." Velasquez seemed to ignore Cindy.

After a few moments of boring agony, Ms. Velasquez began her questioning. Most of the questions were pretty basic, and after a glance at Cindy, Lisa was easily forthcoming. Ms. Velasquez wanted to know how long Lisa and Bobby had been married, how long had they lived at their current address, etc.

Things got a little testy when the questioning turned to net worth and life insurance. Prior to the meeting, Cindy advised Lisa to answer these types of questions, as she was by far the greater bread-winner. She had also brought the most assets to the marriage. And to top it off, Lisa carried an insurance policy with a higher face value for these very reasons.

Ms. Velasquez then moved on to questions about the accident, how it happened, and Bobby's hospitalizations. Lisa reported the dates as best she could recall. Lisa felt sad as she recalled the events that now seemed like they'd occurred ten years ago. She was suddenly jolted back into the present when it came to questions about Lisa's role as caregiver. She braced for the worst.

"Did you notice anything unusual in any of the nurse's routines?"

"During the times I was home, no," Lisa answered.

"Have you been making notes of the feeding times in the absence of the home nurses?" asked Ms. Velasquez.

"Yes," Lisa replied, accurately she believed.

Ms. Velasquez wrote on her legal pad and continued. "How often did you change your husband's diapers?"

Lisa thought for a moment. Because there was no response from Cindy, Lisa felt the question was inane enough for an answer. "When I was the only person there, I guess once or twice."

"Once a day or once, period?" redirected Ms. Velasquez.

"We need to know where this line of inquiry is going," demanded Cindy in a calm, pit-bull-in-waiting manner."

"These are routine questions," Ms. Velasquez said. Nevertheless, she did not press for a clarification.

After a few more questions regarding the general set up of the home for Bobby's care, Ms. Velasquez suddenly dismissed the two women.

"Can't I ask questions about the other caregivers?" Lisa asserted.

"No, Ms. Jeffus," responded Ms. Velasquez. "Those are separate investigations between this office, the home-health agency, and its employees.

"The individual who reported any perceived substandard of care must remain strictly confidential," Ms. Velasquez added.

"Well, what triggered the complaint?" Lisa asked.

Turning to another huge pile of papers, Ms. Velasquez reluctantly said, "The petitioner complained of not enough urine output by your husband."

"Did they not see anything in the diaper, I guess?" Lisa asked further, but Exidor remained in a straight-jacket. Sensing the stone wall, Lisa wasted no time getting out of the sterile public office building.

"Thanks, Cindy," Lisa said, donning her sunglasses. The day was already quite hot, and it was not yet 10:00 a.m. "I can't believe they would accuse me of anything."

"I didn't think she made any accusation," said Cindy, somewhat puzzled. "It's all about the nurses at this point. You said that nurse, Sharon, was her name?"

"That's right."

"Was she pretty much the only person who changed the diapers? A nurse wouldn't turn in her own agency or fellow nurses, that is. The real question is who noticed what and when. And because of Ms. Velasquez's question about the diapers and her detail about the complaint, someone decided that maybe Bobby wasn't being fed."

"There were other nurses, though. At least two others."

"Anyone else? Any other caregivers?"

Lisa thought of Mundy, but she knew she wasn't going to bring him into this because he had accused her of lying. She knew he wasn't the one who turned her in, anyway, because he didn't stick around for the diaper changing yesterday morning. Besides, he was merely making speculation at what she said about the chart.

"What about your mother-in-law?" asked Cindy. "Y'all don't really get along, as I recall."

"I don't think Brenda would. Besides, she was never really there the past week. She wouldn't know what to observe, assuming that new nurse Saturday didn't say something—maybe it was her! I can't remember her name—Terry? Jamie?"

"It doesn't really matter. Just don't answer any questions without me. In the meantime, I checked with the State and with that Masters guy, and they are only to defer to you until this investigation is closed, which it should be in short order."

"Have you talked with Bobby's doctor?" Cindy asked.

"Yes. We finally connected yesterday afternoon. He said that Bobby's eyes opening was a natural response about this time, but that consciousness would still be difficult to measure, especially as the weeks go on. According to that Glasgow Coma Scale thing I was told about, we're kind of entering the PVS or persistent phase of the coma."

"I'm sorry, Lisa," said Cindy. "I really am."

"I guess things could be worse," Lisa said, downcast. "He could be sick or have crippled limbs."

"Was the doctor aware of the APS case?" Cindy followed up.

"Yes. They told him." Lisa became filled with embarrassment for Masters that APS had been called on his agency. She mentally removed him from any fundraisers, at least those where she did the asking. The case also meant his nurses were now in hot water with him. She concluded that if Sharon or the other two girls continued to care for Bobby, they definitely weren't the accused. What was that third one's name?

Lisa only spent the middle part of the day back at the office. Pretty much everything was set for the biotech dinner that Friday. All but two of the DFW invitees had confirmed. Apparently, this Dr. Ranzim was pretty well-known and admired. Lisa had wished she had invited more people. But it was really a get-to-know-you event, so the crowd would be just right. The planning completed, Lisa could get back to Bobby.

Walking in, Lisa found only Brenda and Ron with Bobby. She took a deep breath and prepared for the onslaught.

"That doctor said he needs a minimum of four of those cans a day. Four!" declared Brenda. Ron quickly made himself scarce, telling his wife he was heading home.

"Yes, yes, I heard you, Brenda," Lisa said.

"Four!"

Lisa picked up the feeding chart. She looked across the bed and saw Bobby's eyes still popped open. She went and sat next to him. She caressed his hairline and its short regrowth with her fingernails.

"What do you see, husband?" Because Bobby's eyes glared in one direction, Lisa had to move her head and eyes to connect with his. Even there, however, Lisa just wasn't sure of any true consciousness. She didn't feel a connection.

Lisa knew Brenda was knotted up with pain and anxiety. For all her neuroticism, Brenda was not dishonest. Lisa could only imagine Brenda clinging to her son these past couple of days, straining for the slightest sign of life only to feel the response of a statue.

"Brenda, I am sorry. I know how hard this is," Lisa said. She stepped over and hugged her mother-in-law, who began to cry into her shoulders.

Lisa noticed she didn't feel any emotions. She heard her phone go off in the kitchen. She released Brenda.

"Hey, I called the office, and Nate said Bobby opened his eyes!" said A.J.

"Yes, I'm not so sure. I guess I am engaging in the political art of lowering expectations." Lisa suddenly remembered that A.J. was not that far removed from Mundy via Curtiss. "I may have to find another massage therapist," she said. "I think I made the last one mad." Lisa began to fish for any hearsay.

"Who? Mundy? I've only met him once, but how could he get mad even at a fly, let alone the charming and beautiful Mrs. Jeffus?"

"No, I think I made him mad yesterday morning." Sensing A.J. hadn't heard anything, Lisa lied about what happened to simply end the topic. "I told the nurse to come later, and that messed up his routine with Bobby."

A.J. seemed uninterested in what happened and changed the subject. "Hey look, I have some news. It turns out Curtiss's boss is being named to Oltan's interfaith advisory board. He's going to host a bunch of pastors down here in Dallas for an informal Q&A with the senator before the primaries start."

Lisa was equally as uninterested in what the pastor was doing, but she knew it meant that Curtiss might be moving up in the world. That, in turn, meant that A.J.'s and his relationship might be getting a little more serious. "I know where the senator can find a good campaign manager."

"Well, that was actually why I called. What do you think about me becoming the Texas Director for the Oltan Campaign?" Lisa heard a yelp from the other end of the line.

"Are you serious! That's great! But what about the other candidates?"

"What other candidates? We're going to win!" A.J. shouted into the phone.

Lisa smiled at her friend's celebration. She only wished her own party could find one percent of the same level of energy. "Good luck," she said. "I'll see you on the battlefield."

"Well, I have some bad news to go along with this. I'm supposed to fly to Chicago this weekend for some training."

Lisa immediately knew that meant she and A.J. wouldn't be able to go to the Baby Expo.

"I am so sorry, Lise."

"It's okay," Lisa said. She was disappointed. She had wanted A.J. along to share in the satisfying of a nesting instinct Lisa felt she had been pushing aside due to all the trials of the past weeks. She had really been looking forward to the excursion as a reward for enduring those trials.

Lisa had a sense of judgment come over her. She decided that as punishment for her white lies over Bobby's care, it was justice that her BFF miss the expo. And besides, there would be baby showers in the future she could attend. Lisa took comfort in the thought that God was merciful. "This is a big career chance for you, girl," she said. "God bless you."

Chapter Twenty-five

June 29

Dear God,

Thank you for this day and the trials you've given me. Thank you for seeing the staff and me through to this day. May it be productive and honor you and our country.

And God, thank you for A.J.'s opportunity. Let your will be done in the election to come.

In Jesus' name. Amen.

Lisa closed her prayer journal and finished getting dressed. The situation with Bobby notwithstanding, she had to get her game face on. She had to wear a knock-out ensemble that would survive the day and look good for the biotech group tonight. She chose her black Prada suit with the shorter skirt; it would be snug but still flatter. It hit her that this might be the last time she could wear the suit for the next few months.

She had her hair done, so it was *fabuloso* for the event in which that good first impression would prove key. She dug in her jewelry case and found a gold brooch Bobby had given her. The twisting design reminded her of a DNA strand, so she affixed it to her lapel. She loved those serendipitous moments that seemed to synthesize the moment.

Putting on her watch, she checked on Bobby. No change in his eyes. Cindy had advised not contacting Masters during the investigation, instead entrusting Bobby's care to him per the doctor's already issued orders. Another completely new nurse, Maryann, had shown up Thursday after she and the Jeffuses made do without one Wednesday. A knock at the door signaled that Bobby's help was here. If it proved to be someone new yet again, Lisa knew that her theory about Sharon or one of the nurses calling APS was likely true.

Lisa finally remembered the name of the nurse she had forgotten when she opened the door and saw her—Tami! Remembering that Tami, Jenny, and Sharon had been Bobby's caregivers before APS was called, she began to question her theory.

"Hi," Tami said mousily. Lisa was unimpressed with the dirty-blond waif last Saturday before she left with Stephanie, but now she was even more so. "Did Mr. Jeffus have a good night?" Tami said with the bow-leggedest twang Lisa thought she had ever heard. She doubted whether this thin reed of character would have reported the weather, let alone negligent care.

Lisa did not answer as she let Tami in. "Tami, right?"

"Yes, ma'am."

She led Tami back down the hall. "We changed the sheets yesterday. We're on a more aggressive feeding schedule now." Lisa now gave all those feedings, making sure the chart didn't lie. She did the evening one before Brenda left the previous Tuesday, just to make sure she had a witness.

"Yes, ma'am, my nursing director told me."

"And this is going to be a late night for me, but my in-laws are coming over."

"Yes, ma'am. I'll tell Sharon when she gets here."

That was it. With Tami and later Sharon returning, they were not the ones who had reported negligent care. Why would they risk seeing the patient's wife, if they had been the accusers? Maybe Jenny had been the one, and that Cindy was wrong about nurses not reporting each other. She decided to fish.

"Is Sharon doing okay? I've missed her the past few days."

"Yes, ma'am. I felt kinda sorry for her," said Tami, proceeding to feed Bobby. "We all got suspended early this week 'cause of an APS investigation."

"A what?" Lisa played dumb. She also wanted to reassure Tami and in turn the others that she was not the one who made the call to the State.

Tami looked down at Bobby's abdomen, embarrassed. "I'm not sure if I'm supposed to talk about it."

"No, it's fine," Lisa said firmly. "I won't tell," she demanded. "I could never imagine that y'all would do anything wrong," she said more softly.

"Well, uh, Mr. Masters gives us an automatic suspension if there's a case opened up on one of our patients. That ain't the law—and it ain't right, in my opinion." Suddenly, there was some moxie in the gut of Tami's twenty-inch waist. "But it's how he does business. Anyway, I think 'cuz the diapers on your husband weren't as wet Saturday, that's why we got reported."

Lisa immediately knew that Brenda was the one who had observed something and likely called APS, as the elder Jeffuses were the only other ones with Bobby Saturday. Lisa became livid. Her spiral brooch might have become a throwing star had Brenda been present. "Tell Sharon I'm sorry, but I know she has provided Bobby with the utmost care. I would never have suspected her or you or anyone with Masters of something negligent."

"Thank you, ma'am. We do our best."

"I can be reached on my cell number," Lisa said, storming out to work.

The Tahoe went raging down Highway 78, cutting off a Prius, as Lisa fumbled for her BlackBerry and dialed Brenda's number. No one answered on the cell; she knew, because the dumb old lady didn't keep it charged. She called the house. Still no answer. She called Ron.

"Ron Jeffus," said the soft-spoken voice.

"This is Lisa. You need to get that wife of yours under control! She called APS Saturday because of something she knows nothing about. She got three hard-working nurses suspended and me investigated! Why you ever put up with that miserable old bag is beyond me, Ron!"

"I called APS," Ron said.

Lisa felt suspended in time and space.

"Someone is not feeding Bobby," he said calmly. "This is what happened to my brother, Bobby's uncle. Of course, it was in the hospital back then, not at home, but someone deliberately withheld nutrition from his feeding tube, and he went into kidney failure. We never knew, but I personally think it was a serial killer who worked at the hospital."

"Well, I was questioned by them, too! How could you, Ron?"

"I didn't know they'd question you. I'm sorry, sweetheart. You've been so good to Bobby. We love you."

Lisa held back tears because she didn't want her eyeliner to run. She hung up.

The SUV had slowed to normal commuting speed, mainly due to the morning traffic, which had piled up in North Garland.

She was sorry, even frustrated, about the lying, but Lisa knew what was best. She just couldn't explain it to anyone without getting in trouble. The opportunity to discuss Bobby's prognosis never presented itself with Asitajee. He was too optimistic in his assessment.

Lisa decided that she needed some daily affirmation. She wanted to talk to her best friend, but she knew A.J. was trying to get to the airport. She also felt she was having trouble communicating with her. A.J. was moving on a totally different direction, not in the partisan sense, but in the plain old career sense. The longer A.J. stayed with her new presidential race, the more consuming it would become and the less time she'd have for some Republican fundraiser like Lisa in the reddest of Red states.

As the Tahoe slowed almost to a stop, Lisa thought again of Danny. With the focus on her event tonight as well as dealing with

Bobby and APS, she had been forced to push aside the mystery she and Nate discussed on Tuesday. How was he tangled up with Bailiff? What had he done, or worse, what had Bailiff asked him to do? She remembered how desperate Danny seemed back in May—at least for money. She feared he might pimp himself out for just about anything.

"This is Paul," answered Bailiff on his cell phone.

"Paul, it's Lisa."

"Good morning. I hear everything's set for tonight."

"Yes. I think it's going to be a good event. Listen, I'm sorry to pry, but I think you know we have a contract through Danny Geister—remember?—who used to work for the RNC and the White House."

"Of course, of course, yes. I called him recently actually, asking for his help with a potential contributor."

"You did?"

"Yes. Nate—and don't knock poor Nate for this; I think he forgets he works for the private sector—Nate told me he was doing that contract, and so I tracked him down and got his number to ask him for help with one of our Asian friends. I remembered vaguely—and I don't know how I remembered it—that he spoke Korean. I do remember! It was because Nate had asked me about his dad, Jim, who we saw out in Yale, and I remembered that they were small plane pilots and worked in Korea and all that. Remember when Danny flew us around back in '94?"

"Yes," Lisa said, pensive about the conversation. "But you said you called Danny?"

"Yes, anyway, I called him. Charlie Lin had a—well, I don't know if he was a friend—an acquaintance, who had some kind of INS—"

"ICE?"

"Right, ICE, Homeland Security, whatever issue, and he said he spoke Korean, so I called Danny to translate for my district office."

"You're talking about that Carl Wang who called the office." The traffic along Lisa's commute loosened up.

"Was that his name? Oh, at any rate, for some strange reason," continued Bailiff, "Danny begged off. I think he went and talked to the guy, but then he told me he couldn't help, that his ICE case was too complicated. That's when I went back to Charlie and explained the problem. I told Charlie that you and Danny had been friends and that you might be able to find out from Danny why it was so complicated or what the problem was."

Bailiff was earnest in his voice, and Lisa had absolutely no reason to doubt what he was saying. She was still baffled as to why Danny reacted so strongly at the request. "I guess Charlie was trying to stay out of it; thinking if he were the go-between, it would be too inefficient," said Lisa. "Danny never offered any detailed explanation as to why he couldn't help?" she asked.

"Nothing. Not a word. I just got an abrupt voicemail saying he couldn't help."

"Strange. Danny's usually forthcoming," Lisa said.

"Yes, that's what I remembered about him," said Bailiff. "I thought he would be easy to work with. Oh well."

"If I see him, I'll ask." Lisa didn't want to report that she had already talked to Danny.

"No, don't worry about it. It's not important."

"But what about Lin?"

"No, no. He was just trying to help. He doesn't care one way or the other, I can assure you."

"All right," said Lisa, generally relieved but now wanting to straighten everything out with Danny. "I'll see you later tonight."

"Sure thing. Oh—could you tell Nate to call me? Thanks. I wanted to get his thoughts on one little thing. I really wish he was still on staff."

"Okay," Lisa said, laughing. "I'll tell him." After hanging up, Lisa became more concerned about Danny's psychological health. What could have happened with something as inert and tiresome as an immigration case such that Danny would become so agitated?

She decided it would take more prayer to discern how best to help her friend.

Cara picked up line 1 as she completed a name placard on her computer screen.

"Mockingbird Group. This is Cara," she answered.

"This Carl Wang. I call las' week," Mr. Wang said. Cara recognized the voice and buckled down in an attempt to understand.

"I call…foa Leesa Jeffe-son. I talk to man, he know nothing. Buuut…other man help!" Wang blurted out before Cara could respond. "I so happy!" he shrieked. "Today, woman become U.S. citizen! She go downtown. She raise hand. She say pledge. She become citizen!" As if Mr. Wang's English weren't difficult enough, now Cara was totally lost amid his joyful outburst of patriotism.

"Thank you, Mr. Wang. Did you call Congressman Bailiff's office? They may like to know your woman friend got sworn today. Here, let me give you the number…"

"No, no. I want thank Leesa Jeffe-son. Please let me to speak Leesa Jeffe-son."

"I'm sorry, Mr. Wang, but Mrs. Jeffus is not in yet."

"When talk to her? I give money. I do medicine."

Cara finally figured out who Mr. Wang was. "I'm sorry, Mr. Wang. I didn't have your name down yet for tonight. How do you spell it again?"

"C-A-R-L Wang," he intoned in his dialect.

"Wang, yes sir!" exclaimed Cara. "Like the company."

"Yes," Mr. Wang said, not fully understanding.

"Well, Mr. Wang, did you need directions to the event? It starts at 6:00 p.m. at the Hotel Palomar."

CHAPTER TWENTY-SIX

Lisa walked the length of a King Luxury Suite at the Palomar. The sky was hot but held the vanguard of yet another storm front. She hoped any more rain would hold off until her California guests made it to the event.

She was sorry about offending Ron, but the need to explain herself over the feeding chart had been deftly avoided. She was sorry the nurses had been tattooed as the result of what happened, but she was sure the APS situation would resolve itself; and they wouldn't be in any trouble. Lisa took a deep breath as a means to put the week's hassle aside. She wanted to focus on the business at hand: massaging potential contributors.

Lisa felt a little powerful, back in control as her Gabbana heels clicked across the hotel suite's hardwood floors. She lingered in front of the picture-glass window, which offered an incredible view of Southern Methodist University's Greco-Roman layout. One weekend in DC, she and Bobby visited Monticello and the nearby University of Virginia Campus. Bobby was fascinated by Thomas Jefferson's love of architecture and building design. After some reading about the Founding Father, Bobby discovered that Southern Methodist University had been modeled after the same plan as the University of Virginia's.

Lisa remembered this as she gazed from the Palomar across Central Expressway to the lush island of oaks in the middle of the Park Cities. Though no rumors had been confirmed, in all likelihood the president's library would go somewhere between where she was standing and the school's brick halls. Lisa felt at the center of the universe. Sure, there were problems the White House had burdened the Party with, but she knew that in her heart the President had always done the right thing. And with eyes toward the future, as her dinner here tonight for Bailiff signified, Lisa knew that petty political problems could be overcome, and the Party would restore its appeal.

She was pleased with the event environment. The hotel's style wasn't really her cup of tea, but it was Bailiff's. In fact, the décor was very Bailiff, right down to the dinnerware. Lucy Bailiff had more of a modernist style, and Paul secretly admired innovative architecture—also appropriate given the Jeffersonian themes of the locale. In fact, the Bailiff's modular home had been featured in the *News*'s style section, not just as a unique Dallas property, but also as a model of green architecture. The Bailiffs had purchased their 1940s rambler in White Rock's Peninsula neighborhood, razed it and then built their square-looking house in the hopes that the run-down area south of Lake Highlands would attract new owners and development.

Thus far, the Bailiffs' vision for East Dallas had only been shared by the owners of the Palomar. Lisa had wanted to inspect the suite and go over the seating arrangement with Marcia, the planner. Instead of driving first to the office, Lisa kept going over to 75 then down to Mockingbird Lane.

"I had the intern make the seating placards from a template I sent her," Marcia said.

"Good. Let's try to put Paul here with Ranzim right next to him and then intersperse the California guys with the DFW people," directed Lisa. Her BlackBerry went off.

"Hey, it's Nate."

"What's up?"

"I know you're trying to put this event to bed, but did you want me to start getting the data on Brookshire donors? That's what I meant to ask you earlier this week when I fessed up about Bailiff and Danny. I read that briefing book he gave us."

"Sure. Yes, please do." The Wang case aside, Lisa still knew she had a job to do with Danny's client. "Oh, that reminds me, Paul wanted you to call him."

"About what?"

"I don't know. You're his old flack."

"I promise, Lisa, he won't get it out of me, whatever it is," Nate said.

Lisa smiled as the call ended.

Curtiss dropped A.J. off at DFW for a 5:00 p.m. flight to Chicago. The couple held each other for a minute before A.J. needed to step through security. As they embraced, Curtiss prayed in A.J.'s ear. "Dear Heavenly Father, thank you for the gifts you've given us. Please, please, we humbly ask, comfort us while we are apart. Protect us from evil. Deliver us when our minds may not be on you. Preserve us, if we fall away. Be with your daughter now as she goes to do your work. Guide and strengthen her to do your will."

"Don't forget about Lisa and Bobby, dearest," A.J. said.

"And be with your children, Lisa and Bobby Jeffus. We pray the same for them as for us. Show thy mercy. In Jesus' name. Amen."

"Amen," A.J. echoed. "You are my love," she said. He knowingly but silently nodded in return, waving as A.J. stepped into the TSA line.

"I am so proud of you," Curtiss said. Once he saw his girlfriend make it through the other side of security, Curtiss deliberately walked out the automatic doors to the one-hour terminal parking. In his BMW, he made his way around the turning lanes out the North Exit. He sped his German engine out to Stemmons south. Within fifteen minutes of saying amen with A.J., he was parked in front of the low-brick building that housed Wang and his mistress's parlor.

Curtiss wept as he put the car in park. This was a Friday ritual for him, and he could not control it. Wiping his eyes with a hand-kerchief, he stepped inside.

"Congressman, this is Nate. Lisa said you wanted me to call you?"

"Yes, sir. I need to talk with you about a sensitive client y'all have. Do you have some privacy? Are you using a line other than the office?"

"Yes, sir. I'm on my cell." Nate felt a little alarmed. He was afraid that now with the biotech guys in the air, the dirty anti-life secret of their business was about to be revealed.

"I need you, from now on," Bailiff said, tiptoeing a bit, "to handle everything with George Masters. When he calls, when he gives— just anything y'all do that he has to do with."

"Sir?"

"Just…" Bailiff stammered a minute. His voice dropped into a rare low volume on the other end of the line. "Look, I need your help with him because of your pro-life credentials. There is a real problem with Lisa and her care of Bobby. I don't know what happened, but Masters is very suspicious of Lisa."

Nate hadn't shut his office door, but he hopped up to do so now. "Suspicious…like maybe Lisa is trying to euthanize him? That's absurd!" Nate exclaimed.

"I know, I know, but something is wrong with his care."

"Maybe it's some of Masters' people," Nate insisted. He felt a rush to defend Lisa. He was upset that someone would accuse her of anything. While loyalty could become an albatross in this business, Nate felt a gut desire to take Lisa's name off any blacklist.

"I don't think so," Bailiff discussed. "There was an APS case opened—I don't know who called—and Masters suspended some of his people. But when he called me, he said that they were in tears denying any wrongdoing, almost hysterical. He said he had to sus-pend them, because that was his policy when an APS case is opened, but he did reinstate them. I really think he's telling me the truth when he says his people didn't do anything."

"And you believe him, Pau—I mean, you accept that, Congressman?" Nate now realized his passions were getting into the conversation.

"I know, I know, it's very distressing," Bailiff said. "I was very upset and reacted like you when Masters called me. But after I thought about it some more, I can see where Lisa would maybe want Bobby, you know, to go on. Taking care of someone in that situation is so, so difficult. I'm not saying Lisa is a murderer at all—I am just saying that given all the pressures, being pregnant for the first time, I can see how maybe she'd want Bobby to go home to heaven. She probably thinks it's the right thing, even if only sub-consciously."

Nate remembered seeing Lisa and Danny outside the lobby last week. He became sick at the thought that maybe they had begun an affair. He felt his stomach fall into a pit.

"Anyway," Bailiff said, "I just need you to handle Masters. Go ahead, if you could, and proactively call him and tell him you'll be his point of contact on political matters from now. He's confused also. He knows I can't just up and change my campaign operation—and I won't, especially not until something serious is reported. But APS won't let him talk with Lisa, yet he is still having to provide care.

"It's a mess, really. We need to pray for them."

There was a long pause.

"Nate? Are you there?" asked Bailiff.

"Yes, sir. I will call Masters."

"Thank you."

"But what do we owe Masters, really, sir? I mean, we can replace his contributions, and he's just the boss in a rural county that would never put you below 60 percent, if you lost it," asked Nate. He wanted to at least quell any electoral fears, even if he couldn't get out of his mind Lisa's possible adultery.

"I'm not afraid of George, either, personally. I'm afraid of his network. It gets out down here that my funds are raised by Michael

Schiavo, and I won't have to worry about Election Day totals—my goose'll be cooked in the primary."

"You really think Masters has that kind of influence?"

"I don't think. I know," Bailiff said. "Nate, there's only two ways to run for office: scared as hell or unopposed."

CHAPTER TWENTY-SEVEN

Cara arrived at the Palomar with the name placards about ten minutes before 5:00 p.m. The large round table looked great as she arranged the names, but she had one extra placard for the twenty-one place settings on it.

"Marcia, I have an extra," Cara said, puzzled.

Marcia walked over and took the last unused placard from Cara. "Who is it?"

"Williams?" Cara asked.

"Dr. Mark Williams," Marcia read. "Hmm." Marcia retrieved her portfolio to check the names again.

"I printed the cards in alphabetical order," offered Cara, "if that helps."

"Oh, you just set the cards out," Marcia realized. "We actually have a seating chart Lisa wants to use."

"I'm sorry," said Cara. "I should have asked."

"Don't worry about it. Let's see..."

About a half hour earlier, Lisa had called the front desk to see if any of the biotech visitors had arrived. While Ranzim's staff made the travel arrangements, Lisa recommended the Palomar for their stay, explaining they'd be in the same hotel

for the event. She had been surprised Ranzim and his people would conduct a weekend trip across the country, but then his assistant explained that this day was the best day for him to hold his meetings out at Metroplex Children's Hospital. It turned out that Friday was best for Bailiff also due to the House's voting schedule. But Lisa felt she was expending capital with the potential donors having to burn one of their Friday nights, the local attendees included. Nevertheless, Ranzim was very amenable. He must have felt Bailiff, as an appropriator, was worth it.

Just to make sure everything was smooth, Lisa wanted to try and greet the biotechies when they arrived from the hospital. Upon calling the front desk from the suite, no one had yet checked in, however. She decided to get a jump on the guests and went down to the lobby, passing Cara in the elevator up. She sat down on one of the modernist leather chairs and checked her email with her BlackBerry for a few minutes.

Right at five o'clock, Ranzim and his group of ten associates came crowding in the front door. Lisa recognized Ranzim from a photo of him Nate scoured off the Internet. She immediately stood up and walked over to introduce herself. "Dr. Ranzim, my name is Lisa Jeffus. We talked on the phone."

"Yes. How are you?" Ranzim's voice was more gravelly in person. And while he resembled his photo as that of a man in late middle age, Lisa was quite unimpressed with him physically. While he clearly exuded command, Ranzim was not much taller than she, and he looked kind of frumpy. She concluded it was the trip.

"Welcome to Texas," Lisa said with her trademark cheer. She decided not to ask about the meeting, saving it for dinner and Bailiff.

"Yes, I detect a slight accent, not as strong on the phone, however," Ranzim said, which caught Lisa off guard. Maybe that was his scientific nerd way of greeting someone.

"I hope the airline wasn't too hard on you," she said, thinking of Ranzim's disheveled appearance. She would be gracious, but she would return any comment that seemed like a dig.

"Oh, no, we flew on our jet," Ranzim countered. "This is an interesting hotel."

"Yes, sir. It's new. Dinner is going to be right upstairs, and you'll love it. We have a great view of the SMU campus."

"I look forward to it."

"Why don't you get checked in and relax. We'll have some food and drinks ready at six, but take your time," Lisa said, watching one of Ranzim's entourage already talking with a hotel clerk. She also noticed an eager man making his way through the hotel door and toward her, pushing aside some of Ranzim's people. "Maybe we should move over here a bit—," she said, donning her tour guide cap.

"Leesa Jeffe-son! Leesa Jeffe-son!" declared the pushy man. "You Leesa Jeffe-son!" Wang was confident he had found his target, almost knocking Ranzim over as he stepped before Lisa.

Lisa's eyes glared wide open in semi-panic. "Can I ... can I help you?"

"Yes! I want say thank you. I want say love you!" Wang shouted, grabbing Lisa in an uncomfortable embrace, primarily for the wrinkles she knew he was putting in her suit. Unlike Ranzim, Wang was considerably shorter than Lisa. He also had a European odor.

"Help?" Lisa muttered. She knew she shouldn't scream. Ranzim and two of his people sensed something was wrong and pulled Wang back.

"Security!" shouted another of Ranzim's entourage, followed by another. Immediately, two of the valet workers and a doorman came and grabbed Wang.

"No, no, no! I not criminal! I thank Leesa Jeffe-son! She do good deed! She help woman-friend become citizen of United States!"

"Stop, stop, whoa," Lisa said to everyone in the melee. "Are you Mr. Wang?"

"Yes! I Carl Wang. I call office. I give money. Woman-friend become U.S. citizen."

Lisa got that suspended in time and space feeling again. Only now, one of the country's wealthiest biotech leaders stood two feet away.

"Okay, Okay, Mr. Wang—," Lisa shouted, cutting him off and trying to laugh off the pregnant moment. "That's good. Thank you for coming to thank me! I have some guests right now; why don't you call me later?" She ordered, thrusting a business card from her suit pocket at Wang.

"I no call. Just want to say thank you! You do great thing!"

"These gentlemen will help you outside," Lisa said to the doormen urgently and forcefully.

"I give money for Bailiff to be cong-man! He send man to fix immigration agent! Thank you, Leesa Jeffe-son!" shouted Wang as the hotel workers escorted him out to the edge of the driveway.

"Excuse me, Dr. Ranzim. I need to sit down," Lisa said, returning to the leather chair.

"Are you all right? My heavens!" Ranzim said, assisting her.

Lisa unfastened her suit coat, but before she could catch her breath, her mind was racing about a way to spin the exchange with Wang for Ranzim. She began to breathe heavily. What did Ranzim hear? What did he think? What had Danny done?

Marcia and Cara came running from the elevators over to Lisa, who was obviously in some kind of distress. Yet they had their own problem. "I'm so sorry, ma'am. I think I told someone about the event who wasn't invited!" said Cara, distraught.

"No kidding!" Lisa said, her blue eyes curling at Cara, who instantly broke into tears.

"Are you sure you're all right?" asked Ranzim. "Should we call the police?"

"No! No. Don't call the police," Lisa insisted. "I think it was just a misunderstanding. Yes!" she declared, overjoyed that the right word had popped in her head. Her breathing slowed down slightly. "Yes, it was just a misunderstanding of some kind. As you know, Doctor, the congressman does a variety of casework for his constituents. There is no telling what that gentleman was trying to say," Lisa said, borrowing a form response from days past.

"Oh, there's crazy people all over—that's part of being an elected official. I just want to make sure you're okay, Ms. Jeffus," Ranzim said.

"Please, call me Lisa," she said, her breathing finally returning to normal.

"Why don't we get you upstairs," Ranzim said to one of his group. "You said you had a suite? Is there a place to lie down?" Two of the guests helped Lisa stand and walk toward the elevator.

"Are you Joseph Ranzim?" asked Bailiff's stentorian voice from back by the door.

Lisa turned. "Over here, Paul!" Bailiff had mistaken one of Ranzim's entourage for the CEO.

"Hello, Dr. Ranzim. I'm Paul Bailiff. How was your meeting today?"

"Your assistant here just endured a minor assault," Ranzim stated. "We need to get her to a place more comfortable." By now, the head Palomar director was assisting the knot of guests over to the elevator.

"Lisa?" Bailiff asked, boarding the elevator with her, Ranzim, and his two colleagues.

"It's the ninth floor," Lisa said to the biotechie holding her elbow.

"What happened?"

Lisa didn't respond, because she was still trying to work the political angles in her brain using incomplete information. She was emotionally charged. Danny was involved in this fiasco, some way. She was having trouble breathing, making rapid breaths again. She had to get in front of the spin somehow before—

"An Asian man speaking broken English grabbed her, telling her he loved her!" reported Ranzim.

Now Bailiff was on the speechless defensive. He didn't know what, but he could guess possibly who.

The elevator chimed that it had arrived at the top of the building. "Yes, I agree, let's get you some place comfortable," said Bailiff. "Dr. Ranzim, I'm sorry about this, but if you want to go to your hotel room and unwind, we'll call you when we're ready. I think we just about are," directed Bailiff, seizing the initiative and escorting Lisa alone off the elevator. Not taking no for an answer, Bailiff used part of his body to prevent Ranzim and his colleagues from getting off with them. He also quickly pressed the down button, smiling back at his guests.

Bailiff helped Lisa into the suite. The main room had been cleared out for the dinner table. In the bedroom, Bailiff made Lisa get on the bed. She was still breathing rapidly.

"Take my jacket," she said to Bailiff. "I don't want to wrinkle it." Lisa then lay back on the bed. Shortly, her breathing slowed. A second elevator brought Cara and Marcia back to the suite a minute or two later, although it may have been more accurate to describe their return as Marcia forcing Cara to come back.

"So, what happened?" Lisa asked Cara when the women entered the bedroom. She was calming down. Bailiff prepared a cool washrag.

"I—I'm so sorry. He called this morning later and said he gave money and that he did medicine. I wasn't done with the cards yet, so I assumed he had been invited tonight. So I told him to be here at six o'clock."

"Did you tell him I would be here?"

"No … I don't think so. But he did want to speak with you when he called."

"But he knew I'd be here."

"I guess he assumed that. I did not say you can meet Lisa Jefferson here."

"Jeffus," corrected Marcia.

"Jeffus. I'm sorry," said Cara meekly.

Lisa's breathing had returned to normal. Bailiff attempted to apply the cool cloth to Lisa's forehead. "No. You'll mess up my makeup. It's okay, Cara. It was an accident. Next time we'll be more careful about making sure we know who's calling."

"Yes, ma'am. I will do better," Cara said.

"No, I mean I will. We will." Lisa exhaled deeply.

"Ladies, will you excuse us?" requested Bailiff firmly. The women left the bedroom, Marcia shutting the door behind her. Bailiff sat down beside Lisa on the bed. "Are you dizzy or anything?"

"No, I'm okay." Though she'd only read about them, Lisa concluded she had just endured an anxiety attack of some kind. There was good reason to think so.

"I ... Lisa, I'm worried about you. You have really too much going on." Bailiff's voice was especially elevated.

"I do. But it is manageable, if we can just figure it out. Trust in God, too," she added.

"Listen," said Bailiff, "this is a bad time, but I need to get this out. I had you tell Nate to call me because I, as your client, have instructed him to be the only one who communicates with George Masters."

"I don't care. That sounds perfectly sensible." Lisa felt grateful that Bailiff had anticipated her problem without knowing the details. It was another of those serendipitous moments God provided. She felt she would get better.

"No, Lisa, listen to me," Bailiff said. "Masters is suspicious of you. He knows his people are following the doctor's care orders correctly. And while he knows you, he *knows* you, has his opinions of you. We talked about it. I got upset, but he made some good points. Right or wrong, he sees you as a career woman who might think your disabled husband is now an obstacle."

Lisa did not react.

"He also knows—he didn't say this about you specifically—but he also knows and has seen that some people, when they have an invalid family member, they sometimes justify in their mind that it's time for the person to die naturally, but what they undertake is really murder. They start to withhold things, stop giving medicines. Some even go to an extreme of poisoning the person—all in a rationalized way with good intentions. He didn't say that about you, but he said he's seen it."

"But he said I'm doing it to Bobby for the sake of convenience," Lisa said.

"He didn't say that exactly. But he said he could see how your goals in life might be motive."

Now Lisa became defensive. "Well, did you tell him I'm pregnant? Is that motive to kill a baby's father before he's born?"

"He didn't say anything about that, and I didn't bring it up, because I didn't want to give him any more ammo. I didn't want that to get twisted around, and I was already getting a little mad at him. But listen. There's obviously a political situation here—"

"You're damn right there is, Paul!" Lisa shouted, shooting up on the bed. "Move!" she commanded, kicking her legs against him as she stood up. She marched over to a chair where Bailiff had laid her suit jacket.

"Lisa. Either stay in here or go home," Bailiff said, his voice returning to its booming volume.

"What? I planned this whole thing out there. I am fine, and we are going to work." Lisa found some makeup in her purse, which one of the women had brought in. "You're gonna go out there, Congressman, do what you do, and then I'm going to follow up with each of them and take their money in your name. You're going to do that, not because you need the money to beat down some stooge Masters may or may not put up in a primary," Lisa exclaimed, "but because you work for me! This is the way it is in the whole stinking country. Insecure fools like you decide to acquire the love they need by running for office, but they manipulate the people who are successful in their own right in order to do so.

"You would be nothing without my grandfather or me!" Jacket on and buttoned, Lisa swung the bedroom door open to the gathering crowd, including Ranzim. "How is everybody?" she asked with a toothy smile. "A little excitement down there, huh?"

CHAPTER TWENTY-EIGHT

During dinner, Lisa sat on the other side of Ranzim from Bailiff. Ranzim said nothing more about Wang, immigration, or the assault. He thought she looked pale, but Ranzim never asked again. Before sitting, Lisa spun the story of a confused constituent successfully, she felt, to the other biotechies who had witnessed the weird encounter. The remaining DFW-based attendees stayed necessarily clueless.

The meal was four courses: salad, soup, entrée, and dessert. Bailiff usually gave his group pitch in between the last two. This was not a bald solicitation of funds but rather an impromptu-feeling "let's-hold-hands" speech, where he explained how he was impressed or moved or whatever, and that he would do everything that was necessary for the micro-cause about which the group had gathered.

Lisa felt a sharp stomach ache after the soup and only picked at her entrée. As a result, her plate was the last to be removed by the server. Upon seeing that all the entrée plates were now gone, it was Ranzim who stood up ahead of Bailiff. He motioned to one of his associates, who brought over a midsized box wrapped in expensive metallic-blue paper and a silver ribbon.

"We wanted to make a small gesture here in gratitude to our host," Ranzim began. Lisa felt light-headed again, mainly because she had to turn her neck up sharply to look at Ranzim as he spoke. "We would like you to have this, Congressman. I assure you it complies with the gift rules."

Bailiff was a bit surprised but took the stylishly wrapped box. One of the guests voiced for him to open it, which Bailiff did. Inside was a long, multicolored, straplike item with leather ends. Ranzim reached over and took one end of the shotgun sling, while Bailiff, mesmerized, kept holding the other.

"Your campaign director," said Ranzim, "our lovely and vivacious hostess, Mrs. Jeffus, informed us that you were recently given a shotgun."

Bailiff looked at Lisa, who shook her head in ignorance. She would have smiled, but now she felt a dull pain, not just in her stomach but in her lower abdomen. Even her lower back hurt. She felt like she was starting to cramp but knew that shouldn't be possible if she was pregnant.

"This shotgun sling is to remind you of us," said Ranzim. "In the building that houses our laboratory, we have along the halls mosaics put together more than one thousand years ago by Byzantine monks.

"The mosaics—after which this sling is patterned—are an inspiration to us to pursue God's map of life, the genome. May this modest strap and its pattern inspire you, Congressman, as you blast away at ignorance in the halls of government."

Lisa felt a shooting pain in her gut. She started breathing heavily again, but this time it was sudden and from her diaphragm, not short and fast from her rib cage.

"Hear, hear!" shouted one of the guests, raising his wine glass.

"Hear, hear!" said everyone, raising their glasses.

Lisa felt weak and strange with the pain in her lower abdomen. The discomfort was well beyond cramping. She stood up during the toast, trying to use it as cover for an exit. Bailiff nevertheless noticed her hurry into the suite's bathroom, even as he stayed at the table.

Lisa shut the bathroom door behind her. She raised up her skirt, pulling her hosiery down her legs around her Gabbana shoes. She fell back onto the toilet at the sight of a large collection of blood.

Nate wandered into the ER of Presbyterian Hospital of Dallas off Greenville Avenue and Walnut Hill Lane. The air outside was humid, ready for the downpour the weathermen had been predicting all day. He thought the blast of cooler, drier air from the hospital doors might frost over his phone.

As he updated his wife over the cell line, Nate could hear Stephanie's voice crack. He felt weak in his knees and fell into a seat in the hospital lobby. He paused after explaining what he'd been told.

"Nate, are you all right?" asked Stephanie. "Nate?"

Collecting himself, Nate replied, "I hate this business." He stood back up and made his way to the elevators.

He found Lisa on the third floor. The room was dimly lit for night—and empty. Bailiff had come and gone. Lisa watched Nate come in as her head with its fallen auburn hairdo rested against the elevated bed back and pillow. He noticed that she still had most of her face on. By the way Lisa looked at him, Nate sensed the greater chill to be up here in the general ward, not in the lobby. He awkwardly moved to sit in the room's lone chair.

"Don't sit down," Lisa ordered without lifting her head up.

"I am not the enemy."

"You and Bailiff were hatching this takeover ever since he asked you out to Black County that night."

"Lisa, don't," Nate complained.

"It wasn't going to stop with the biotech group. It was going to be Masters. His doctors, and in time his bankers, lawyers—the rest of the Indian chiefs. Then, when he felt you had the core group, he would've broken you off to handle his operation exclusively. Then without me, he could cut the percentage. In time, he would prejudice other clients against me, all to save his ass with who he thinks are his grassroots."

"That's a lie! That is all nonsense!" Nate declared, making sure his vocabulary didn't stray into unchristian territory. "And you know it. You know how reluctant I am. And this is why I hate this business: all you people are constantly afraid of each other, plus the enemy. I'm no super-Christian, but I know fear isn't God's plan for us." Deeply upset, Nate hurried out and home. If Lisa and Danny had begun an illicit relationship, it was but a symptom of the paranoid self-deception that now seemed to exist in Lisa's heart. Nate felt sick to his stomach, heading onto the elevator.

Next to the closing elevator doors, the large stairwell door creaked open. Danny stepped onto the third floor and down the hall, the heels of his reptilian Tony Lamas tapping the linoleum.

Dr. Thorpe had visited earlier. Lisa would be hospitalized for a couple more days yet, as the spontaneous abortion she had endured resulted in heavy blood loss. She didn't care that she was bedridden. She felt defeated and angry, unable simply to stand and brush her teeth. Even the sight of Danny's massive silhouette in the wide doorframe failed to move Lisa out of her inner rage.

"Bailiff told me." Danny crossed over to the chair in which Lisa had forbidden Nate to sit.

"How long have you been working all these shady deals?" Lisa asked.

"Since before I went to the White House," Danny answered, sitting down. "I didn't begin in earnest until I went to the RNC."

Lisa sighed.

"I'm sorry that you've been shown what goes on behind the curtain," Danny said. A grim freedom emerged as he spoke; there was no longer this dark pall that would come over him—his words were from the other side. "All these guys. The money. The women. The corrupt bargains. And all this crap you read online or in *The Washington Post*—just the tip of the iceberg. Miniscule. And nothing has ever changed. There's no amount of laws, regulations, anything that can be passed. In fact, the new rules are just new ways for them to have their cake and eat it too.

"A lot of these poor rich dummies think they're 'ponying-up' to stop things. They never stop to think that the shyster they're contributing to actually sees lawmaking as a way to shake them down. Democrat or Republican—it doesn't matter.

"Our republic is broken. It's like a pro-athlete with high-blood pressure and high cholesterol—a ticking time bomb waiting to die. And only guys like me—like you, too, whether you know it or not— are the ones who only barely maintain order. You feed the system its junk food; I clean out the clots in the blood. I'm the agent of wrath it talks about in Romans 13. Not the magistrate, the judge, nor the officeholder. Me."

"I can't believe Bailiff had it in him. He seems like such a goof-ball," said Lisa. As bleak as Danny's perspective was, she took a per-verse delight in wallowing in it. "And a liar, too. Wow. What a liar."

Silence filled the space between the two souls.

Danny pulled out his cell phone and selected photos. He called up the one of Curtiss's BMW. "This is what happens when God's people start worshiping power, government. It's the spirit of the Baal that Elijah called down fire against in the Old Testament," he said to Lisa, extending his phone to her.

"This is Curtiss Small's car." She chuckled. "I recognize the license plate. The building looks seedy. Where is this?"

"It's at an Asian massage joint up off Stemmons. A brothel. It is a brothel," Danny bluntly explained.

"I don't see any signs," Lisa said.

"Of course you don't," Danny said, taking back his phone. "I know it is because it's next to Wang's office. The woman we greased ICE for was his mistress, the madam who runs that place.

"See, even God's people are reaping the whirlwind in our sick republic."

Lisa was a little skeptical of the photo, but it had been a night of revelations.

"You know, Lisa," Danny said. He stood up. "We could end it. I think we should."

Danny walked over and kissed Lisa on the forehead. She trembled, and chills came over her as she watched him leave.

Lisa began breathing heavily again like the anxiety attack. She wasn't on an EKG. No nurses were monitoring her. Lightning flashed outside the window of her room.

Dear God… Dear God… Hear my cry!

"Lisa!" called A.J., moving quickly to her side. "Lisa, calm down! Where's the nurse's button!"

"No, I'm fine," Lisa's breathing returned to normal the instant she heard her friend's voice. "It's all right. It's all right. Don't call her in here. I want to talk. Thank you, God. Thank you for sending my friend."

"What happened, dear? Oh, my goodness!" A.J. was disturbed to see Lisa where she was. A.J. stepped back to the door and moved her suitcase out of the way, having left it upon hearing Lisa's breathing.

"I miscarried."

"What? What happened?"

"How did you know?" Lisa asked. "I thought you were on a plane."

"I was. As soon as I landed in Chicago, my phone lit up with missed calls and voicemails. They were all from Congressman Bailiff."

This news struck Lisa such that her head began to hurt.

"He said you had an accident at the hotel. I guess this was right around 7:30 p.m. I got on the very next plane back to DFW, which was right next to my arrival gate… I couldn't get a hold of Curtiss, though, for some reason. I took a cab here. But girl, I'm so upset!"

"I'm so glad you're here," Lisa said, tears forming in her tired, now grayish-blue eyes. "I'm so confused." With weariness and sorrow in her voice, Lisa then told A.J. about the encounter with Wang, and how Danny just alleged to her not fifteen minutes earlier the level of Bailiff's corruption. "But I can't believe Bailiff called you, too?"

"Maybe he just called your friends for you," said A.J.

"Why would he do that? He and Nate have been working to undo the entire Mockingbird Group."

"Why do you say that? That's the most ridiculous thing I've ever heard. Who is putting these things into your head? Nate only barely knows what to do because he's told," A.J. insisted. "And Bailiff—look, you should take whatever Danny says about him with a grain of salt. I don't know what he just told you, but…well." A.J. wanted to be sensitive to her friend's condition. "I'm sorry, Lise, but Danny is just not right at all. I was never going to tell you this, dear. I was going to take this to my grave. But now's the time. I just think you need to know this. So much of your trouble has been since the day that man walked into your office."

"What are you saying?"

"Do you remember that FBI agent I dated for a little bit up in DC?"

"Neal, right? Was that his name?"

"O'Neal, yes. Ty O'Neal. Anyway, even though we weren't that serious, I asked him to check on the police reports when Danny's wife had that accident."

"And?"

"He said that there had been a second person in the vehicle."

"Danny never told me that," Lisa said.

"The other person wasn't killed, however. He walked away. O'Neal also said," A.J. paused.

"What is it? Tell me."

"He also said there were no skid marks."

"Was she drunk?"

"There was alcohol in the autopsy report but not a lot. Ty saw that the Maryland State Police closed the report, but he tracked down where the totaled car was towed. He personally went by there and did some of his own checking. The first thing he looked at were the brakes, and the pads had been loosened."

"Are you kidding me?" Lisa said, astounded. Then, as if by an unseen power, her memory recalled how Danny refused to shake her hand the previous month, saying he had worked on his brakes.

"Do you remember those two Senate candidates on our side, the one in '02 and the one in '04—both who died in plane crashes?"

"Yeah, um…it was Harper in Kansas and then another one in Indiana, I think."

"Danny was assigned to each state in those races on your side."

Lisa had started to give A.J.'s smear campaign against Danny credence with the brake job, but now she could not believe what she was hearing. "A.J.... I, I've heard stuff like this before, about the plane crashes. Nate actually believes some of it. I think... I just don't believe what you're saying." As with the feeding chart, Lisa's heart led her once more into denial and rationalization.

"In fact, I think you're being partisan," Lisa said to A.J., laughing incredulously. "Yeah. You're being partisan! You're being petty."

"Lisa—"

"You're being partisan, because you just don't like Danny; because he wins! You know what? Thanks for getting on that flight back, but your agenda isn't going to make me feel better."

"Lisa," said A.J., now equally stunned.

"Why don't you go home now to that pastor of yours, who, by the way, visits a massage joint up here off Stemmons when he's not with you!" Lisa heard herself shout. "That's probably why he didn't answer your phone calls!" Lisa's breathing picked up again.

A.J. stood up. The large woman staggered from Lisa's words.

"I think I should leave," she said. Normally fearless and confrontational, A.J. stumbled out the door, as if a rail spike had been driven through her heart.

"Just stay away!" Lisa tried to shout, choking on her own breath. Tears poured from her eyes. "Bye, A.J.," she muttered, short of breath. "Bye..." Lisa mashed repeatedly on the nurse's call button before blacking out. Thunder boomed outside the hospital as the unstable summer air churned itself.

Danny's Durango made its way over to Abrams through the massive downpour and the flashes of the static air. As midnight approached, no pawn shop or Wal-Mart would have available what he needed for the job he was about to do. Besides, he wanted to add a little poetry to his task by stopping off at the Mockingbird Group. Bailiff would be judged with the perfect symbol. Danny took pride in the syncretism he was going to achieve between the poetry of the prophets and the images of the pagans.

Danny had lifted Lisa's keys out of her purse when he went to kiss her good-bye at the hospital. He didn't feel for her the way she felt for him, he knew. Yet, insofar as he recognized feelings at all anymore, Danny wanted to vindicate Lisa's heart. She was one of the good ones. She came from Texas royalty, but she was never pretentious. She knew the value of property and money, but she was never greedy. She understood freedom and independence, both for herself and others. In short, Danny believed the republic had been designed for people like Lisa. It would be punished for letting her down.

The ailing republic, starting with the local congressman, would be condemned for taking the life of her unborn child.

Danny stepped off the elevators of the Commerce building and unlocked the doors of the Mockingbird Group. Because politicians could never receive a donation in cash, Lisa had never sprung for an alarm. Guided by a single, recessed light over the copier in the center of the suite, Danny made his way to the corner office.

He switched on a brass lamp on Lisa's credenza. Danny then stepped up to the shadowbox containing the pink baseball bat and removed it from the wall.

"Mrs. Jeffus! Mrs. Jeffus!" shouted the nurse. "Lisa!"

Lisa opened her eyes. She had only fainted for a moment after the panic attack. While her breathing was normal again, she still felt a busy heart. A second nurse was checking her blood pressure. She felt streaks of tear-borne moisture down the sides of her head.

"I'm calling the doctor and ask for a sedative," said the nurse. "Are you allergic to any medications?"

Lisa could only nod her head no.

After a moment, the nurses were out of the room. Lisa stared at the joint between the wall and ceiling. The anger was gone, but she felt spent and numb. Never before in her life had she felt so alone. She felt a dull pain in her chest.

For twenty minutes, she felt as though she were hanging in a vacuum. The storm outside was the only sound.

The nurse returned with some Valium, which Lisa waved off, still staring ahead of her. Busy, the nurse set the small cup of pills on the bedside table next to Lisa's pink water pitcher.

Lisa's earlier tears had run down her temples and into her ears. The streaks now felt dried. Not looking, Lisa reached for her purse, which had been placed on the shelf beside her bed. She fumbled past her prayer journal, finding her compact. In the small mirror, the streaks, which felt like Central Expressway, were not near as large.

A few seconds after returning her compact back to her purse, she retrieved her prayer journal. She opened it randomly to an entry the day of Bobby's accident:

Dear God–

Though I walk through the valley of the shadow of death,
Thou art with me ...

Lisa took a deep breath. She took her BlackBerry from her purse. Someone had turned it off.

She restarted it. Several emails and missed calls appeared, but she ignored them as she dialed down to past messages. Lisa found A.J.'s text with Mundy's phone number. She selected it and dialed it.

"Potter's Hands Massage Therapy," spoke Mundy's groggy voice after several rings.

"Mundy?"

Mundy recognized Lisa's voice immediately, in spite of his sleepiness. "It's kinda late for a massage, isn't it, Mrs. Jeffus?" He sat up on his bed, his glasses removed.

"I'm not sorry for calling you so late, Mundy," Lisa said. "But I'm sorry I lied."

"How is your husband?" asked Mundy after a pause.

"He's the same. His doctor upped his food intake. And I make sure and give it to him."

"What about his eyes?"

"What about them?"

"Are they still opened?"

"Yes. But he can't see anything."

"Yes, he can," corrected Mundy.

Lisa stayed silent for a bit. "I'm actually in the hospital myself. I miscarried our baby."

"I'm sorry."

"I guess—" Lisa didn't think she had any more tears left, as she wept through her words. "I guess its God's judgment," she sobbed.

Mundy only listened on the other end of the line.

"I tried to kill my husband. Oh, God," Lisa groaned. "Oh, God. I tried to kill my helpless husband. I have alienated everyone who cares about me, and I care only for someone who has become evil. God help me," Lisa muttered into her BlackBerry, which by now was coated in tearful moisture.

"You know," Mundy said, after the sobbing ended on the other end, "lots of people think God's grace is the thing that gives us the good stuff, the blessings, or whatever. But really, it's the thing that preserves us when we embrace the darkness."

CHAPTER TWENTY-NINE

Danny drove his Durango out to a point along White Rock Lake's eastern shore in Lake Highlands Park. The pouring rain only made the night darker. He donned his rain jacket and pulled the hood over his head. He also fastened a pair of waterproof boot covers over his Tony Lamas. He would dispose of these in a dumpster down off Buckner Boulevard after he made his getaway.

Danny had parked as far down the park road as the flooded shore would let him. He would avoid walking down Lake Highlands Drive, upon which the Bailiffs' modernist home was located, as even at this late hour a vehicle or two might come driving down it. He hiked through the park along Dixon Branch, now also greatly swelled with all the spring rain.

Sure enough, a car headed his way down Lake Highlands. Danny ducked into a stand of trees slightly above the creek and almost even with the Bailiff house. His boots sank in the mud and water, which were backing up into the trees and the slick runoff they covered. Drainage from the low knoll that Bailiff's home sat on came pouring into the runoff. Danny slipped once but caught himself as he made his way up the short slope.

Most of the downstairs den lights were on as Danny approached the front door. He saw Bailiff moving around inside clad in a bathrobe over his slacks, not completely undressed from the dinner earlier that evening.

216

Bailiff had finished a fourth glass of red wine before fastening the multicolored "mosaic" gun sling Ranzim had given him to his Remington 870 pistol grip. He thought the event went well, all things considered. He felt he had connected with Ranzim, and Bailiff called his new friend briefly to update him after leaving Lisa at Presbyterian. Bailiff knew that given his and Lisa's exchange before the dinner, his continued presence at the hospital would be unwelcome.

The congressman was home before ten o'clock, eager to unwind from the stressful evening. He and Lucy opened a bottle of Cabernet, as Bailiff updated his wife on the anxious events of the past few hours. Bailiff returned from the kitchen with a glass of water to drink before going to bed as Danny approached the front door with murder in his eyes.

Bailiff noticed that his new sling had leather shell holders in it. He just couldn't go to bed without trying out his new gear. He deserved to at least hold his toys after what had happened. Bailiff fished through a drawer for some shells. He found two Magnums. He was attempting to fit them into the leather shell holders when he heard a knock at the door.

The light buzz in Bailiff's head prevented him from becoming afraid of an intruder, but his heart did leap for fear it was someone with bad news about Lisa. He set his shotgun on a sofa close to the foyer. He went to the door and opened it. The noise of the rainstorm came into the Bailiff house.

"Danny Geister," Bailiff thundered with the aid of the wine. "Tell me what's wrong."

"Everything." Danny thrust the fat end of the bat into Bailiff's belly, buckling the congressman and causing him to let out a gasp. As Danny pulled the pink bat above his head, he hit the low ceiling of the Bailiff foyer. Still bent over, Bailiff stumbled toward the sofa as Danny readjusted for a second hit.

The pink bat came down on Bailiff's back right as he reached his Remington. In one motion, he seized the pistol grip and pointed the barrel at Danny. Not knowing it was unloaded, Danny dove behind a wall between the sofa and foyer. Still breathless and unable to call to Lucy, who was upstairs, Bailiff pulled the two Magnum shells from the sling and loaded them into the gun.

Danny gave a glance back at Bailiff and realized the weapon was not loaded. Bailiff cocked the pump. Danny leapt at Bailiff's head, swinging only to have the blunt instrument meet the barrel and bang it away. The first shell went off. Its shot smashed into the foyer drywall behind Danny. The two men reeled through the smoke and smashed sheetrock, deafened by the blast.

"Paul! Paul!" screamed Lucy from upstairs.

Through the still open door and rain outside, dogs barked noisily. Danny made another swing at Bailiff's head, striking it the instant Bailiff completed pumping the barrel a second time. Shotgun still in his hands, Bailiff fell back against sofa.

"Paul!" shouted Lucy midway down the stairs, not fifteen feet from Danny as he reared back for a finishing blow. Danny turned to see her.

Still stunned from the hit, Paul feebly extended the gun toward Danny's exposed abdomen. Danny lunged away toward the front door as the second Magnum shell went off, filling the foyer again with smoke and debris. Danny's boot covers, soaked and muddy, scampered out the door and toward the street.

Lucy grabbed the gun from her injured husband and pumped it again. She ran outside into the storm. Her vision limited by the few street lamps, she pulled the shotgun trigger at Danny's sprinting shape as it neared the distant stand of trees he used as cover earlier. The chamber empty, only a click sounded. Getting drenched, Lucy returned inside and dialed 911.

CHAPTER THIRTY

The day after the attack on Bailiff, the storm having passed, the Dallas Police Department blanketed Lake Highlands Park with its investigations unit. And because a U.S. Congressman had been assaulted, the FBI got in on the act. After waiting for the waters to recede, however, all that was found in the stand of trees was a shorted-out camera phone. A serial number check revealed the phone had been purchased with cash ten months earlier at a mall in Shreveport, Louisiana. The mall had never fitted itself with security cameras around the carrier's kiosk, and a number assigned to the phone at the time of sale had been registered to a name not Danny's. Even the FBI lab in Virginia couldn't reactivate the phone's ruined circuits or memory card.

Bailiff was subjected to a couple of rounds of questioning, first by the Dallas Police then by the Feds. He was too hurt in his head to tell Lucy not to dial 911. As a result, detectives and agents sat him through discussions about who his assailant might be.

"I don't know," Bailiff answered. "He was a late-night intruder. Clearly, a very troubled young man," became his pat reply.

"But you opened the door for him?" one agent asked. "There's no sign of breaking and entering."

"My campaign fundraiser had a miscarriage earlier that evening," Bailiff said. "Between news related to that and some extra wine I drank, I unwisely opened the door."

And that was that. He said the same thing to *The Dallas Morning News* and the Capitol Hill newspapers. He never responded to requests from *The Washington Post* or television media. Bailiff would never report the true identity of Danny Geister.

Lisa also knew the true identity of who took her baseball bat, and she would never report it. But she could support her newfound honesty of soul with the luxury of never being asked about Danny. She noticed her keys were missing when she was discharged from Presbyterian the following Sunday, but she kept it to herself, suspecting Danny. She then made sure she was the first one at the Mockingbird Group Monday to see what Danny had done at the office. With only the baseball bat missing from its shadowbox, she contacted her IT support company herself. Within a short time, Lisa received from them a report that no data had been compromised. In fact, the computers stayed off all weekend, and the office server was never accessed. Only Marcia noticed the bat was missing, and that was a few days later. Lisa simply explained to her, laconically, that it had been removed and that its memory was too upsetting given the miscarriage.

Losing the keys also meant asking Ron and Brenda to let her in to her own house. It was Ron she called first, anyway, on Sunday to ask the elder Jeffuses for a ride home. She asked Brenda to step outside when they arrived at the hospital, and Lisa begged Ron for forgiveness. Choking, she confessed to Ron what she had tried to do to his son. She owned up to her angry words about his wife. The gentle man sensed her brokenness and granted her clemency with an explanation that he knew how she felt, having experienced similar emotions with his brother those years ago. After a brief explanation that he had promised to himself never to let a loved one become a victim of such emotions, Ron stayed himself, remaining silent about the trouble for the rest of his life.

Lisa knew that the things Danny said about Bailiff and the things Bailiff said about Danny and the affair with Carl Wang could both be true. The same went for Bailiff and Nate. She called Nate

Sunday night, after arriving home, and explained that what she said was wrong, but she didn't expect things to be the same. Lisa told Nate he could stay on paid leave as long as he liked. Nate said that he appreciated it and that he was already talking with one of Texas's senators who wanted to come home and run for governor and who needed help with Christian conservatives.

Nate knew he had to get away from Bailiff, given all the history now. He just didn't think Bailiff was on the up-and-up. Nate would later find out about the actual earmark in the Labor and Health Appropriations Bill, which would stay in the federal budget into perpetuity. Nate was grateful he didn't have to glad handle the bio-tech donors. He admitted to himself that he didn't have much stomach for the legislative sausage making. Maybe that was hypocritical for the Christian to be comfortable with some things about politics while accepting—or ignoring—others. Nate thought he would be more at home on the front end of a true campaign, where all he had to do was worry about headlines. Lisa agreed.

Lisa waited a week before contacting Bailiff. She told him that she had thought about it and prayed about it, and that depending on how her presidential clients fared in the primaries, she was going to shutter the Mockingbird Group. In the interim, she would move her clients, including him, off to other fundraisers. She had enough money nested away, both earned and inherited, to take some courses for a teaching certificate and support herself and Bobby for a few years at least. She wanted to teach government to teenagers. She felt everyone, all around, needed to start over. Bailiff was frustrated by the news, but he took it in stride, making plans to rebuild his operation.

A week after the miscarriage, Lisa made a private appointment with George Masters at his twenty-acre country home just across the border in Black County. Only Masters greeted Lisa at the door of his three-thousand-square-foot brick home with its English gables. Leading her into his study, Lisa was struck by a massive bookcase packed with just about every evangelical pastoral book ever printed.

Amid the books and hanging on the walls were photos of Masters with various elected officials.

"I know this might not go over well with APS," Lisa began after Masters showed her the seat across his desk, "but I appreciated you taking my call about Bobby's care."

"I don't care what they say," Masters quickly said. "There is just too much they can't get right. Bureaucratic fools. Did you know they closed our case? They didn't have any evidence. What a surprise."

Lisa shifted uncomfortably in her seat. She remembered when she and Danny had rented *Born on the Fourth of July* and the scene where the soldier had to tell his best friend's parents that he was the one who killed him with friendly fire.

"I didn't come out here to be vindictive," Lisa said. "But Bailiff said you called him with your concerns about what was going on at our house, is that right?"

"Yes. Please don't, Lis—"

"It's all right, George. Let me explain." Lisa took a deep breath. She wasn't going to lie, but neither did she want to implicate herself. She didn't really trust Masters, but Lisa decided her freedom was more important than what might happen. "I wanted to tell you that my confusion over how to care for Bobby was why my father-in-law called APS. It's my fault that Bobby's care declined there for a little bit. I think on some level, I didn't want to care for hi—"

Masters held up his hand, stopping Lisa, before he thought she might say something he didn't need to hear.

"Do you know why I'm a radical?" he asked after a second. "More than thirty years ago, right after college, I got my girlfriend pregnant. This was before I found the Lord but right after Roe versus Wade.

"I paid for her to have an abortion," he confessed. "It was safe, and she went on to marry someone else and have beautiful children. I went to seminary. I married a Christian girl, but I quit being a pastor, because I just couldn't overcome the guilt. I support pro-life causes, not just because of the innocent little lives, but because I don't want anyone else to fail like I did. I believe the government must protect people from themselves, and we must impose morality when we can, wherever we can—to the utmost. We had our chance with the Republican Party. But I am afraid our time to speak is coming to a close. Maybe now is a time to be silent. Maybe now we can only surrender the country to God. It's really his, anyway. I know a lot of our people affirm that, but not many truly believe it."

Lisa only listened. She heard her BlackBerry vibrate in her purse.

"The American Christian's problem is just that. We're American Christians."

July 23

Dear God,

You know my every need. It is hard for me to understand the mystery of brokenness when we have already been taught your grace, yet I am grateful for it. It is really a gift. I remember all of your blessings, but it is your strength that I can only now see by being broken for which I am most thankful. Truly, as the Psalmist says, "the lines have fallen for me in beautiful places."

Lisa heard the doorbell ring. She set down her prayer journal and made her way to the front of the house.

"Thanks for coming over," Lisa said to A.J.

A.J. smiled, aloof but happy to see her friend. The two women sat in the Jeffuses' living room.

"How's Bobby?" A.J. asked.

"Unchanged. You can go visit him, if you like."

"I will in a minute. I called you because I wanted to tell you I was sorry," A.J. said.

Lisa teared up and took her friend's hand. "No, love, I'm sorry. I'm so sorry for everything. The lies, the accusations, all of it."

"Curtiss has a problem. He is trying to get through it with his boss, the pastor, but I think there are still issues. We broke up, anyway. I'm going to be in Chicago most of the time now from now through the primaries at least. I just … I called because it can't be this way. When there's a hurt relationship, I have come to wonder why we experienced the bond in the first place."

"For me," responded Lisa, "the good bond is proof enough that goodness will endure."

A.J. nodded. The two women looked at each other for a moment. "Let's go see your husband," A.J. said.

Arm-in-arm, Lisa led A.J. back to Bobby's room. He still lay motionless on the bed. Tami sat quietly in a chair nearby, nodding at the two when they entered.

"I thought his eyes opened?" A.J. asked.

"They did, but the doctor said to close them, so they wouldn't get dry. He can't blink. But here," Lisa said, moving up to the head of the bed, "I can open the lids."

Lisa gently raised Bobby's eye lids. She looked into his eyes, moving her head to the position of that one stare she could connect with.

"What is your name?" mumbled Bobby. "You have the sharpest eyes."